# Hidden Allies

## The Living Oracle

### Book Four

## Melissa McShane

# CHAPTER ONE

An oracle, in my experience, rarely gets spontaneous visions for her own benefit. Usually my prophecies direct me to help others. The transit from the climate-controlled Gunther Node to the outdoors access point made me wish this wasn't true. The February night was unusually cold, slapping me with a full-body shiver that came close to being painful. I'd worked up a warm glow during my martial arts training session, so I was in shirtsleeves. That was a mistake. I could have used a warning about the drop in temperature.

I fumbled into my hoodie and ran to my car, the enormous Tahoe I referred to as my land yacht. Sergio, the night attendant, strolled forward to greet me. "Hey, Helena, you look cold."

"Sergio, it's a good thing I like you, because otherwise I would say something really rude." Sergio wasn't wearing anything heavier than a windbreaker over his coveralls, but he looked comfortably warm.

"I don't believe you," Sergio said. "You're, like, the politest person I know. How do you do it?"

I hit the ignition and sat shivering in the front seat, waiting for the heater to wake up and do its job. "You only see me when I'm in public. I promise I'm not always this civil."

Sergio chuckled. "Uh-*huh*. Right." He winked and walked around the rear of the land yacht to open the rolling gate. The Gunther Node's access point near the Columbia River had been destroyed in a missile attack, and the new access point was in this auto repair shop in Gresham, deep in an industrial neighborhood. It was, in fact, a legitimate business, though it was unusual in being the only one in the area open at all hours. The smells of motor oil and gasoline filled the chill night air.

Warm air finally flowed through the vents, and my seat warmer—ah, seat warmers, the high-water mark of automotive decadence—kicked into gear. I flexed my cold fingers and put the land yacht in gear. Waving to Sergio, I backed out of the yard and headed for home.

I glanced occasionally at the map on my land yacht's screen as I maneuvered the Tahoe through the dark and winding streets of Portland. Exactly one month ago, Malcolm and I had moved our little family into our new home, and the secluded neighborhood was enough off the beaten trail that I still wasn't totally familiar with the route between the house and, well, anywhere else.

I liked the new house, and I liked the seclusion, which struck me as typical of Portland—little overgrown, forested neighborhoods in the heart of the city—but I still missed my old home, destroyed in the same missile attack that had taken out the access point, and I was reluctant to give my whole heart to the new one. Still, things could be worse. There's nothing like having your house blown up by a secret paramilitary organization to make you appreciate what you have.

I sped past the Ogilvys' house, or rather the mailbox at the end of their long drive. Their house, like ours and the other five houses nearby, was far enough from the road to be hard to see thanks to the many trees and bushes obscuring it. I guessed visibility would be almost nonexistent during the summer, when everything was in full leaf. We'd met Chase and Debra Ogilvy once, and they were nice enough, but I'd felt their personalities matched their secluded, somewhat distant house. None of our neighbors had been outgoing in welcoming us, which was another thing I missed about my home... and now I was done thinking about it. No point dwelling on the past.

The old-fashioned street lamp at the foot of our drive glowed a warm welcome. The lamp had appealed to me from the start, even before we'd seen the house: a tall iron base supporting three lanterns at different heights, all of them casting mixed shadows over the driveway. The mailbox flanking it wasn't so appealing, because the neighbors had told us the sturdy brick structures that looked like tiny pizza ovens were necessary to protect against casual vandalism. The reminder that there were people in the world who delighted in destruction ruined the mailbox's whimsical charm.

The arching branches of rows of maple trees, black against the moonlit sky, curved over the driveway. Ahead, the carriage lanterns hanging on the carport and the garage joined the streetlamp in welcoming me home. I parked in the oversized garage and turned off the ignition, then sat for a moment, enjoying the dimness and stillness. I felt the warm, stretched-out sensation that came after a good workout, all my muscles pleasantly relaxed, my mind calm. These training sessions with Sibby Gonzalez were having an effect on my ability to defend myself, but they also were improving my stamina and strength.

I collected my purse and workout bag and went inside. The house was quiet except for the distant sound of conversation I quickly identified as coming from the television. It was after eight-thirty in the evening, so the kids would all be in bed. "Asleep" was probably too much to hope for, but as long as they were quiet, I was satisfied.

Nobody was downstairs, so I followed the sound of the television upstairs, checking in on each of my children as I passed their bedrooms. Alastair was huddled under the blankets with a flashlight, reading. He wasn't trying to hide—he knew we didn't mind after-hours reading because he never stayed awake past nine—but he'd said he liked how it felt to be in a cave of blankets at night. Duncan was asleep, sprawled across his bed like he meant to colonize enemy territory. Night-Noon, our elven caracal, curled up beside him. She was a cat the size of a German shepherd who believed she was an ordinary housecat, and she didn't mind scrunching up in what little space Duncan left available.

Jenny was also asleep, clutching one of her new dolls. Almost everything we'd owned had gone up in the fire after the missile attack. Some of those losses, like the children's Christmas ornaments or the boxes of photos from my own childhood my mother had given me that weren't yet digitized, were devastating. In general, though, our wealth made replacing most things easy.

But word had gotten out in the Warden community that the Campbell children had nothing, and at Christmastime, the presents had poured in. Dolls for Jenny, Lego for Duncan, piles and piles of books for Alastair. Nothing so outrageous that they were spoiled, thankfully, but enough that when we bought the new house, their rooms didn't look bare and sad.

I paused for a while outside Jenny's door, watching her small face relaxed in sleep. I savored Jenny's peaceful moments. She was an empath, someone who felt the emotions of others as if they were her own, and although she was making progress in her ability to control what she felt, there were still far too many episodes (my word, not that of her doctor Loretta Deveaux) for me to relax my vigilance.

Sighing, I walked to the end of the hall. Malcolm was sitting up in bed, dressed for sleep in black boxers and T-shirt, watching *His Girl Friday* on the television screen above the fireplace. "Good, you're home. Did the workout go all right?"

"As ever." I sank onto the bed and leaned in for a kiss. "I mean, I wouldn't want to take *you* on, but I'm more confident that I could take out a random mugger."

"It's a good start."

I sighed again. "I know. The goal is for me to be able to defend myself against a Savant, though they seem dormant these days." The Savants, the paramilitary organization that had destroyed my home, hadn't done anything to bring themselves to the Wardens' attention in the three months since their last, devastating attack. I knew better than to assume that meant they weren't a threat anymore, but I'd stopped looking in my rear view mirror as often as I used to.

Malcolm put his hand around my waist and pulled me closer. "Go get changed and join me. I'm in the mood to hold you."

"I love that mood."

I'd showered at the Gunther Node, so I just tossed my clothes into the hamper and pulled on my cutest pajamas, in case holding turned into something more active. Out of everything different in our new house, the dressing room attached to our bedroom had taken the most getting used to. It was easily the size of the bedroom itself and had more cupboards and closets than Malcolm and I combined could use. The rose-colored walls and nut-brown floorboards made the cupboards look like a high-end couturier's boutique, not exactly welcoming. Maybe someone more committed to fashion, like my best friends Judy and Viv, would appreciate it. I just felt out of place.

The feeling halted me where I stood, and I closed my eyes and breathed in the faint scent of lavender from the diffuser on a high shelf where Night-Noon couldn't reach it. I needed not to indulge those feelings. I'd been the primary decider when we chose this house, and it was better for me to dwell on what I loved about it than to focus on the ways in which it fell short.

An alarm jerked me out of my reverie. It wasn't the fire alarm or the carbon monoxide sensor, both of which would have been a relief by comparison. The dull *braap braap braap* was something worse. It was the proximity alarm that said someone was trespassing on our property.

My heart ratcheted into overdrive. I dashed from the dressing room to find Malcolm pulling his gun from beneath the mattress. It was magically keyed to him so it would only fire if he was the one to squeeze the trigger, but the kids all knew not to touch it anyway.

"Helena, watch the doors in case this is a serious incursion." Malcolm didn't bother putting on warmer clothes aside from his slippers, which were soled to allow for walking around outside.

I ran with him down the hallway, pausing at Alastair's door to say, "Don't worry. We'll see what it is," to Alastair. He was sitting up in bed with his book clutched to his chest.

"Is it intruders?" he asked. He didn't sound worried, just curious, and I briefly cursed the circumstances that had led to my children being blasé about being in danger.

"We don't know. Dad will find out. You stay put until I call for you, okay?"

Alastair nodded vigorously. I knew him well enough to realize he hoped I'd call him to help fight. Nine years old and already dreaming of being a warrior for justice.

Malcolm had already clattered down the stairs to the great room, where he turned on the television using the special remote control. That one turned the TV into a monitor revealing the many protections layered over this house. The proximity warning attached to the invisible perimeter fence. The shrouds, also invisible, that deflected magical attacks, human or elven. The tiny explosive devices that could be armed with a push of a button once we determined an intruder meant us harm and wasn't just Chase Ogilvy coming to borrow a cup of sugar. A handful of lesser defenses. And, of course, dozens of security cameras that meant no inch of our property was free of surveillance.

Malcolm brought up the view that showed all the display windows as little tiles in a grid. "There," he said, shoving the remote into my hands, and ran for the back door.

I hadn't seen anything out of the ordinary, so I scanned the little windows until I saw movement. The cameras represented the pinnacle of the glass magus' art, and the views showed the yards and the driveway in perfect clarity, though without much contrast. I pressed the button that would change the display. All the little windows turned green with traditional night vision resolution. I found it easier to interpret, but even so, it took me a while to perceive what Malcolm had reacted to. Something moved in one of the squares, a lumbering shape low to the ground. A bear, maybe. How a bear had gotten this far into the city, I didn't know, and instinct told me this wasn't the whole story.

I checked all the displays showing approaches to the house. Nothing moved except Malcolm, who came into view near the carport. He cut across the rear lawn, gun at the ready. Belatedly I hit the cancel button, and the alarm shut off. If there was more than one intruder, I wanted the warning of the sirens going off again.

Malcolm left one square for another. The creature he was stalking had stopped moving, but I couldn't make out more than that, even with the night vision setting. Slowly, Malcolm came into view in the same window as the intruder. I made myself check the other windows. If this was an ambush—but nothing else moved.

Malcolm stopped with his back to the camera, his body blocking the view of the intruder. He shoved his gun into his waistband and, to my surprise, picked up the creature and strode back toward the house. I followed his progress in the windows until a tap at the French doors brought me to myself. I hurried to unlock the doors and let Malcolm in. "Malcolm, what is it?"

"A puzzle," Malcolm said.

He laid his burden down on one of the sofas. It looked like a furry monster at first glance, but a second look told me it was a person wrapped in a heavy fur coat or cloak. Malcolm folded the coat back, revealing an unconscious woman.

No. Not a woman. I took in the unnaturally pale skin, the lank, tangled white-blonde hair, the shadows of her cheeks and brow ridges that were almost blue. It wasn't a woman.

It was an elf.

My heart again lurched, fear battering at me. Elves had been trapped in their realm of Faerie for a thousand years as the barrier humans had erected to protect themselves poisoned their land and, eventually, them as well. Now they wanted revenge. If the Savants were dangerous, elves were a hundred times worse. "You brought her *inside?*" I exclaimed. "Malcolm, what if this is a trap?"

"If she was booby-trapped, the wards neutralized any hidden bombs. And she made no effort to disguise herself. I think the shrouds worked as advertised and stripped her of most of her defenses. If this is a trap, we would already see more elves coming through the slip she made."

"That's not possible," I said. "We're protected. No elf can open a portal anywhere close to here."

"Like I said, a puzzle." Malcolm leaned over the elf. "I don't know if she's breathing. She didn't move when I lifted her."

The elf's eyes opened. Quick as a cat, she grabbed Malcolm's wrist, her pale, undead-looking skin making his healthy tan look unnatural. Malcolm let out a hiss and broke her grip with some effort. He again trained his gun on her head.

The elf licked cracked and bloody lips. Her mouth worked a few times like she was trying out words. "Don't let him take us," she said in perfect English. She exhaled deeply, and didn't draw another breath.

Malcolm and I stared at each other. "What was that?" I said.

"She took language from me the way Gabriel Roarke always talks about," Malcolm said. He flipped the fur coat open, adding, "I'll try to resuscitate her."

"Malcolm! Look!" I exclaimed.

The elf woman wore a harness strapped around her torso. I knew what it was for even before the child clinging to its dead mother opened deep-set, vividly blue eyes and let out a thin, frightened wail.

# CHAPTER TWO

Malcolm and I again stared at each other. An elf baby. One whose cries were growing louder and more insistent. The sound cut me to the heart. Without thinking, I fumbled with the straps until the baby—no, the child; it looked to be about eighteen months old—was free. Then I gingerly picked it up. It kicked and cried more, wordless pleas for comfort.

"Helena, be careful," Malcolm said, alarmed.

"You said any traps have been neutralized. This child isn't any danger to us." I examined it. The child wore a long shift or dress or something, shapeless and not very feminine, and I didn't want to make assumptions about its sex based solely on its clothes. It looked more human than its mother, its skin pale but flushed with its crying, its silky blond hair lacking the lank, dry appearance most elves' hair had. The only indications that the child was an elf were its strange thinness and its impossibly blue eyes.

Malcolm muttered something under his breath and moved the elf woman to the floor to start CPR. Her body jerked helplessly with the chest compressions, but otherwise she didn't react. I held the child gingerly, resisting the impulse to cuddle it. This could still be a trap.

"Mom? Is that a baby crying?" Alastair stood in the doorway to the great room.

"Alastair, I told you to stay in your room."

"Yeah, but I heard crying and I figured—"

"Your mother is right, Alastair. You need to stay where we tell you to unless there's imminent danger, like a fire." Malcolm gave up on resuscitation. His voice was sterner than mine. "I understand curiosity, but part of being a Warden is following orders."

"Okay. I'm sorry." Alastair made no move to leave. I was suddenly very conscious of the dead elf woman on the floor, concealed from Alastair by the couch's high back. Alastair had seen dead bodies before, thanks to his oracular gift, but I didn't think that meant we should expose him to death in his own home if we could help it.

The child I held threw its head back and screamed. I couldn't bear it anymore; I cuddled the child close to my chest, stroking its head. "There, there, shh," I murmured. "You're safe."

"Helena," Malcolm said.

"Malcolm, it's a child. It doesn't matter if it's an elf or a human—"

"An *elf?*" Alastair exclaimed. "Where did an elf baby come from? Don't we have wards against elves?"

"We don't know where it came from," Malcolm said with finality. "I want you to go to your room now. There isn't anything you can do about this situation now, and morning will be soon enough to talk about it. Understand?"

"I can prophesy," Alastair persisted. "I can find out where it came from."

"This is not your responsibility." Malcolm crossed the room and put a hand on his son's shoulder. "I know you want to help, and I admire that about you. But you won't be able to act on anything you see in vision. You need to let us investigate, and in the morning, when we know better what we face, we will want your help. Now, go back to bed."

Alastair nodded and ran back up the stairs.

"You are so much better at handling him than I am when he gets stubborn about prophesying," I said with a sigh. The elf child in my arms had relaxed, and its violent weeping had subsided to sniffling sobs.

"He knows you are sympathetic to his desires," Malcolm said, "which means he knows how to play on those sympathies. Genius or not, he's still only nine, and nine-year-olds can be manipulative. I find it remarkable that you rarely give in to his wishes."

"Well, I do know what is too much for his age." The elf child was falling asleep, I realized from how its body was relaxing. "But I don't know what an elf of *this* age needs beyond the basics. I mean, Gabriel Roarke has the same basic anatomy as a human, so I assume this child needs to eat and sleep and pee like anyone—"

Warmth spread across my midsection just then, a sensation familiar to any parent, and I let out a hiss of dismay and held the child away from me as it finished urinating. "Okay, so the child isn't potty trained, which tells me it might actually be the age it appears. I need to find her, or him, a change of clothes. Too bad we don't have any more disposable training pants." Jenny had been a little late to potty-training, I thought in an attempt to remain the baby of the family, but any remnants of that stage were gone with the old house.

"Can I leave the child to you? I need to call the Gunther Node and see about taking care of its mother." Malcolm covered the elf woman's face with her fur coat, then unfolded a throw blanket draped over the back of the couch and covered her whole body with it. "I intend to figure out how she got here, and if that turns out to be impossible, we will need the oracle."

"I agree." My mind was already preoccupied with taking care of the child. No portable crib—also destroyed by the Savants. Damn them. I could at least get one of Jenny's nightgowns so the child didn't have to lie around in wet clothes.

I carried my wet, smelly burden upstairs to Jenny's room without turning on her light and rooted around in her dresser for her smallest nightgown. The child, straddling my waist now, stared at me in silence, its enormous eyes less alien in the darkness. I decided against underwear, which would almost certainly be too big, and retreated to my bedroom.

I ran a shallow bath while I removed the wet shift. Again, the child didn't fight me and didn't cry. I tried not to think about how unnerving its silence was after its loud but justifiable screaming. The child was male and wore no underwear, which suggested he was in the middle of potty training or whatever it was elves did with their children at that age; if you didn't have training pants, you wanted as few barriers between your child and the toilet as possible.

I set the little boy in the tub and gently rinsed him off. Night-Noon wandered in somewhere in the middle of the bath and nosed the water, probably hoping there was room in the tub for her as well. Elven caracals loved water the way housecats generally did not. When her attention moved to the child, I started to push her away, but the little boy reached out his hands to her. When I saw he didn't grab her ears or the sides of her head, I let Night-Noon nuzzle him. He smiled, but petted her in perfect silence.

Again, the absurdity of the situation stunned me. I was giving a bath to an elf child whose dead mother lay in our great room, waiting for removal by the Gunther Node. An elf child who didn't look all that inhuman, certainly not by comparison to the undead appearance of all the adult elves I'd ever seen. The boy continued to watch me impassively. I'd expected him to eventually demand his mother, but he seemed content to let me care for him.

Once he was dry and dressed, I carried him to my bed and said, "Let me see what I can do for you. You're past the stage of rolling out of a crib, but you shouldn't sleep with us." We had a couple of recliner chairs in the bedroom, and I opened one up to its fullest extension and went in search of sheets and a blanket. After some thought, I also grabbed a twin-size fitted sheet with a mattress protector. I wasn't inclined to risk another potty incident.

When I returned to the bedroom, the boy lay curled up on my bed, sleeping, with Night-Noon reclining next to him. I quickly assembled a makeshift bed on the recliner and carefully transferred our small guest to it, shooing Night-Noon gently away. He didn't do more than clutch the blanket to himself and immediately fall deeper asleep.

I changed my own clothes, swiftly sponging myself off, then returned downstairs. That had felt like it took much longer than it did, because Malcolm was still alone in the great room, without any other Wardens there fussing over the dead elf. He was talking on his phone, but he finished his conversation when I entered. "Lucia is coming herself, along with a handful of others. They'll take the body to the

Gunther Node for examination. I should get dressed." He made no move to put this suggestion into action.

"I need to call Gabriel. He will know if there's anything special we need to do for an elf child."

Malcolm frowned. "Helena, they'll take the child to the Gunther Node, too. You don't need to worry about it."

I wasn't sure why that statement made my heart ache. I'd cared for the boy for all of half an hour. That wasn't enough time to grow attached. "I assumed he would stay with us."

"I don't see why. Lucia's people are more than qualified."

"Because his mother sought us out. She asked us for help. And it's not like I'm unqualified after raising three children of my own."

"There's more to it than that. If the boy's mother was fleeing something, that something or someone might still be searching. We could bring danger on our family."

Normally, this was the kind of argument I responded to. "You're the one who said we were protected. Malcolm, I think this goes beyond practicalities. I think that elf came here on purpose, which means her little boy is tangled up in whatever she was fleeing. She said 'don't let him take *us*.' Which further means that the oracle is going to be involved, and it's inefficient for me to be called on to prophesy for Lucia on the boy's behalf when I could prophesy about him directly."

"Ah." Malcolm turned as if he could see through the ceiling to our bedroom. "Then I think you should prophesy now, because Lucia is going to make the same argument I did."

I settled myself on the couch and ran through a series of possible queries before settling on *Why did the elf woman come here, of all places?*

The rushing, swooping sensation of a prophecy overtook me, and I flew with it, relaxing into the understanding it conveyed. I expected to see the viewpoint of someone fleeing through a dark forest; I'd seen into Faerie a couple of times and entered it once, and all those times it had been heavily forested. Instead, I got flashes of faces, all of them elves, none of them familiar. This reassured me, because of the two elves I'd seen multiple times in vision, one of them terrified me. If he was involved, I might rethink my stance on keeping the child with me.

The glimpses of faces gave way to a series of images of padlocks, all of them the kind that required a key rather than a combination. Lock after lock clicked open. The vision whirled around me, dizzying me, and then I saw a picture of my house, small and perfect in the oval of a locket pendant, and the vision receded.

I blinked to moisten my dry eyes. "I was partly right and partly wrong. She did come here intentionally, but not because she knew about us or the oracle or anything. She had some kind of key, maybe not a physical one, but it opened a specific slip—one near our house." My hands were shaking, and I clasped them to still them. "I thought that was impossible."

"So did I, and it disturbs me, too." Malcolm uncovered the dead elf and began searching her. I watched, feeling numb. Passage between our world and Faerie happened at places called slips, where the membranes between the worlds were very thin. Most slips were located in wilderness or remote locations, and no slips could form in large cities, which Portland was. I'd asked this question when we were looking seriously at this house because of the wooded area it was located in, and everyone from Lucia to Gabriel Roarke, himself an elf and a master of elven magic, assured me the city's protection was in place no matter how the neighborhood looked.

Malcolm grunted and held up something the size of a walnut. "Look at this."

I joined him. The red lump, up close, was a flattened sphere, more oval than round. Its surface was intricately carved to look like two serpents entwined with each other. A closer look told me it was actually hollow; gaps here and there revealed empty space behind the serpents. "What is it?"

"I have no idea." Malcolm brought the sphere closer to the light. "It feels like stone. Ruby, maybe?"

"That's a big ruby." I held out my hand to take it. "Let me see what I can learn." I didn't need a physical focus to prophesy, but sometimes I was able to direct the oracular gift to tell me something about an object I held.

Clasping the sphere in my hand, I sat on a nearby chair and leaned back. Normally I could simply gather my attention wordlessly, falling into the state from which I prophesied, but this time I asked a simple question: *what are you?*

This time, the vision came sluggishly, like I was pulling it physically from wherever the oracular gift drew them. Objects swam into view: a red apple that gleamed as if waxed, a woman's hand with short-trimmed nails, a large kitchen knife. The hand drew the knife's blade across the surface of the apple, cutting a deep gouge through the waxy red skin. In a flash, the apple became the red stone, gleaming with inner light. Then it was the apple again. With an effect like a movie being run backwards, the cut sealed over, but now the red surface was marred by a thick growth across the place where the cut had been. The hand with the knife reappeared. This time, when the knife passed across the apple's surface, it bumped over the rough, ridged growth without making so much as a dent.

I rose out of vision, blinking away the last sight of the knife. "This thing is what caused the slip to open. But it was a one-time event. It's like what Rick Jeong said about forcing slips to open—they seal over thicker than before. If there was a place inclined to become a slip somewhere near here, it's impassable now." This didn't reassure me as much as I'd expected. The idea that elves had objects that could open slips from Faerie to our world, anywhere they wanted, frightened me. Suppose those slips couldn't be tracked or identified?

"This is something we should investigate," Malcolm said, gently taking the sphere from my hand. "If there are more of these, keyed to particular places, particularly if those places aren't ones where slips can form naturally, we have a problem."

"That's what I thought, too."

I followed Malcolm upstairs and stood watching the little elf boy while Malcolm dressed. He really didn't look inhuman, just thin. His appearance roused in me the same inappropriate guilt I always felt when I thought about the barrier to Faerie that had poisoned that realm for a thousand years. Inappropriate, because not only hadn't I been responsible for it, I'd been the one to remove the barrier. But despite how all elves hated humanity and wanted us destroyed, I felt sympathy for them in this one small way: no matter what they'd done in the past, they didn't deserve to be poisoned and corrupted.

"I wonder if the corruption happens over time," I said.

"What was that?" Malcolm emerged from the dressing room, pulling a sweater over his head.

"I was just thinking how this little guy doesn't look sickly and emaciated the way adult elves do, and whether that means elves don't start out corrupted. How awful, if your babies start out looking normal and gradually change."

"That is sad, I agree, but it doesn't change my feeling about elves in general." Malcolm clasped my shoulder lightly as if comforting me. I nodded. There wasn't a lot we could do about elf hostility.

The doorbell rang. The little boy stirred in sleep and opened his enormous eyes. "You might as well bring him down to meet Lucia," Malcolm said.

I bent over the little boy, who focused on me with an unsettling intensity. Then he reached out his arms to be picked up. My breath caught. Keeping my back to Malcolm, I lifted the child into my arms, blinking away unexpected tears. Maybe it was true that the trust of small children and animals meant something special.

The child locked his legs around my waist to support himself and looked around alertly, as if curious about where we were going. "Let's go, then," I said, relieved that I sounded calm. But I let Malcolm lead the way.

# CHAPTER THREE

I waited in the formal living room rather than the great room while Malcolm went to answer the door. I didn't think the little boy should have to witness his mother's body being taken away, even though after his initial screaming, he hadn't seemed overly worried at being separated from her. That got me thinking: suppose this wasn't his mother? We had no way of knowing what her relationship to the child was, and supposing she'd kidnapped him, or was his nurse, or something?

The complications made my head spin. So many possibilities, all of them with terrible implications. What if this child was someone important, heir to a throne or something? The Wardens were already entangled with the elves in what was fast becoming all-out war, and suppose the boy mixed us up with some faction within the elf community and made things worse?

Distantly, the door opened, and I heard voices. I quickly leaned back in my chair with the little boy balanced on my lap and willed myself to find an answer to this question: *who is this boy?*

The whirling, floating sensation of vision caught me up immediately. Again, faces flashed past me, but this time, they were all the same face: the blonde elf woman who'd carried the child into our house, repeatedly speaking the same short syllables in letters that flew around her head like butterflies. Rather than the stillness of death, she appeared now in many moods, many expressions, happy, angry, afraid, sad. She was rarely happy, but when she was, it was in the presence of the little boy, who appeared at many different ages from newborn to how he looked now. It looked like my theory was right, because in his very youngest appearances, he was rosy-cheeked and plump like any healthy newborn.

Another face joined those two, this one male. He looked as irritated and unhappy as the woman, though aside from how they were both blond, they didn't look related. After a few seconds, the images merged, and the baby disappeared, leaving the man and the woman together, shouting, crying, silently raging, both repeating the same syllables I'd heard before, though now the letters were spiky and bat-winged.

When the vision ended, my ears rung with the sensation that someone had spoken to me and was waiting for a response. I never saw or heard anything from the real world while I was in vision, but some part of me registered input. It wasn't a pleasant sensation, and I had to work at not replying sharply. "Lucia," I said. "His name is Connvuir—I saw it spelled 'convooeer' but it's pronounced 'connver.' I don't know if he's important, but I think his parents fought a lot. My guess is his father is the one his mother fled."

"And hello to you, too," Lucia said in her usual acerbic way. "I don't suppose you know why that elf woman came here?"

"I did explain about the device, if I can call it that," Malcolm said. "Helena couldn't tell why the elf had that particular one. We believe it was coincidence. Far more worrying is the possibility that there are others of the same type, capable of opening slips in places we believe impregnable."

"Yes, yes, right, I see that." Lucia waved Malcolm's words away. "We need to figure out how to send the kid back. The last thing we need is to get tangled up in elf politics more than we already are."

"Send him back? How? He's not even two years old—" I began.

"As far as he looks, sure, but elves live to be nine hundred years old. Who knows what their maturation looks like?" Lucia sounded even crankier than usual.

"Even if he's actually five or even ten years old, he's at a developmental stage matching a year and a half old child," I shot back. "We can't just shove him through a slip and hope for the best."

"Nobody is suggesting that," Malcolm said, glaring at Lucia and daring her to make him a liar. "But I agree, and I think Helena does as well, that we can't afford to risk whatever danger he poses."

"I did think, what if he's a prince or something," I admitted. "Somebody the elves will want back, anyway. We need to be careful. But this latest prophecy suggests that his parents fought constantly, and combined with his mother's last words, I think we might actually have saved his life. If his mother was fleeing danger at his father's hands, I mean."

"We're not in the business of protecting elves, Davies," Lucia said. "They can take care of themselves—fine, yes, I know we're talking about a child here, but as it happens, I was referring to the adults who got him into this situation. I don't know that we're obligated to remedy the problem."

"I can try to find out our best course of action." I settled Connvuir more comfortably on my lap.

"Wait a minute before you go charging off to prophesy," Lucia said. "This can't be allowed to take precedence over the bigger picture. We are still in the position of gathering information about the elves. It's past time we stopped reacting to their incursions."

I glanced at Malcolm. "I thought, after the destruction at Callann, the elves hadn't made any other big attacks."

"They continue to probe our defenses," Malcolm said. "Lucia is right that it's bad strategy to be constantly on the defensive."

"And I'm not yet ready to call on the oracle for specific guidance, so don't complain that I don't keep you in the loop." Lucia rubbed the heels of her palms against her eyes and groaned. "Fine. Let's at least see if we can resolve this new problem."

I closed my eyes and sorted through possible questions before settling on *How do we restore Connvuir to his people?*

The rush of prophecy was faster this time, like a raging whitewater river moving too fast for me to make sense of what I saw. I glimpsed a memory, a tiny clearing in a forest carpeted with new grass. It was a slip

I'd visited in person, the one where Night-Noon had escaped from Faerie. By the time I processed that, more images had flashed past faster than I could comprehend. Another coherent image, this of the gate to Faerie the Savants had built, matte-silver and twinkling with Christmas lights.

That one, I held onto, though it quivered like it wanted to escape. A silver blade cut through the image at the center of the gate, as if it was theater backdrop, and a figure lunged through. I screamed at the sight of the terrible dark-haired elf, his face hauntingly white, his body corded with muscle, and wrenched myself out of vision.

I came to myself with Malcolm's arms around me and the little boy, who cried fearfully. "Sorry," I gasped. "Did I scream? Or was that the vision?"

"It was most certainly not the vision," Malcolm said. "What happened?"

I didn't answer at first. My heart pounded painfully, and my breathing was ragged. "It was him," I finally said. "The elf we saw in Seattle. The one Jenny calls the scary elf. I don't know if I wish we had a name for him or not. He's a danger to Connvuir somehow. But the important part is that you're right, and we have to figure out a way to send him back into Faerie. I couldn't see anything more specific than that the slips are important."

Now that the terror had passed, I could remember the images that had passed too fleetly for comprehension at the time. Slips, lots of slips, more than just the few I had personal knowledge of. "That's as much as I got. The vision didn't say how to do it, just that he needs to return. Shh, shh, I'm sorry." I cuddled Connvuir close and rocked him as his sobs abated.

"We'll figure it out," Lucia said. "I'll take him back to the node."

I held the little boy closer as if Lucia had threatened to remove him from me bodily. "I think he needs to stay here. If I have more prophecies about him—"

"And if your scary elf comes here looking for him?" Lucia said.

"He can't get in here any more than he can reach the Gunther Node. If I have prophecies clarifying the boy's situation, it will be more efficient if I can act on them immediately." That sounded reasonable, though in my heart I knew my decision had nothing to do with logic.

Lucia looked at Malcolm. "And you're on board with this?"

"Helena feels certain about this course of action, and I support her." Malcolm rested a hand on my shoulder.

"Of course you do." Lucia scowled. "Give me the stone, or whatever it is. I can at least get someone to analyze it and see what kind of a threat it poses—it and others like it. Gives me the illusion that I'm in charge around here."

I didn't feel the need to respond to that.

Malcolm handed Lucia the carved stone sphere. She tossed it once in the air and caught it like it was an ordinary rock. "I want to know the instant you see anything else, Davies. Don't go thinking you're the only one who can handle this, right?"

"I'm not stupid, Lucia. It's not like I want to adopt Connvuir. I want him returned to his people." Though at the moment, that seemed like a bad idea, if Connvuir's "people" consisted of a father who might be dangerous to him. I was already resolved not to hand him over to random elves who might not care about him as a person.

"That goes for you as well," Malcolm said. "Campbell Security is ready to take action against the elves. We just need to know what that action should be."

"Of course." Lucia looked very tired all of a sudden. "My informants are having trouble penetrating Faerie. It's not that we don't have access to slips—our tracking combined with the information the adepts give us means we have a thorough map of all the naturally occurring ones, and Rick Jeong's 'slip key' device for opening new ones means we can go through in places the elves won't suspect. The problem is that the elves have some way of identifying our presence in their world the way we do with them in our world. My people get in, but they don't get far before they're tagged and have to return. That's if they aren't killed."

"I didn't know Wardens were being killed by elves," I said.

"It's been less than a week since we started pushing. This is all still new territory." Lucia gently took Connvuir's chin in her hand and tilted his head so she could meet his gaze. Connvuir stared back at her silently. "Does he speak?"

"He hasn't yet. He might not be old enough. I don't know if he acquired English from me the way his mother did Malcolm, there at the end."

Lucia grunted and released the child. "Don't bitch at me when he keeps you up all night. Remember I offered to take him off your hands. Campbell, I'll call you tomorrow morning. I want to borrow some of Campbell Security's analysts. We need to crack this problem."

I followed Lucia to the front door. Two of the Gunther Node's signature little white vans huddled under the carport against the drizzling rain that had started to fall. I hoped that meant someone had removed the body. I wasn't afraid of death or reminders of death, but the dead elf felt like a weight on my soul and I wanted my house back.

"You should maybe look into why you're so committed to keeping him with you, Davies," Lucia said abruptly. Beyond her, headlights flashed, and Connvuir turned his head away from the brightness. "If he's influencing you somehow, that might not be safe."

"I don't feel influenced. All my reasons are, um, reasonable." It wasn't the whole truth, and I could see why Lucia doubted me. I *had* been awfully quick to step up to care for the child. But I felt, deep in my heart, that taking care of Connvuir was the right thing to do.

"Be sure of that," Lucia said, and climbed into the passenger seat of the nearer van. The other had already reversed down our long driveway. I watched Lucia until her van, too, was gone.

"It's too late to call Gabriel, but we really ought to. In the morning," Malcolm said. "If elf children require special care, he will know."

"I agree." My eyes still focused on the spot where Lucia had been. She'd been watching Connvuir, not me, I was convinced, and her regard made me unexpectedly nervous and inclined to question my own motives. "Is it just me, or was she testier than usual?"

"It's not just you," Malcolm said. "She didn't tell you about Rebecca Greenough?"

"What about her?" I remembered Rebecca Greenough all too well. She was custodian of the biggest node in London, and back when the oracular bookstore Abernathy's still existed, she'd tried to convince the Board of Neutralities to move it back to its original home in Charing Cross Road. Part of that had involved slandering me personally. I hadn't thought of her in years, but the mention of her name brought it all back.

"Since the dissolution of the Board, there's been a lot of conflict over who should lead the Wardens worldwide. With the threat of the elves, there's no question we need to be united. Lucia is the obvious choice, but Greenough has pushed back against her. She thinks she's a better choice because London is more central."

"That's stupid. It's a globe. There is no central point."

"A fact many Wardens have pointed out. But Greenough has just enough power that Lucia has had to divert some of her attention to the challenge she poses. Attention that can't really be spared." Malcolm touched Connvuir's head lightly. "And this little guy represents yet another problem that Lucia will ultimately be responsible for solving, if it turns out he's someone important."

"Then I'm glad I insisted on keeping him here," I said. "That should ease Lucia's burden a bit. Stupid Rebecca Greenough. You know she only wants to lead to gain personal power."

"I wish more of the Wardens who follow her realized that," Malcolm said.

We walked upstairs, Malcolm turning off the lights as he went, and I settled Connvuir on his makeshift bed again. He gazed up at me for a few seconds, so alert I was sure he understood at least some of what was going on, then rolled to his side and closed his eyes. I stood watching him for a moment, remembering the visions I'd had. His mother, and father, and the scary elf, and all those slips. It felt like less than nothing to build a plan on.

Malcolm drew me into his embrace. "Promise me you're not acting on impulse."

"What? No, of course not. Well, maybe a little, if by 'impulse' you mean the direction of the oracle. Instinct might be a better word. It makes more logical sense to send Connvuir to the Gunther Node, but I'm certain this is the right path." Saying that sent another pang through me, and I suppressed it. I shouldn't get attached to the child.

"You know I'll stand by you, whatever you decide. But I am concerned about our family becoming personally entangled in whatever elf business this little boy represents." Malcolm's warm breath brushed my forehead.

"That worries me too. If I wasn't completely convinced there's no way an elf can access the slip that woman used, I would send us all to ground in the Gunther Node until we were sure this place is safe. But I'm certain that stone represents the only access Faerie has to this location, and I'm equally certain that path is closed for good." I sighed. "This is, sadly, the best outcome. Imagine if someone intent on killing us had used the stone, instead of a dying woman."

"That occurred to me as well." Malcolm nudged me in the direction of the bed. "You should sleep. I'm going to have a talk with Alastair."

"Is he still awake?" I felt silly the moment those words passed my lips. "Of course he's still awake. I hope you can convince him he doesn't have to save the world."

"His instincts are sound. I think he wants to act because this situation, elves threatening our world, frightens him, and he deals with fear by fighting. He'll learn other ways of coping eventually." Malcolm kissed me. "I love you. Thank you for trusting me."

"Always."

I curled up in bed and turned off the lights, leaving only the small night light burning around the corner in the dressing room in case Jenny had a frightening vision during the night. I felt so conscious of the elf child sleeping nearby I was sure I wouldn't sleep, but in no time, the weariness of all the excitement combined with my body's exhaustion won out, and I slept before Malcolm returned to bed.

# CHAPTER FOUR

"He doesn't look like an elf baby," Duncan said at breakfast the next morning. He sat staring at Connvuir, who currently occupied Jenny's high chair. Fortunately, she'd mostly outgrown needing it—more of that wanting to stay the baby, I guessed. She hadn't pitched a fit when I plopped her on the bench beside Alastair.

"His eyes are strange," Jenny said. "They look like doll eyes. Big and blue." She put a chunk of banana I'd cut up for her on the high chair tray. Connvuir prodded it with his finger, knocking it off the tray to the floor, where Night-Noon gobbled it up. Jenny giggled and put another banana piece on the tray. This time, Connvuir carefully scooped it up and took a small, dainty bite I wouldn't have thought a baby capable of. Seconds later he crammed the rest into his mouth and chewed enthusiastically, smearing mushed banana over his lips. That was more like it.

"Why doesn't he look like an elf, though? They all look scary and white and stuff." Duncan offered Connvuir another chunk of banana.

"I don't know, sweetie. There's a lot we don't know about elves. Now, everyone keep an eye on our guest while I talk to Mr. Roarke, all right?" The phone had already rung several times, but I was used to Gabriel not answering immediately. His wife, Cassie, had told me he often put his phone down absentmindedly and then had to search for it when it rang.

"Shouldn't he talk? He looks old enough to talk." Alastair's bowl of cereal lay untouched before him.

I suppressed impatience. I was tired of answering all their questions with "I don't know." "Babies start talking at different ages. Maybe he doesn't understand our language. Or maybe we're all talking enough to satisfy him—oh, hi, Gabriel." I waved at the kids to keep Connvuir entertained and walked away from the dining table. "I have kind of an unusual request."

"Not to be snarky, but your requests are rarely usual." Gabriel chuckled. "All right, stump me."

"I had an elf child land in my lap last night, and I have many, many questions about caring for him. I don't even know how old he really is."

Gabriel said nothing. I waited. Finally, he said, "Sun and Moon. *You* have questions? How on earth did an elf child—Helena, this is impossible!"

"It's only mostly impossible. Malcolm went to the Gunther Node early this morning to see if we can figure out the rest." I filled him in on the details while keeping an eye on the children. They were fully engaged in offering different foods to Connvuir and seeing what he'd accept. "I've been treating him like a human child because I don't know what else to do, but there have to be differences. Are elves allergic to any foods? Can he have milk? Apple juice?"

"I'd say there aren't many differences as far as digestion goes, but a thousand years of corruption must have had some effect. Unfortunately, I'm not in a position to know what those differences are." Gabriel paused. "You say he looks to be about eighteen months old? That probably means he's not quite three. Elves do mature more slowly than humans, but not as slowly as you'd imagine. Babies are weaned at age two, we enter adolescence by the time we are sixteen, and we're adults at age twenty-seven."

"He's not potty-trained yet, either. And he doesn't speak."

"That's unusual. A three-year-old elf ought to be verbal. Maybe he's in shock from everything that happened."

I poured a cup of milk for Connvuir and helped him hold it. He drank without spilling. "I thought maybe he didn't understand us, but wouldn't he have absorbed English through his skin?"

"He's too little for that. That's an ability we develop during adolescence. Just a minute." Gabriel's voice became too muffled to understand for a moment. "Sorry. You don't know anything about his parents? His name?"

"All I know is that his name is Connvuir. My visions didn't tell me a family name—oh, unless that is a family name?"

"No, it's what we call a birth-name or milk-name. It means 'little rabbit.' Birth-names tend to be simple and sweet, nothing that would impress a personality on a baby. Elves know names have power, so we are careful in what we call ourselves and each other. My birth-name, Shantein, means 'fox.' I had a full head of red hair when I was born."

"That's so interesting." It had never occurred to me I would ever be in a position to care about elf culture, given that so many of them were only interested in killing me. "So, birth-name, and what else?"

"Parents choose the birth-name. We choose our use-name at adulthood. Then we have our clan names as surnames. So my full name is Leichtir'Shantein Mevair. But I also have a private name I share only with my wife and close relatives or friends." Gabriel laughed again. "Quite the mouthful, I know. Your little fellow isn't so complicated."

"Except that he belongs to a clan who might want him back. I wonder why my vision didn't reveal that name?"

"It wouldn't help, unless the Wardens have discovered who the clans involved in the invasion are."

"True." The meal at the table had devolved into a mess, which meant nobody was eating anymore. "Thanks, Gabriel. I'll keep you informed as things go."

"Thank you. I was going to ask that very thing. I know I am well and truly separated from the clan of my youth, but I still care about my people and I'd like to know about the fate of such an unexpected gift."

"You think of Connvuir as a gift?" I ran a washcloth under the faucet, wrung it out, and washed the elf child's messy face and hands.

"I realize it's probably hopelessly optimistic, but suppose he is a bridge between our people? If his clan sees that humans cared for him instead of hurting him, they might question whether all humans deserve death."

"That is pretty optimistic. Everything I've seen says Connvuir's father and mother fought and argued viciously. And that terrible elf we keep seeing is also a danger to him. But I would like you to be right."

"Stay safe, Helena."

I hung up and stuffed my phone in my back pocket. "All right, let's clean up, and I'm going to pretend you all didn't behave like savages over breakfast. Having a guest is no reason to ignore basic good manners."

"We were showing Connvuir how to use a spoon," Duncan protested.

"He is perfectly capable of using a spoon, as I saw, but I appreciate your concern. Now, you boys get dressed for school while I figure out a wardrobe for our small friend. No groaning! He'll be here when school is out." Fridays were late start days for Monument School, the boys' new elementary school, but I maintained our usual schedule for breakfast rather than change things dramatically just one day out of the week.

I set Connvuir on Jenny's bed while I went through her drawers, searching for clothes that could be adjusted to fit a male child two-thirds her size. Fleece pants, sweaters, socks—Connvuir's feet were too small for Jenny's shoes, so I'd have to carry him if we went anywhere, but the rest, we could manage.

Connvuir didn't try to dress himself, but he also didn't fight me, so I called it a win. "There. Warm feet," I told him as I put socks on him. "I hope you're more comfortable."

Connvuir stared at me silently with those big blue eyes. His mouth moved like he was about to speak. Then he held out his arms to me to be held. Automatically, I picked him up and was about to carry him out of Jenny's room when he put his arms around my neck and rested his head on my shoulder.

I froze. It was a gesture I remembered each of my children making at that age, that trusting desire for closeness and security. Instinctively, I cuddled Connvuir close and stroked his silky hair. "You lost your mom," I whispered, "but now you have me."

I'd spoken almost without thinking, and the words replayed themselves in my head like a chastisement. Connvuir wasn't my child. He wasn't even human. Sure, I could take care of him, because I'd promised I would. But getting attached wasn't just a bad idea, it was actively irresponsible. I had my own children's welfare to think of, and Connvuir might be a danger to all of us, if only because of the adult elves who might want him back. Even so, cuddling this sweet, innocent boy took me back to when my children were babies. I couldn't care for him without developing some level of affection. I ignored the little voice that said I was rationalizing again.

I took Connvuir to the bathroom and encouraged him to go, but he just looked at the toilet like it was alien furniture. I hadn't thought to ask Gabriel about elven toilet etiquette. Time for a trip to the store.

My phone rang when I was helping Jenny with her shoes. "Everything all right?" Malcolm asked.

"Fine. We're about to leave for school, and then I'm going to pick up some things for Connvuir. Do you have any news?"

"Rick identified the stone as corundum, of which ruby is a variant. He's doing something he hopes will locate other, similar stones—something well beyond my comprehension, naturally. He was more concerned about the dangers it poses than any of us were, which is unnerving."

"No kidding." Rick Jeong was the most laid-back man I knew, so when he got worried, I got worried. "Did he have any ideas about how to get Connvuir returned to Faerie?"

"Not yet. The problem with the stone took precedence. We should be prepared to host our guest for a few days, at least."

Jenny brought me her coat, and I held it while she put it on. "It's not a hardship. He's very well-behaved. But this afternoon, I'll prophesy again."

"I was going to suggest it. Thank you for taking this on. I will be home by lunchtime."

"I look forward to it. I love you."

When I hung up, I realized Connvuir was staring at my phone. On a whim, I offered it to him. He held it gingerly, then raised it to his face. I was about to snatch it away so he wouldn't chew on it when he sniffed it, made a face, and sneezed. "I guess plastic has a smell you wouldn't be familiar with," I said with a laugh, and took the phone away. "Or maybe elves make something similar to plastic. I'm sorry I know almost nothing about your people. Come on, let's get in the car."

With some juggling, I managed car seats for all those who needed them, and we were out the door very nearly on time. I listened as the children talked at Connvuir—it really did feel as if they were battering at him with their interest, but not in a bad way, just a potentially overwhelming one. Connvuir continued to be completely silent, though I caught a glimpse of him now and then in the rear view mirror, and he smiled sometimes at things the children did. His smile relieved my mind. The idea that he'd been traumatized by the events that had brought him to us had taken hold of me, worrying me more because there was nothing I could do about it except provide him with security and comfort. I hoped, if he could still smile, it meant he wasn't permanently damaged.

It was a rare dry day in February, and I dropped the boys off in the designated zone and waited to be waved through to the exit. Monument School was enough different from their old school, Talbott Academy, that I never felt maudlin about missing the place. In fact, I'd decided to look at the change positively; this gave Alastair a chance to leave behind his reputation as a fighter and troublemaker. This kept me from dwelling on how the boys no longer had Wardens for teachers, something that had been a real blessing in the past. They would just have to adapt.

We stopped at a local shopping center for a few necessities, including a box of disposable training pants and a pair of sneakers in Connvuir's size, and made it home without incident or potty accident. Once I had Connvuir's needs met, I set him down in front of the television with Jenny for half an hour of cartoons and quickly cleaned the kitchen. When I came back to the great room, Connvuir and Jenny were rapt in contemplation of an episode of *Bluey* and paid me no attention. I sank onto a nearby chair and idly filled myself with a desire to know more about Connvuir.

The prophesy whirled me away into a series of images that at first made no sense. After a second or two, I realized I was again seeing faces, this time many different elf faces. I caught a glimpse of Connvuir's mother here and there, and his father, and shied away from the scary elf when he appeared. A family, maybe? If the scary elf was related to Connvuir, no wonder the boy was in danger.

This was one of those visions that felt as if an outside force was trying to communicate. After a short time, it seemed that force believed I'd seen enough, and the images changed. Instead of faces, I now saw locations, fields and mountains and forests, all of them subtly wrong. Faerie. I had no idea what it all meant, couldn't even tell if I was seeing the cuivuirskeen, the places in Faerie where slips opened. My best guess was that this was, again, a message about returning Connvuir to Faerie, but it still told me nothing useful.

As if my frustration had communicated itself to my oracular gift, the vision faded, and I was staring at the television screen again. So, Connvuir had a family, an extended family, and he needed to go back— but that didn't fit with my earlier prophecies about the danger Connvuir's family posed. Or was it just his father that was the danger, and there were other family members he could be restored to? I didn't want to consider the possibility that I didn't want Connvuir to go back to Faerie, and I was subconsciously sabotaging myself. I wasn't so attached as to be irrational.

I massaged my temples as Jenny said, "One more, Mommy?"

"One more for you. I think Connvuir needs a nap." The elf child was leaning back against the couch cushions, his eyelids drooping. I picked him up and settled him on my hip. "I'll be back."

I took the little boy upstairs and settled him in his makeshift bed. I could have bought him a portacrib, but I'd shied away at the last moment, and I wasn't sure why. Possibly that was too permanent an action? Connvuir wouldn't be with us forever.

Connvuir settled in to sleep with the boneless, heavy look I remembered all my children having at that age, that look of total relaxation. He still hadn't made a fuss about missing his mother, and while that was a relief in one sense, in another it was disturbing. What if I wasn't the only one becoming attached?

I told myself to stop borrowing trouble and returned downstairs just as the back door opened and shut and Malcolm entered. I hugged him briefly. "I'm trying not to worry, but my visions aren't helping and I feel increasingly like they should."

"Meaning, you don't know how to return the boy?" Malcolm hugged me back. "Don't take on the whole world's burdens, love. We have everyone at the Gunther Node working on the problem as well."

"I know, I just thought I'd get there first."

Malcolm chuckled. "That's very like you. Think instead that you're caring for Connvuir until he can go home—that's more than enough support."

"That's true."

A cry from upstairs startled both of us. It didn't sound like a terrified or pained cry, but I hurried up the stairs anyway. Connvuir was sitting up in his bed, his eyes red with tears. When he saw me, he wiped his eyes and held out his arms to be picked up, all in silence.

I remembered all the times my own children had reached out for comfort, and my heart ached again. "All right, it's okay," I murmured, picking the little boy up. "You're safe here. Did you have a bad dream?"

Connvuir laid his head on my shoulder and sighed. His soft, silky blond hair was matted on one side where he'd lain on it. I finger-combed the tangles. "I wish you could talk."

"The elves took his voice," Jenny said from the doorway. "They scared it away."

I turned, startled again. "Jenny! Did you see something?"

Jenny nodded. "He was afraid, but I am not afraid. There's a fence. His mommy ran with him away from the bad elf."

I exchanged glances with Malcolm, who stood behind Jenny. A fence meant Jenny had successfully distanced herself from Connvuir's emotional reaction, but I still felt sick. I hated it when Jenny saw that monster in vision. "Did the bad elf scare you?"

"No. He didn't chase me, only Connvuir. I think he is the daddy, but daddies don't chase their babies, right?"

That was different. "Not usually, no. Did the bad elf have dark hair?"

"Nope, nope," Jenny said firmly. "That is the scary elf. I didn't see him."

I wished there weren't so many elves intent on harming humanity.

Jenny's vocabulary at three years old wasn't up to distinguishing easily between them. "Okay. So Connvuir's father chased him and his mother?"

Jenny nodded again. "And Connvuir's voice got lost when they went through the line in the air."

"I see." I didn't, really, but Jenny wasn't likely to know the answers to all the many questions I had. "Did you see anything else? Maybe how Connvuir can go back to Faerie?"

"No. I think his daddy wants to hurt him." Jenny's lips trembled. "Daddies shouldn't hurt their little boys."

Malcolm scooped Jenny up and hugged her. "That's right. And we will make sure Connvuir stays safe, right?"

Jenny buried her face in her father's shoulder and nodded vigorously. I controlled the usual surge of anger I felt when Jenny witnessed something too awful for a three-year-old to see. "Let's go have a snack," I suggested, hoping to distract her.

But as Malcolm got out cookies and milk, I was the one distracted. My earlier assertion that Connvuir was as safe here as at the Gunther Node now felt like it verged on arrogance. Yes, I was confident in our protections, but how safe were we, really? If elves really had taken Connvuir's voice, and that wasn't just Jenny's interpretation of normal trauma, that was an ability they hadn't demonstrated before. We might be facing things we didn't know to expect—which meant being more on the watch than ever.

# CHAPTER FIVE

"I'd be worried if I were you," Judy said between bites of spaghetti and meatballs. "If this little boy is a missing prince, the elves are going to be out in force looking for him."

It was girls' night out, and we were at Giuseppe's, my choice that evening. Nothing bad had happened in the six days since Connvuir's mother had appeared in our backyard, but I hadn't stopped feeling tense about it. "I know that. We're as protected as we can be."

"You're protected at your house, but you can't hole up there forever." Judy pointed her fork in my direction. "What about when you're at the store, or on the way to school?"

"Are you trying to make me more worried than I already am?"

"It's not about being worried, it's about being prepared. You need to have a plan for all the possibilities."

"You can't plan for *every* possibility, Judy," Viv said. "Some things just happen."

"You can be mentally prepared. Envision scenarios, that sort of thing."

"It's fine," I said. "And I have thought things through. But I can't stay alert forever. That's how you lose your edge, Malcolm says." I speared a bite of lasagna and ate it like it was my worst enemy.

"Malcolm's right," Viv said. "Try to relax. While staying alert."

I laughed. "Okay, that helped."

"I'm sorry, I'm not trying to stress you out," Judy said. "I'm worried. You'd think someone would know *something* by now."

"I've given up on prophesying about Connvuir because the answers are all the same generic view of Faerie, which means I'm not asking the right questions. I've decided to let things go for now, give my subconscious time to think about it." I didn't say I suspected I wasn't asking the right questions because I was afraid of the answers.

"What about the Wardens, though? Shouldn't they have figured things out?" Judy leaned forward, intent on Viv. "The glass magi at least."

"We can see into Faerie, but it's a big place and we don't know what we're looking for. Not to mention Noden's Scope is limited in range and duration." Viv scowled. "And even when we do see something interesting, like a war group mobilizing, we can't watch them for long enough to know where they're going unless we get lucky and see them right before they enter our world. Finding Connvuir's family is impossible."

"What about the other thing, the elf incursions?" I asked.

"That, I'm not sure about. I'm not on a hunting team. But I know Lucia has our forces gathering information so we'll have more warning about elves entering our world, with the goal of learning where in Faerie *we* can strike to stop them." Viv looked uncharacteristically serious. "And I think she has someone working on the possibility of detaching Faerie from our world entirely."

"Can that be done?" Judy asked. "It's an entire, what, reality? Dimension?"

"Nobody knows," Viv said. "The only person who even tried to shift realities was Darius Wallach, and the attempt killed him. But he succeeded well enough to prove the theory wasn't totally wackadoodle. Between us, I think the fact that Lucia is even considering it means things are more desperate than it sounds."

I shivered at the thought. "But we're holding our own. No elves have gotten in to destroy anything, the way they did the village of Callann."

"That's true, but it's not enough. I mean, it's not enough to build a victory on." Viv returned to eating fettucine. "This is war, and it's not the sort of war where a partial win will be enough. The elves won't stop until we're eradicated."

"Are we sure of that?" I said. "How much do we know about their intent? I've been assuming that's true, that they want us destroyed—I'm asking if Lucia has learned more to prove it."

"Still above my pay grade." Viv shrugged. "I think we have to act as if it's true, because the alternative is death."

Judy groaned. "I feel like this conversation is my fault. Can we talk about something else? How are the boys doing at their new school?"

"They're doing all right. Duncan has already made a lot of new friends. Alastair is struggling. He lost both his closest friends when we moved, and he isn't the type to enjoy casual relationships." I made sure he had play dates with his friend Kenny, but that wasn't the same as Alastair seeing him every day. "Their teachers are very good, though, and I feel confident that they're committed to helping the boys adapt."

"But no Wardens for teachers," Judy said.

"No. We couldn't justify manipulating the school staff to that extent. I think Lucia is looking into a long-term solution. But Duncan is more comfortable with spontaneous prophecies than he used to be, and Alastair is determined to build a better reputation than he had at Talbott."

"I hope so. It's hard to have a reputation as a troublemaker," Viv said. "I know all my elementary school teachers had conversations about me, every time I moved up a grade. Warning each other about my 'little problem with authority.' It's not my fault most of them were humorless and unappreciative of sideways thinking."

"Viv, you painted your name on the walls of three separate classrooms."

"It was an experiment in color theory. They should have been impressed." Viv tossed her magenta-dyed hair flip airily.

"You haven't changed much since then, have you?" Judy teased. "Since I know your vast collection of glitter gel pens is so you can write your name inside everything you own."

"You say that like it's a bad thing."

I ate a final bite of lasagna and washed it down with water. One beer wouldn't be enough to incapacitate me, but I superstitiously didn't want even the smallest possibility of inebriation, not while things were so uncertain. So I was sticking with water tonight. "How about we go back to my house for dessert? I made Chocopocalypse cake yesterday and it's just sitting there uneaten."

"I approve of this plan," Viv said.

Judy had driven all of us to the restaurant from my house so we could have more time to talk, so we piled into her CR-V and waited for it to warm up a bit. Viv, who always claimed she was part lizard, punched the button to turn the passenger seat warmer to max. "I swear I'm moving to Phoenix."

"You are not. Who would you go places with?" I said.

"And don't say we'd all move with you. I like the cold," Judy said.

"You're crazy. Both of you are crazy." Viv huddled deeper into her overstuffed parka. "I wish Clarence had heated seats." Clarence was her battered old Lexus GX.

"Why did you choose that name, anyway?" Judy asked.

"You know, Clarence. From *It's a Wonderful Life*. My guardian angel. Helena's not the only one allowed to make ancient movie references."

"I'm so proud," I said.

Judy put the car in gear. "We really should do a retro movie night soon. And by 'retro' I mean 'something from before 2010,' not black and white."

"You need to be less resistant to the power of the classics," I said. "*Casablanca. The Philadelphia Story. Bringing Up Baby.*"

"I'm not saying they're not great, I'm saying they'd be better with one hundred percent more car chases."

I laughed and leaned back in the rear seat, watching the night streets slip by. Judy bypassed the road to my house—no, that was the way to my old house, my destroyed house, and I felt the tiniest pang of sorrow. Not enough to qualify as regret, which I had told myself I was done having about what I'd lost, but the kind of feeling you get when something is over and you know you no longer have a reason to take that route.

Instead I made myself look forward to making this new path the familiar one.

I listened to Judy and Viv talking about some new designer I'd never heard of. I didn't have anything to contribute to that conversation, but I liked their enthusiasm, and I was always interested in learning something new, even if it wasn't about anything I cared about. Now we were on the Banfield, where traffic was unusually light, and I made a game of identifying car makes and models. I was terrible at it, but it was something Jenny loved.

"Helena?" Viv said.

"Huh? Sorry, I was distracted. Did you say something?"

"I asked how Jenny is doing. Is she affected by the elf baby at all?"

"Oh." I sat up straighter. "He's pretty calm, surprisingly, and she hasn't had any emotional episodes that weren't about prophecies. Dr. Deveaux says it's too early to declare victory, but Jenny is doing well deflecting other people's emotions."

"Maybe—sorry. I was about to say 'maybe she'll grow up normal,' but that's not what I meant. I've been talking to the adepts who are learning glass magic, and they're all extremely pessimistic about the chances of an empath staying sane. But I don't think any of them are aware of Jenny's special circumstances."

"An oracle with an elf genetic heritage for empathy," Judy said. She changed lanes for the exit ramp. "She's unprecedented."

"Where are you going?" I asked. This wasn't my usual route.

"I'm following the GPS. It's good at routing me around traffic congestion."

"You'd follow that thing off a cliff if it told you to," Viv said.

"Which it never would. I'm telling you, you need to get on board with twenty-first century technology."

"I like picking a route and sticking with it," I said. "Then I can find my way if something happens to the onboard computer."

"That's how the assassins get you," Judy said. "Predictability."

"There aren't—" I paused. "I would like to tell you assassins are impossible, but then I remembered the world I live in."

"That's right," Judy said. "You need to think like a rogue."

"Helena is still not great about RPG classes," Viv said. "She's only good at thinking like a paladin."

"I *am* good at roleplaying game terminology! I could follow that discussion Jeremiah and Mike had the other night at the Kellers' house. All that stuff about quests." I didn't say it was because I'd asked Duncan to explain it later.

"It's fine, Helena, nobody expects you to like everything." Viv turned around to look at me. "Though I really think you could use a hobby. Something to relax with that isn't movies or martial arts."

"You think so? It never occurred to me. Like what?"

Judy muttered something under her breath and made another turn. We'd entered the overgrown, forested area surrounding my house, and the road seemed darker than usual. "Is something wrong?" I asked.

"Just all this construction. It's taking me miles out of my way."

A chill washed over me. I looked past her through the windshield. There was nothing but forested road—road I was sure I'd never seen before. "Judy. I don't see any construction."

Judy glanced at me, her face horrified. She stomped on the brake, bringing us to an abrupt, jolting halt. "No construction?"

"We have to get out of here, now," Viv said.

"I don't know where to go! It all looks like blocked-off roads to me!"

I unfastened my seatbelt. "Let me drive."

Something moved in the glow of the headlights, tall and thin and white. I sucked in a breath. "Elves. Drive, now!"

Judy swore and put the car in gear, stomping on the gas. The CR-V lurched forward. "I don't see elves!"

"There's one right ahead of you!" Viv exclaimed. She'd dug her illusion-piercing glasses out of her bag and held them to her face. "Go, go, don't stop!"

Judy accelerated. The elf in front of the car vanished with an effect like someone jerked off stage in an old vaudeville act. More elves converged on the car from all sides. "Did I hit it?"

Viv abruptly pressed the glasses to Judy's eyes. "I should have thought of this before—keep driving!"

Judy cranked the wheel to the right. The car veered sideways and took the next curve at high speed. Overgrown bushes scraped against its sides, sending up a *skree* of tortured metal. Judy didn't slow. The new road curved back and forth like a snake, but she rode the center line, completely unconcerned about other traffic. It occurred to me that we hadn't seen any other cars for a while now, and I was certain we weren't anywhere near my home. This felt like wilderness, untamed and terrifying.

Something struck the roof of the car, and we all shrieked as long white fingers inched across the windshield. An elf crawled impossibly down the screen, clinging I didn't know how. Judy viciously jerked the wheel back and forth, but she didn't dislodge the elf. He stared at us with enormous black-ringed eyes, the irises so pale they were almost white. Then he drew back a fist and smashed the windshield.

Judy braked hard, ducking her head. Viv and I shrieked and covered our faces against the million tiny cubes of safety glass showering us. When I dared look again, the elf was ten feet away, picking himself up off the ground where our momentum had flung him. Judy put the car in reverse and sped backward. She hit something hard that jolted all of us, a tree or something, but she'd already revved up and gunned the engine, hurtling forward directly at the elf.

Again, the elf vanished. Judy spun the wheel. "I don't see the road!"

"I dropped the glasses," Viv said.

"It's ahead and to your left—just go!" I shouted.

Judy stomped on the gas again. The car again lurched into motion, but this time its movement wasn't smooth. "Something happened to the rear tires. The axle, maybe. I don't know how much farther we can go."

"Worry about that later," Viv said. She rose with the glasses in her hand and once more held them to Judy's face. "I don't see any more elves—"

They came at us from both sides like white, emaciated spirits, arms outstretched as if they were zombies, the fast kind that scared me most in horror movies. I screamed again as one grabbed hold of the door handle on my side and tried to work it. Judy pressed on the gas, and the car sped forward, not as fast as before, but still leaving most of the elves behind.

All except one. The female elf's long black hair streamed in the wind as she was dragged along with us, clinging to the door handle. "Judy!" I shouted.

Judy swerved as if she was in an action movie and scraped along the row of trees and bushes on the driver's side. Amazingly, this didn't knock the elf woman off. She dragged herself up so she was eye to eye with me. I couldn't look away from the terrible depth of her eyes.

A peculiar weariness came over me, the kind of tiredness that comes from a day of hard labor and is impossible to fight. Distantly, I realized Viv and Judy had gone silent, and the car was slowing, but I was too exhausted to remember if this was strange or not. My head sagged against the cold glass, and everything went dark.

# CHAPTER SIX

The smell was the first thing that struck me when I swam back into consciousness. Not a terrible smell, but not a pleasant one —musty and faintly bitter, like old smoke mixed with sandalwood. It wasn't a strong scent, but it was nothing like the cold, wet, green smell of the Pacific Northwest. I inhaled, sneezed, and opened my eyes on darkness. My whole body ached with exhaustion, enough that when I tried to sit up, my arms and legs merely quivered. Whatever I was lying on was padded lightly, so I wasn't uncomfortable, but not being able to move made my heart rate speed up.

I made myself lie still and focused on what my other senses told me. The complete darkness suggested I was indoors, that and how I didn't hear anything like the wind or insects or passing traffic. The smell had already faded to insignificance in air that was close and still, no drafts, just a chilly pressure against my face and hands. I wriggled my fingers and felt smooth, velvety cloth covering the cushion beneath me. My mouth tasted like metal, and I ran my tongue around the inside of my cheeks to moisten them. I heard no other movement. Wherever this was, I wasn't in immediate danger.

That knowledge started another train of thought, one I shied away from contemplating. But avoiding it made no sense. The elves had captured me and taken me somewhere, and I couldn't imagine their ultimate purpose was a good one. Either I'd been kidnapped because I was an oracle, or someone knew I had Connvuir and wanted him back, and neither of those options thrilled me.

Someone coughed nearby. "Who's there?" I said, my heart accelerating again.

"Helena?" It was Judy. "Where is this place?"

On my other side, Viv said, "So they took all of us. Does anyone remember anything?"

"No," I said, "but we have to assume the worst. I think we're in Faerie."

"The worst would be that the elves have enough presence in our world to have a secret stronghold there," Judy said. "Faerie is kind of a relief, in that sense."

"I feel like I've been kneaded like dough and rolled out flat," Viv moaned. "I can barely move. Do you suppose they paralyzed us?"

I shifted my weight, and this time, my arms moved freely, though I didn't think I could lift anything heavier than a pillow. "I think they put us to sleep. Gabriel Roarke said some elves have that ability. They put us to sleep, and brought us through a slip into Faerie. But we didn't leave Portland, I'm sure of it, no matter what illusions they put on the road, so how did they manage that? No slips in the city."

"The same way Connvuir's mother did?" Viv suggested. "Another stone like the one she had?"

"Let's not worry about it," Judy said. "If that was how they did it, we can't go back that way, right?"

"Any slip they made with a stone would seal over too thickly to break through again," I confirmed.

"So for our purposes, it doesn't matter." Judy's voice strained like she was exerting herself. "We have to get out of here and find our own way back."

I didn't want to dwell on that. I didn't think any of us had the kind of magic that could open a slip, even if the oracle guided us to one we could use safely. I got my arms beneath me and pushed myself up. The velvet slid beneath my palms, but I managed to sit. "Let's start with getting out of here."

Viv groaned again, but now her voice was coming from higher up, so she'd made it to her feet. "Keep moving. The weariness goes away the more you work your muscles. I'm going to see if I can find a door, or a window, or something."

I let her search and stretched my arms and legs. She was right; I already felt more alert. With the brain fog clearing, I was ready to prophesy. I closed my eyes out of habit and centered myself, letting my brain drift for the moment. I acknowledged the chill in the air, felt a moment's gratitude that the elves hadn't taken my coat, and let the feeling pass. Then I focused my attention on the question *How do we escape?*

Nothing happened. No swooping sensation picked me up and carried me away in vision. Instead, I felt the dull blankness of a question the oracle couldn't answer. Usually that meant the question was so broad there were any number of possibilities, or it could mean I was thinking about the question the wrong way. So I tried again, a little differently: *How do we get out of this room?*

A whirl of images struck me: my own face and Viv and Judy's, a warm, oddly greenish light illuminating a round room with stone walls like a medieval tower, and a door standing open. That struck me as unhelpful, but I clung to the implied promise that there was a door that could open and blinked away the images. "Okay, that's a start," I said.

"What is?" Viv asked. "This room is round, and I haven't found any windows, but there's a door here that's locked. It's fitted too closely to the wall for me to sense what's outside."

A small, bright light suddenly illuminated Judy's face as she turned on her phone flashlight. "I must really have been out of it not to think of this before."

Viv laughed and turned hers on, too. "And to think I crept around, feeling my way in the dark... let us never speak of this again." She shone the light on the wall, which looked as it had in my vision. "The door is locked, but I think I can do something about that. Helena, do you have any insights?"

"I don't know what to ask," I said. "I need more information. Like, where exactly are we in Faerie? It's like how a map that shows a destination is useless if it doesn't also show where you currently are. But I saw the door standing open, so that's a start."

Viv clicked off her flashlight. "Judy, hold your light over here."

I stood with Judy behind Viv, who knelt in front of the door. It didn't match the medieval-looking stones; it was a smoothly planed slab of wood with bronze hinges and a bronze lever handle. The door itself looked like anything you'd buy at a home improvement store, but the hinges and handle were oddly ornate, in a design that didn't quite match any human era of décor. If I squinted, they might have looked like a fusion of art deco and art nouveau.

Below the handle was a keyhole. Viv shifted back and forth, trying to see into the keyhole without her head blocking the light. "This would be easier if they'd kidnapped us with all our stuff. Trivial, even, with the glass magus supplies I carry with me. I need just a glimpse inside... got it. Okay, stand back."

Judy and I obediently stepped backwards. Viv laid a hand flat against the wood beside the keyhole, framing it within the circle of her thumb and forefinger. She gripped the handle with her other hand. Her lips moving silently, she bowed her head and didn't move for a few seconds. Then she pressed down on the handle. The lock disengaged with a faint *click*.

Viv let out a deep breath. "Maybe I should be the party rogue. Are we ready?"

"Sweep the room one last time before you open the door," I suggested. "Maybe they *did* kidnap us with our stuff."

Checking the round room with our flashlights yielded nothing new, but I'd mostly expected that, so I wasn't disappointed. I considered prophesying again, but I still didn't feel I knew enough to be effective, so instead, I said, "All right. Let's see what's out there."

Viv opened the door, revealing a corridor that passed perpendicular to the room of our captivity, made of the same rough stone. Light shone from a fist-sized sphere affixed to the opposite wall, greenish-yellow light like I'd seen in my vision. A purple carpet ran the length of the corridor, out of sight in both directions.

And a very startled elf who'd had her hand on the door handle gaped at us in astonishment.

I didn't think, I just reacted. I grabbed the elf by the wrist and hauled her into the room. She was off balance from leaning forward, and between that and the fact that she barely weighed anything, my attack sent her flying over my hip to land in a sprawling heap on the floor. The key she held fell out of her hand and skittered away across the stone floor.

Judy snatched it up. "Go, now!"

We all piled out the door, which Viv slammed behind us. Judy swiftly locked it and pocketed the key. "Which way?"

I checked both directions. To the right, more greenish light illuminated the corridor. To the left, the light was cooler, more blue, like moonlight. "That way," I gasped. "It's open to the outdoors."

We ran, our feet nearly soundless on the purple carpet, passing a few more doors, all of them on our left and widely spaced. The wall to our right was blank and unbroken by windows. "I feel like the hall is curving," Viv said. "Like we're in a round building or tower or something, except the outside wall doesn't have windows."

"And we're gradually going downhill," Judy said. "It's a spiral."

The cool light was growing brighter. "I know there's an exit," I said, and then we came around the curve to find a window set in the outer wall. It was huge, at least ten feet tall and twice that wide, like someone wanted to compensate for the lack of windows elsewhere. Blue-tinged, murky light poured through the sheet glass from a full moon twice the size of our own.

We all stopped to stare. The impossible moon lit up the streets of a city, but no city on Earth would ever look like this. For one thing, it was nearly vertical, with ramps connecting different levels of buildings that clung to a mountainside like those shelf mushrooms growing on tree bark. Dreamlike white aqueducts and tunnels spanned the levels, passing over and beneath stone buildings that looked like they'd been extruded rather than built. And yet their material didn't look like concrete, which was the only stony substance I could think of that could be poured into those impossible shapes.

Very few lights burned in the windows of those buildings. The moon painted the whole city dull silver and illuminated a white plain beyond. It looked snow covered, but the air didn't feel cold enough for that, even accounting for how we were indoors. A forest encroached on the plain, as dark as the plain was white. And it all looked dim, as if there were a thin, dark mist filling the air, like soot from a wildfire or black gauze. I blinked, but my vision didn't clear. If this pall was the residue of the former barrier's taint... well, we couldn't do anything about it, so there was no point in wondering.

I dragged my attention back to our immediate surroundings. "Okay, so it's not an exit, but we know we're definitely in Faerie."

"I can see a door, sort of," Judy said. Her face was pressed against the glass as she craned to see the base of the building we were in. "It looks like a short tunnel extending from this building. I think it's a full loop around this spiral, though, so we've got a ways to go."

"Let's hope our luck holds," Viv said.

We ran faster now, with Viv in the lead so her long legs wouldn't trip her up following us. We passed more doors, but no more giant windows. I silently hoped the time was as late as I imagined, based on the moon and the darkness of the houses. If we could just make it to the bottom without encountering any elves...

We'd passed yet another door and were out of sight around the curve when I heard the click and scrape of it opening and, terrifyingly, the sound of voices. "Keep going!" I whispered. Stopping to find out if the two men having a loud conversation in the hallway were coming our way was stupid. Our only chance was to stay ahead of them.

Viv stumbled to a halt as the hall came to an end at another door. This one looked nothing like the wooden ones we'd passed. It was made of a metal I couldn't identify, copper with a silvery sheen to it, and had no visible hinges. It didn't have a latch; instead, a lacquered wooden knob the size of my doubled fists lay at the exact center of the door.

Viv tried turning it. It didn't budge. "Um."

"There's no other way out," Judy said. "There must be some way to open it. I'm sure it leads to that tunnel."

That sparked a memory, something Alastair always said about space stations and ships docking. "An airlock," I said. "That's why the tunnel."

"That's not good," Judy said. "That means the environment outside is dangerous. We might not survive."

"Well, we're definitely not going to survive whatever the elves have in mind," Viv said. She was patting the door frame all over, running her hands across wood that matched the knob. "Okay. This is different." Part of the frame slid open, revealing a row of four tiny knobs that looked like irregularly-faceted quartz. "We don't have time to crack the code."

"We don't need to," I said. I closed my eyes and willed the knowledge to rise up inside me. Images of flashing lights in a row and hands touching the knobs appeared and vanished. I gently pushed Viv aside and rapidly touched the knobs in the pattern I'd seen. Each lump of quartz lit up as I touched it, red, gold, silver, blue. There was a clunk, and the door quivered.

I grabbed the central knob with both hands and twisted. "Everyone inside!"

We darted through the gap, and I shoved the door shut and heard the same dull clunk as the lock engaged. This was, in fact, a short tunnel leading to another door identical to the first. The air inside was damp by comparison to the hallway and even colder than before, making me reconsider my assumptions about snow on the plain. Instead of the greenish-yellow light or the cold blue moonlight, this place seemed lit by black-light bulbs, though I didn't see any set in visible fixtures. It just had that odd, purplish radiance I was familiar with from Judy's Halloween décor.

"Look at this," Viv said. A row of hooks ran along the side of the tunnel at eye level. Dark fabric, coats or cloaks or something, hung from many of them. Viv fingered the material. "Feels like that weird stuff your designer friend Dolores wanted to make popular, Judy. The burlap-weight fabric with a linen finish."

I took one down and examined it more closely. It was a cloak with a hood, lined with satin dyed the same dark color, and it did weigh a ton. "I bet it's warm."

"*I* bet it's environmental wear," Judy said. She dangled another, smaller item of cloth at arm's length. "This is a mask, but it's not cloth, or not just cloth—it's got vents sewn into it. I'm guessing they wear these when they go outside."

The door shook as if someone had tried the knob. We all stared at each other. "It's fine," I said. "The airlock won't open if there are people inside."

"You want to bet there's a failsafe for if someone gets stuck?" Viv said. "They won't wait around forever."

"Then let's get out of here." I slung the cloak around my shoulders. It had a row of toggles up the chest rather than a single hook at the neck, keeping it securely fitted across my shoulders no matter how I moved my arms.

"Can I reiterate my concern about the environment out there?" Judy said. "You saw the mist. We don't know how corrosive it is. The barrier may not be actively tainting Faerie anymore, but clearly the taint didn't go away with the barrier." She fitted the mask to her face, blunting her objection. The mask made her look sinister, the visible vents resembling the air slits of some monstrous alien's face.

"We'll have to get back inside quickly, is all," Viv said.

Nobody said anything about how impractical that might be.

The mask didn't have straps or ties. I pressed it to my mouth and nose and nearly shrieked at how it automatically fitted itself to my face. Once the moment passed, I turned my head back and forth and marveled at how it didn't shift. I could breathe easily, too, without feeling hot and smothered. The mask's weight was almost unnoticeable.

"I'm trying not to think about who might have worn this before me," Judy muttered.

"Don't worry about it," I said. I crossed to the outer door, which had another array of crystal knobs. I tapped them in reverse order from before, and the door lock clunked open. "Let's get out of here before our luck runs out."

# CHAPTER SEVEN

The air outside was much colder than indoors, with a bite to it that spoke of a storm to come. Having seen the thin mist, I expected the street to smell of smoke. But the air smelled of nothing, not of automobile fuel the way a human city would or of animal waste and smoke the way I imagined a preindustrial city would. It was eerie, like despite the evidence the city was unoccupied. Or maybe it just meant nobody spent any more time in the murk than they had to. There certainly wasn't anyone else on the street with us.

"We have to move," Judy said. "Where to?"

"No idea," I said. "Let's get away from this door before those men come out, find a corner to hide, and make a plan from there."

"Then I guess it doesn't matter where we go." Judy turned right and strode off down the street.

We passed a number of other short tunnels extending from the buildings, all of them ending in doors made of that strange silvery-copper metal. Lanterns hung from poles at intervals too distant to provide continuous illumination, so we moved from puddles of grimy light to patches of darkness and back again. The lights shone on tall buildings, some of them with flat faces, others cylindrical like the one we'd exited. Even close up, I couldn't identify the material all the walls and the street were made of. It reminded me of stone one moment and matte-brushed metal the next. I couldn't tell if that was my perception or if the buildings really were changing by the minute.

The narrow street curved rather than making a straight line, reminding me of medieval towns in Italy, barely wide enough for a car to pass and so tall it felt like walking through a canyon. The walls bulged oddly around the oval glass windows at ground level, like the builders had pressed the glass into soft clay and left it lumpy. All the windows were dark, reflecting our imperfect images as we hurried past.

Ahead, movement warned us an instant before a figure walked out of the darkness, heading our way. I slowed, but Judy kept walking as if she hadn't seen the person. I remembered then what she always said—if you walk with purpose and carry a clipboard, you can go practically anywhere without being stopped. We didn't have clipboards, but those would likely have drawn attention here. So, after that brief hesitation, I hurried after Judy and Viv.

The figure was robed and masked like we were, with the cloak's hood pulled down over their eyes. I kept my head ducked and focused on Viv's back. If there was some elven protocol for passing someone in the street, some greeting or other, we were screwed.

The person drew even with us and continued walking, staying far enough away our cloaks didn't brush against each other. I listened to our mingled footsteps until the elf's were gone and let out a deep breath that warmed my face. "That was lucky."

"We can't count on luck," Judy said. "There, I see an alley between two lights. Let's hope it's not occupied."

"You are so pessimistic," Viv said. "Which is probably going to save our lives."

The alley was even narrower than the street, not even as wide as my outstretched arms. I started to lean against the wall and thought better of it when I got a close look at the "stone." The grimy murk clung to the material with an unhealthy sheen that looked like it would rub off easily. Even with the cloak between me and it, I didn't want it on me.

Viv pushed her hood back slightly so her eyes and the edge of her pink hair were visible. "Okay. So we're free, at least for the moment—"

"Don't you be pessimistic too. I've got that locked up."

Viv chuckled. "All right. We're free, but we're in a strange city and we don't know how to get back to our world. The elves either took our stuff or left it in the car, but either way it means I don't have the tools I could use to find and open a slip."

"I didn't know you could do that," I exclaimed.

"Sure. I've been working with some of the adepts, learning their method for opening slips and adapting it to Warden magic. We hoped to eliminate the need for frameworks made of trees. Which we did, but we haven't figured out how the elves do it, with no materials at all. So if I had my bag, and Helena could find us a slip, I could get us home. No idea where it would let out, but we'd be out of Faerie." She patted her hip. "All I have are my illusion-piercing glasses."

"That's something, at least," I said. "But it means I shouldn't try for a vision leading us to a slip. We'll need a different exit."

"Or find tools Viv can use instead of her own," Judy said. "Either way is dangerous, but it's not like we have a choice."

"I think I should start with seeing if there's an exit we can use." I again almost leaned against the wall reflexively, scowled behind my mask, and planted my feet wide in a stance I'd learned in my martial arts instruction. When I closed my eyes, they stung as if rinsed in brine, and I had to blink several times before the pain vanished. Momentary fear struck, the thought that Faerie's air might already have contaminated us. I pushed it aside and focused on my question, a wordless inquiry I let sink into my bones as I willed the oracle to find us a way home.

Instead of being swept up in vision as usual, knowledge welled up around me like waves pulling me deep into a warm ocean. I saw the streets of the elven city from above, tangled like spaghetti into a maze I couldn't follow. The city began to rotate, too slowly to make me dizzy, but fast enough to confuse my eye further. More images appeared, those oddly familiar shapes part art deco and part art nouveau, their motifs outlined in black like someone had drawn over them with a Sharpie. One after another, I saw them presented for my understanding, and I did my best to memorize what I saw, though I didn't know what use I'd make of the memory.

When the final shape, a sun impaled on a wiggly blade, vanished, I swam out of the depths and drew in a deep breath before I remembered my fears of contamination. The chilly air struck me, colder than before by contrast to the ocean of my vision, and I wrapped my arms around myself and shivered. "It's okay," I said when Viv and Judy exclaimed, "it's passing."

I pulled out my phone's stylus and opened a note, where I drew in order the images I'd seen before I could forget them. "I think the vision means we should look for those drawings. They might be a map or a guide. I know I couldn't remember a path through these streets. They're much too complex."

"But if there are markings at key intersections, that could help," Viv said. "I say we go for it."

"I agree," Judy said. "Though I don't know how we'll find the first one. I guess we wander?"

I shook my head. "Visions are either helpful or not, and since it showed me all those emblems, or whatever they're called, without showing a bigger landmark, that means the first one is nearby."

Judy made us wait while she peered around the end of the alley, looking for elves strolling past. When she gestured that the coast was clear, we gathered outside the alley and examined all the nearby buildings. "The first image was a trapezoid with two wavy lines across it," I said, pointing at the phone screen.

"There," Viv said. Across the street, carved into posts flanking one of the tunnel-doors, were two identical trapezoids. The wavy lines were more spiky than I remembered, sort of like the stylized waves my children drew in pictures, but I was sure it was right.

"What's the next one?" Judy asked. I angled the phone to face her. "Looks like a Chinese temple dog. I didn't know you were such an artist, Helena."

"The real thing looks more like a poodle, so I'm not all that great an artist."

"There are carved animals on the walls above where the tunnels connect to the houses," Viv said, ignoring our banter. "I don't see any dogs, poodle or otherwise."

"The other way," I suggested. "Back the way we came. That would fit our luck, if we started out going the wrong way."

Viv again adjusted her hood so it didn't block her eyes. "I think that's it!"

A wind came out of nowhere, not a very strong one, but colder than the air surrounding us. It brought with it a dry, papery scent, reminding me of Abernathy's and the days when the oracle was separate from me. The cold wind numbed my hands, and I stuffed my phone into the back pocket of my jeans and massaged my fingers. "We need to keep moving or we'll freeze. I don't see a dog, Viv."

"Trust me, it's there." Viv headed back the way we'd come. I followed her, wrapping my hands in the heavy cloak. The fabric didn't bend easily, and I remembered what Viv had said about burlap with a soft surface. It kept out the cold well, so I didn't care that it wasn't velvet.

Viv came to a stop in front of a tunnel flanked by posts topped by ornately carved spheres and pointed. There, above the lintel, was a much better drawn dog than what I'd produced. I pulled out my phone. "A row of circles crossed out, and then a bell shape."

Judy hissed. "Someone's coming. Put it away, quick!"

I tucked my phone away as two people came into view ahead. We'd already passed the exit we'd taken, so I didn't think it was the same men we'd avoided, but it didn't matter. This time, I took the lead, tugging my hood over my face and walking with purpose. I hoped I looked unconcerned, because behind the hood I was listening for footsteps and taking surreptitious looks at the pair. The enveloping cloaks made it impossible to tell male from female, though again, that didn't matter.

The footsteps grew louder. The two elves drew closer. Then, to my horror, one of them approached us. In a high, feminine voice, she said something in her own language, a few melodic words that sounded like a musical phrase.

I froze. Tilting my head slightly, I peered at the elf. She was hooded and masked as we were, but her too-large eyes, solidly dark with only a hint of whites, clearly focused on me. I had no idea what she'd said. By her relaxed demeanor, it had been something simple like a request for the time, not a demand that we explain ourselves for breaking curfew, but that wouldn't last long.

I grunted and shook my head, then took a few steps away. Immediately her companion put his hand on my shoulder and sang more words. The light but insistent touch told me we weren't getting out of this undetected. My mind was blank. No clever plans came to me fully-formed and ready to implement.

Viv stepped forward and wrenched the elf's hand away from my shoulder. "Run," she whispered.

I broke into a run for a few steps, followed by Judy, but I stopped when I realized the elves were blocking Viv's way. Viv bodychecked the male elf, who grabbed at her shoulders. He got hold of her cloak instead, twisting it so the hood fell back. Viv's pink hair shone purple in the weird moonlight.

The elf backed away, speaking rapidly in that musical language. His companion grabbed his hand. Both stared at Viv without moving further. Viv didn't bother with the hood. She ran, darting past us, and I jerked into motion and sped after her.

Behind us, something howled.

We didn't speak, saving our breath for running. My heart pounded with exertion and fear. Even if that howl had come from one of the elves and not some hideous monster, it had alerted the neighborhood, and those elves could tell their friends how they'd seen humans loose in the city. It wouldn't take long at all for that news to reach someone involved in our kidnapping, and then...

Viv came to a halt in another of those dark alleys and bent with her hands on her knees, gasping. "I don't know where we are. I figured this was at least the right direction, since the vision wouldn't have us double back."

"There will be more elves on the streets now," Judy said. "We have to move faster. Any more encounters like that one could be the last."

"Let me see if I can get better direction now that we've made some progress," I said.

But this time, my vision simply repeated what I'd seen before: all those abstract pictures, ending with the sun impaled on a serpentine blade. The only difference was it left off the symbols we'd already found. "Viv's right that we went in the right direction," I said, "so let's keep moving, and hope nobody else wants to talk to us."

I didn't see a row of circles, but the next symbol, a bell with an over-long clapper, greeted us the moment we emerged from the alley. It was carved, not above a tunnel-door, but at the corner of an intersection of five roads. I took it as a sign and crossed the street to take that turn.

The new road curved and circled back twice with no new symbol in sight. We did see more elves, though, all of them cloaked against the night with their heads tilted to protect their eyes. There weren't enough for me to call the street thronged with pedestrians, but we never had the street to ourselves. Fortunately, none of them accosted us. None of them showed any interest in anyone else, in fact. I tried not to feel too relieved at this. Complacency was our enemy.

Finally, I saw the bisected torus my vision had showed me, carved on another building at a crossroads. One more down. "Turn right," I muttered, though there weren't any elves within earshot. Then I felt stupid. I knew Gabriel Roarke had uncanny hearing, and what did I know about the range of a modern elf's senses? But none of the elves showed surprise at hearing a foreign language.

I was about to cross the street when I saw a commotion some distance down the road I intended to take. Five or six elves marched in a loose group, taking up most of the narrow way. They wore face masks but no cloaks, and their long hair, some dark, some nearly white in the dim moonlight, tangled in the wind that blew increasingly hard through the canyons of the streets. The elves all wore leather shirts and trousers decorated with bronze plates a few inches across that clinked when they walked. The hilts of swords sheathed low across their backs bobbed in time with their marching.

Viv grabbed my hand. "They're stopping people."

The elves were, in fact, stopping people, grabbing their shoulders and wrenching their hoods back, then releasing them and moving to the next person. It was all done in eerie silence, with no shouts or accusations from the squad and no protests from their victims. I glanced at the symbol that until seconds ago had meant freedom, then back at the squad. "We're going to get lost."

"Beats getting caught," Judy said. "Keep walking. Not too fast— don't run. Take the first right and we'll see if we can't circle around behind them."

I followed Judy this time, resisting the urge to look behind me. The back of my neck itched with the knowledge that those elves were almost on us. I was sure they would reach the crossroads before we got off the street, see us moving furtively, and give active chase. But nothing happened. We hurried once we were out of sight, still not running. Judy led us in a circle and waved me and Viv back while she peeked around a corner. "This is the street, and those goons haven't looked back. Come on."

We walked, and ran along stretches of road when no one else was there, and walked again, following the symbols of my vision. The surreal light, the bizarre architecture, the sound of footsteps echoing off the high walls all gave me a detached feeling, like this was part dream and part reality. Twice more we nearly ran into patrols, the second time escaping only because someone they accosted fought back for once.

When I finally saw the symbol of the sun and dagger, it took me a moment to remember this was the end of the line. I blinked my aching eyes. We were in a narrow cul-de-sac with four houses and their tunnel-doors. Directly ahead, at the dead end, the enormous moon rose behind the tallest of the houses, casting its moonshadow across the three of us.

"I don't see a sun," Viv said, turning on her heel to observe the four lintels.

I pointed. "It's scratched into the wall." It was the only symbol that I thought hadn't been intentional. It lacked the depth and regularity of the others. In fact, I thought it might be graffiti. It said something about elves that even their graffiti was beautiful; the circle surrounded by rays indicating sunlight, the serpent-shaped dagger impaling it from beneath, all had a graceful elegance I didn't think vandals ever displayed.

"That's weird," Judy said. "I haven't seen graffiti anywhere else in the city."

"But there's nowhere to go," I protested. "Maybe one of these doors leads to an escape."

Judy drew back abruptly. "How sure are you that vision was right?"

I opened my mouth to defend myself and stopped at the sound of footsteps. Many footsteps. *Marching* footsteps. Behind us, blocking our exit, appeared a double squad of elves in the funny bronze "armor."

Some of them had drawn their swords, which were also made of bronze rather than steel—well, of course elves couldn't use cold iron. All of them were intent on us.

We drew close together. "I'm out of ideas," Judy whispered.

"I could fight one of them if he was unarmed," Viv said.

I glanced at the sun and dagger graffiti. The lamp burning near it deepened the grooves, making it seem for the moment as intentional as the others. Then I looked at the elf in the lead. With his face concealed by the mask, his expression was invisible, though I wasn't confident in my ability to read elf faces in any case. But his heavy black brows, stark against his pale, bluish skin, were furrowed in a way that suggested violence was an option. I stared at his sword and remembered another bronze weapon, dripping with blood, held by an elf in a clearing outside Seattle. I thought of my children and Malcolm, who might never find out what had happened to me in Faerie.

Then I drew in a deep breath and squared my shoulders. "I don't know how this is the exit, but I'm sure it is," I said, and I stepped forward to face the elf, pulling back my hood.

The elf came to a stop and held up a hand, commanding the others to fall back. He held his sword across his body, ready to attack. My heart pounding, I stared him down. I knew there was a solution, but he was going to have to be the one to offer it, or my ploy wouldn't work. Behind me, Viv and Judy were completely still.

Finally, the elf gripped the sword's sheath in his left hand and thrust the sword into it with a finality that felt as violent as if he'd plunged it into my heart. He took two steps forward, putting himself within arm's reach of me, and extended his right hand, again forcefully. With no hesitation, I clasped his hand in mine.

A shiver ran through me, a full-body tremor like someone had brushed a feather against the sole of my foot. The elf tensed briefly, his grip crushing my hand for a second. Then he released me, flinging my hand away like it was a dead rat. I resisted the urge to rub his touch off my skin, not because I cared about offending him, but because I didn't want to lose the edge I was sure I had.

The elf tilted his head from side to side, cracking his neck in a gesture so unexpectedly human I nearly laughed. He must have sensed my amusement, because he stiffened the way someone does when they've been mocked. In a deep, resonant voice, he said. "You will come with us. The king would like a word."

# CHAPTER EIGHT

"The king?" I exclaimed. The king of the elves had arranged our kidnapping? The passing thought that it had been our enemy the scary elf, and the king was taking advantage of it, only gripped me for a moment before a more terrifying thought replaced it: what if the king of the elves *was* the scary elf? Then I came to my senses. The scary elf wouldn't have bothered with a kidnapping, he'd have just killed us outright. But if it was the elves' king, that narrowed the reasons for our abduction.

"So, this doesn't have anything to do with the elf child? With Connvuir?" I exclaimed.

The elf's eerie, pitch-black eyes narrowed. "Connvuir? Connvuir Tionn?"

I wanted to kick myself. This elf recognized the name, and I'd just given away what might be valuable information. "Never mind. Why would your king kidnap us?"

The elf smirked. "You should be honored, human, by the king's condescension. Show respect."

"I don't show respect to kidnappers, *elf*," I snapped. How dare this elf act like I should be grateful at being snatched?

The smirk faded. "It's hardly kidnapping if you make yourself unavailable to a civilized invitation. Follow me."

"You've got a strange definition of kidnapping," Judy said. "And we're not going anywhere. If the king wants to speak to us, you won't force us."

"I have my orders, human," the elf said, as disdainfully as a prince. "The king would prefer you come as guests, but he insists you do come."

"Really?" Viv held her illusion-piercing lenses to her eyes and surveyed the arrogant elf. "If we're guests, then you ought to give us your name."

The elf's pale lips thinned. "You don't have the right."

"It's that, or you provide us a way home." Viv held herself ready to fight. "We're not completely ignorant."

*I* felt completely ignorant, but I stayed silent. Wherever Viv had gotten her knowledge about elf customs—all right, it was probably Gabriel Roarke—it looked like she'd scored a hit. Beside me, Judy had crossed her arms over her chest and looked irritated, without a trace of uncertainty.

The elf glanced at his companions, whose expressions didn't change, all but one elf woman off to the side whose lips quirked in a tiny smile that vanished immediately. So, at least one of them was enjoying their leader's consternation.

Finally, the elf ground out, "My use-name is Carth, human, and my family name is Ailmach. You will learn to respect it."

"I don't think that's true," Viv said. "Well?"

It took me a second to realize she'd addressed me, and another second to register that she'd deliberately not used my name. "Carth Ailmach, huh? The king sent you specifically to find us?"

"I do my duty," Carth said. "And you're delaying the inevitable."

I felt like needling him further. I was still on edge from our frightened journey through the city, and I was mad at the oracle—and therefore, mad at myself—for giving me this "exit." But that thought brought me to my senses. An elf king might have the power to stop these incursions. I wasn't Lucia, with the power to make binding treaties on the part of humanity, but I was an oracle, and I wasn't powerless.

"Okay, Carth, lead the way," I said.

He didn't move. "It's tradition that you return the gift of a name with your own."

"Screw tradition," I said. "You people kidnapped us. You get nothing. When I meet the king, maybe I'll reconsider."

That seriously pissed him off. I remembered thinking, after watching the *Lord of the Rings* movies, how elves were elegant and noble and self-controlled. This guy looked like he wished he could use his fancy bronze sword on the rude human. I glanced at the elf woman, who now wore an expression of extreme amusement she didn't bother hiding. Carth didn't notice.

He got himself under control and gestured, saying, "Form up." The double squad, twelve elves in all, moved with precision to put me, Judy, and Viv in the center of a protective square. At least, I chose to see it as protective and not as a prisoners' guard.

With Carth at its head, the square marched us through the streets, almost immediately taking us beyond the places I remembered searching. Cloaked and hooded elves backed away from the guards, most of them keeping their heads ducked so I couldn't see their eyes. It was easy to read their fear in the furtive, scuttling way they retreated from Carth's squad. That annoyed me further. The king of the elves employed jackbooted thugs to terrorize his people—well, it wasn't as if I was predisposed to like him, but that certainly didn't help.

We crossed a number of ramps, always moving upward. Occasionally I heard rushing water as we passed aqueducts, all of which were covered with a fine mesh preventing debris getting into the water supply. I didn't know what to make of how the water wasn't fully covered to protect against the murky grime, but I was sure I didn't want to drink it.

Finally, we came to a copper gate, and recollection struck. I'd seen this gate, or rather one like it, in vision: two big doors made of copper polished bright as a new penny. Either this was a tiny version of that, or my vision had been metaphorical, but either way I was now certain we were in the elf city I'd seen a few times. Probably if we'd been brought here in daylight, I would have realized the truth sooner.

This left me feeling conflicted. I had a guess as to who the king was, because in those visions of the city, I'd also seen an elf who saw me as well. But I'd felt strongly that that elf didn't mean me harm—that he might even be someone I could work with. If he was the one who'd ordered my kidnapping, that changed everything I thought I knew.

Carth shouted something in Elvish, and a responding shout preceded the gate swinging open. Beyond lay a round courtyard with a statue at the center. The statue was of an elf riding a horse, though since the horse was rearing up I couldn't tell if the rider was proudly standing in the stirrups or trying not to fall off.

The building beyond the courtyard was the largest one I'd seen in the elf city, six or seven stories tall and with three separate tunnel-door entrances. It gleamed darkly in the moonlight, its windows all lit, unlike every other building we'd passed in our flight. I could barely make out a pennant, or maybe a flag, flapping in the sharp wind from a pole over the biggest of the doors. Carth led the squad to that door and shouted another command. The squad broke apart like a clod of dirt dissolving in a puddle. I caught the eye of the elf woman, who looked me over once and then turned away. So much for solidarity over our mutual dislike of Carth.

Carth slid back a panel on the doorpost, revealing two rows of quartz lumps. He glanced once at me and then ostentatiously moved so he blocked my view of the lock, or whatever they called it. I rolled my eyes, though with him facing away from me, it was a useless gesture. Still, it made me feel better.

The door lock clunked, and Carth pushed it open. "You will follow me. Stay close together."

I thought about taunting him further with some comment about how he couldn't stop us doing anything we wanted, but I decided I didn't want to interact with him any more than I had to. As fun as taunts were, I needed to be alert to my surroundings, not play games with a smug elf.

The tunnel was identical to the previous one, down to the rows of hooks with cloaks hanging from them and the masks in baskets hooked to the walls. Carth removed his cloak and mask and put them away. Now that I could see his face, I liked him even less. He had narrow, pinched features and too-pale skin and a long nose that came to an unnaturally sharp point. It was the kind of face that gets cast as the humorless principal in a movie about teenage rebellion.

Carth didn't bother looking to see if we followed his example, but I saw no reason to maintain our concealment, so I hung up my cloak and dropped the mask into a basket. Again, the idea of wearing something someone else had breathed heavily on so close against my skin gave me the creeps. What if elves didn't know about germs?

The door on the inner side didn't have a crystal array. Instead, Carth pulled a handle attached to a dangling rope and spoke three words into a metal mesh grille at head height—head height to Carth, which meant I would have to stand on tiptoe to reach it. Again, the door lock clunked, and Carth pulled the door open.

Beyond, a hall with a vaulted ceiling extended into the distance. It wasn't much warmer than the outdoors, but I still felt relieved at being out of the oppressive dankness. It was beautiful in an alien way. Beams carved with fanciful shapes in that weird style came to a point at the ceiling's peak, the carvings filled with glimmering silver. More of the greenish lights clung to the walls and hung suspended by chains from the roof peak. They turned Carth's undead-pale skin an even less healthy color, though I couldn't imagine the lighting that would make him look normal.

Carth didn't pause to give us time to appreciate the hall; he strode forward, not looking back, and we hurried to catch up. I looked around as we walked, making note of everything—the oracle worked best with plenty of information. The hall's dark stones lacked the unhealthy gleam of the ones in the street, and a second glance told me this was real stone, not whatever the other buildings were made of. A third glance convinced me this place was really old. The rounded edges of the paving stones suggested many thousands of feet had worn them down over centuries. It also smelled of damp stone and, more distantly, fresh water, two scents that were so normal they seemed out of place in Faerie.

We passed stone frameworks that looked like doors should be there, but there was nothing but blank walls. There weren't any exits at all. I toyed with the idea that there were secret doors, but anything the elves hid with illusions would be visible to me, thanks to my genetic difference, and if they were just really well concealed doors, that did us no good.

I hadn't been thinking about my ability to see through illusions, but now I couldn't think of anything else. I had that ability because I was descended from an elf, and some aspect of that ancestor's "elfness" had manifested in me. Now that I was in Faerie, some of my old curiosity returned. Who was that elf ancestor? Did he, or she, have elven descendants who were alive today? Would the elves care that I had that connection? Gabriel Roarke had told me that elves wouldn't care about my heritage in any way that mattered—I couldn't inherit an elf fortune, for example—but now that elves and humans were in conflict, I couldn't help wondering if I could use that heritage to my benefit.

We were coming up on the end of the hallway, a peaked arch like the empty ones I'd seen in the hall, but bigger. It had no door, and past the opening I saw warmer light, yellow and flickering like candles. Carth didn't stop at the opening, so neither did we, even when we saw the room beyond was full of elves.

A strip of carpet led from the door to the foot of a dais three steps high. It divided the crowd of silent, watching elves, none of whom encroached on the carpet. They all turned when we entered, making a rustling sound like wind across dry leaves. I met the large, pale eyes of one elf and held his gaze for a moment. He showed no emotion, not fear or anger, and I had to look away out of discomfort and the feeling that he could read my mind. I knew that wasn't an elf power, but the size and depth of his eyes made the illusion convincing.

Carth strode to the foot of the dais and went to one knee, bowing his head. He said a few words in Elvish, and suddenly everyone in the room knelt and repeated those words. Judy, Viv, and I remained standing. I felt more awkward than I had back in grade school when a teacher called on me for an answer I didn't know. Then, I'd felt everyone was staring at me. Now, no one was, but that left us open to be the focus of the elf standing on the dais.

It was, in fact, the elf I'd seen in vision next to the copper gates. His hair was almost pure white, but his face was unlined, reminding me that I had no way of knowing how old an elf was by his appearance. He wore clothes similar to Carth's, but without the bronze plates that clinked lightly when Carth moved. His head was bare, his hair tangled, and if I'd seen him on the street I wouldn't have pegged him as a king. And he looked directly at me with that same soul-piercing gaze I'd seen in the other elf.

I met his gaze directly, hoping elf hearing wasn't so supernaturally good that he could hear my heart racing. None of us moved. I didn't dare break our connection to see what Viv and Judy were doing. I almost spoke, but then I realized only Carth understood English, and I might be giving up some advantage by speaking first. I really wished Lucia were here. She understood politics and negotiation.

Without looking away from me, the elf king said something long and uninflected, like ritual. This caused the elves to stand and Carth to walk away out of sight. Two elf women near the front of the crowd bowed to the king and walked in the other direction. Still the king didn't look away. My eyes watered like we were in a staring contest. Maybe we were. I hated not knowing what was going on.

After a few seconds, the two women returned. One held an unadorned glass chalice with a shallow bowl. The other carried a hairy sack with a teardrop shape that sloshed like it was full of liquid. The first woman handed the chalice to the king, who held it in front of him with both hands cradling the bowl rather than gripping the stem. The second woman tipped the sack over the chalice. A stream of water flowed into the bowl, filling it to within a quarter inch of the brim.

The king spoke again and drank, swallowing deeply. Then he walked down the three steps and extended the chalice to me. Confused, I didn't take it. The king said nothing, just continued to hold the chalice in my direction.

"It is a demonstration of purity of intent," Carth said from where he stood to the side. "Pure water is a gift. The king drinks first so you can see there's no poison. Then you drink to show you trust he doesn't mean you harm."

"We're not elves. Something that is harmless to you may be poison to us," Judy said.

*That* hadn't occurred to me. I'd been remembering the murky water of the aqueducts. And yet... "You wouldn't bring us all this way to kill us now," I said. I took the chalice by the stem. When the king released his grip, the chalice sagged—it was unexpectedly heavy—but I managed not to spill any of the water. I raised it to my lips and drank.

It was the best water I'd ever tasted, sweet and delicious and cold. All thoughts of rejecting it left my head, and I had to stop myself from gulping all of it down. I restrained myself and only swallowed twice before passing the chalice to Judy. Then I thought that might be a mistake, that maybe the king had to offer it himself to each of us, but he didn't react.

Judy drank without showing any sign that the water surprised her and handed the chalice to Viv, who did the same, draining it. Carth returned to take the chalice away. I watched the king instead of Carth. His attention was on me, his eyebrows drawn together in the middle as if in thought. I reminded myself that elves didn't have to have expressions or reactions in common with humans, but it was hard to imagine that look meaning anything other than "what do I do with you?"

When Carth carried the chalice away, the king said something that made the kneeling elves all stand with the same rush of noise as before, but more ragged, like it took some of them longer to stand than others. The king rolled up his right shirtsleeve. He already didn't look very regal, and this gave him the appearance of someone preparing to do hard labor. But I knew what he had in mind before he finished, and when he extended his right hand to me, I was ready.

Part of me shouted that this was stupid, that the elves were our enemies and I ought to give the equivalent of name, rank, and serial number and nothing more. But that wouldn't get us anywhere. If I wanted to find out why they'd kidnapped the three of us, if I wanted to learn what was going on, I had to take a chance.

I clasped the elf king's hand.

# CHAPTER NINE

The same rush I'd felt when touching Carth passed over and through me, and I shivered. The king closed his eyes briefly, as if the moment had affected him physically as well. Maybe it had. I was tired of not knowing things—well, that ended now.

Before the king could speak, I said, "You kidnapped us. I want to know why."

The king focused on me, frowning slightly. "It is tradition—"

"Not our tradition," I snapped, "and if what you want is a civil conversation, you're starting in the hole. I want to know what makes you think you can snatch us out of our world and expect us not to be pissed off about it."

It occurred to me as I was speaking that I'd used a couple of English idioms, and although the king now understood that language, he might not be fully fluent. Suppose the magic only gave him translations of what he already spoke? But I was mad enough not to care.

"I see." The king inclined his head, just a bit, but enough that the gesture showed respect—if that was a thing elves had in common with humans. "I wanted to speak with you, but since we don't—didn't—share a language, I could hardly explain myself. And you fled before anyone could speak to you."

"That's a reason, but it's not an excuse," I said, falling back on something I said to my kids when they tried to get out of a justified punishment. "Why us?"

"My people didn't know which of you is the visionary, so they took all of you." The king glanced briefly at Judy and Viv, then returned his focus to me. "But I have seen you before. You are the one I wanted to speak to."

If he'd meant to throw me off my rhythm, he'd failed. Things were starting to fall into place. "I'm an oracle, yes. Does that matter to you?"

"Of course it does. Those of us who have the visionary gift are honored. Myself included." The king inclined his head again. "My use-name is Taelinn, and my family name is Ailmach. I am king over all of Faerie. And I apologize for bringing you here in such an abrupt way."

That surprised me. I figured kings probably didn't apologize for much. I was still angry, but it occurred to me that refusing to accept the king's apology would mean not getting very far in any negotiations he had in mind. "My name is Helena Campbell, and that's as close to a... a 'use-name' as humans get. I accept your apology."

The king said something in Elvish that made the crowd murmur. "I explained to them that our human guests accepted my apology and are to be treated with respect," Taelinn Ailmach said in response to my protest. "Since none of them speak your language, some talking in mine is necessary. I realize that's impolite, and I hope you'll accept that I don't mean any disrespect."

"It's understandable." I half-turned to look at the crowd behind me. "Should we let them acquire English? Our language?"

"That's unnecessary for now. Most of them are wary of humans and don't have a need to speak your language. If you don't mind, there are some who will want to accept your gift. But that comes later. Now that the witnessing is done, I'd like to speak to you in private." The king gestured toward a side door, the one the women with the water and chalice had used.

"Well?" I asked Viv and Judy.

"You're the oracle. It's up to you," Judy said, giving me a look I recognized. It meant she would let me do the talking while she observed our surroundings and watched for danger. Viv ran her hand over the pocket holding her illusion-piercing glasses.

"Okay, we'll talk," I told the king.

"Then, join me in my study," Taelinn said, waving a hand gracefully at the door again. Again, I reflected that all my assumptions about elves were wrong. These elves didn't act like vicious killers, but they also weren't dressed elegantly or possessed of an elevated vocabulary and British accent. Of course, they might still be vicious killers, and since Taelinn and Carth had learned English from me, it made sense that they'd talk like me as well. I strode ahead of the king, covering my confusion with a firm step and, I hoped, a determined expression.

The chalice women flanked the side door. There was no sign of the chalice or the waterskin. One opened the door and gave it a firm push so it swung inward without her getting in my way. I didn't pause for Taelinn to precede me. Start a meeting on your own terms, Lucia always said, and channeling my inner Lucia seemed like a good idea now.

The king didn't act as if he minded that I'd barged ahead. In fact, he stood to the side and bowed to Judy and Viv as they followed me. That politeness threw me, but I controlled myself and took a seat on the circle-shaped backless couch at the center of the room. The little room looked as old as the hall, the stone walls pitted with age, small piles of ash worked into the corners of the unlit fireplace like no one had thoroughly swept it for decades. It also lacked all the little touches that made a room comfortable, like rugs and throw pillows. Though throw pillows would be a mistake on this couch.

Taelinn walked around the couch, brushing a fat braided bell rope that hung next to the fireplace, and touched a long reed to the lamp on the mantel—a real fire, not the greenish light sources. He lit the kindling in the fireplace with the reed, then, when the logs caught fire, tossed it into the fireplace and joined us. Judy and Viv sat close beside me, with Taelinn opposite us, and for a moment, no one spoke. Having come this far, I couldn't think where to go next.

"I apologize again for our abruptness in taking you. I hope it won't interfere with our coming to an agreement," Taelinn said, taking the decision out of my hands.

"What agreement?" I said. "You've entered our world and killed innocent people. I'm not open to any agreement beyond you stopping these incursions."

"Ah." Taelinn leaned forward, resting his elbows on his knees, and bowed his head. "Let's set aside agreements for the moment in favor of an explanation instead."

"I hope you're not going to offer me excuses."

"No." He raised his head and fixed me with those overlarge, dark eyes. "I was not responsible for those incursions. Will you let me tell you something about our politics?"

I gaped. "But all those elves—"

"Are not under my control." Taelinn straightened. "This is a long story, but I hope you'll accept my promise that it's all necessary for you to understand. Back when the barrier first appeared—"

"A thousand years back. No wonder it's a long story," Judy muttered.

Taelinn ignored her. "We didn't at first understand what had happened, and it took a few years for the taint produced by the barrier to become perceptible. Over the centuries, there was some argument—a lot of argument—about what to do. One faction declared war on humans, swearing that when the barrier was gone, they would eradicate humanity. They were a minority, but a very loud voice.

"In the last seventy years, though, that faction gained a new and charismatic leader. Clissach Lachma made many promises to his followers about being able to claim the human world once its inhabitants were slaughtered. When we discovered the barrier was gone, I forbade all elves from entering your world. Lachma didn't consider himself bound to obey."

"Did he claim the kingship, or something? Try to overthrow you?" I asked. My irritation had started to fade. The knowledge that not all elves wanted the same thing seemed like a possibility we should have considered. But it didn't matter now.

"Yes, and no. Lachma declared himself the true leader of our people, but he didn't push to convert everyone's loyalty. He wants to rule an elf kingdom in the human world and abandon tainted Faerie to me and my followers." Taelinn grimaced. "The prospect of cleansing Faerie struck him as boring work with no possibility of gaining glory."

"*Is* it possible?" Viv asked. She held her illusion-piercing lenses in one hand and tapped them idly against her thigh.

"I think it is. Not everyone agrees with me. But it's the sort of thing that can't be done if poison continues to pour into our world, so it's only been a short time that we've been able to work on proving it. I admit we've had little luck so far."

"I see." I wasn't sure how much I could trust this elf. Even if he was telling the truth about factions among the elves, he might be lying about not having control over the one entering our world to cause havoc. But I couldn't see how that would benefit him, particularly since he knew I was an oracle and could, I hoped, prophesy to learn the truth.

Taelinn smiled, a rueful expression. "You don't believe me."

"I would like some evidence beyond your word, yes," I retorted, controlling my instinct to reassure him that yes, I believed him. Just because he'd been friendly was no reason to lower my guard.

"Then I invite you to summon a vision. Ask any question you like. I'm confident the answers will prove my veracity." Taelinn spread his arms in a welcoming gesture.

I eyed him suspiciously. "You're sure?"

"Of course. Lying to you would ruin my intentions—and don't react like that. You wouldn't believe me if I said I was doing this out of the goodness of my heart."

"I guess not." Feeling awkward and conspicuous, I closed my eyes and centered myself. I didn't usually have an audience for my oracular gift, and I'd never deliberately prophesied in front of a stranger before. I hoped that wouldn't be a problem for the oracle. I really wanted answers.

But I couldn't at first think of a good question for the oracle—or, more specifically, I couldn't decide which of all my many questions would prove or disprove the king's assertions. After what felt like a full minute of delay, I finally settled on *Who is Clissach Lachma?*

Vision swept me up, and out of the whirlwind emerged a figure. It was what I'd mostly expected, so I was prepared to see the scary elf. His face was contorted with anger as he shouted at someone who wasn't present in the vision. I watched him with more detachment than I'd been capable of before. So, my enemy had a name. It was a start.

I dragged myself out of the prophecy before Lachma could see me. I didn't think that could easily happen, but Lachma had noticed both me and Duncan when we'd had prophecies about him, and I hated the thought of him intruding on my vision. Not to mention I didn't know what use he could make of seeing us. "Is Clissach Lachma also a, um, visionary?" I asked Taelinn.

Taelinn didn't react to the abrupt question. "He is not. But he is uncannily perceptive. Are you satisfied?"

"Not yet." I willed another question: *Are Taelinn Ailmach and Clissach Lachma enemies?*

This time, the vision came more swiftly, and I saw one scene after another of the king and Lachma facing each other. There were no sounds, and I saw no fighting, but my instincts told me their rigid stances meant anger and opposition. So that much was true. Still, none of it convinced me I should trust Taelinn Ailmach to act in my best interests. We might be able to make common cause—the enemy of my enemy is my friend, sort of thing—but I wasn't going to give away any more than I had to.

I opened my eyes. "All right, I believe what you've told us. Lachma is the one who's been invading our world, and you lack the power to stop him."

Taelinn's face tightened. "I'm not interested in starting civil war in Faerie. My obligations are to my people, not to humans. If I acted to stop him, it would mean war."

"Then why should we care about your problems?"

"I think humans and elves have things they can offer each other." Taelinn leaned forward as if in emphasis. "If Faerie is cleansed, many of those who follow Lachma will change their allegiance. I already have an advantage in numbers, and if that advantage is great enough, I can force change without it coming to war."

Beside me, Judy shifted her weight. "And you want humans to help with that."

"I've seen in vision that humans have magic that can accomplish that cleansing, yes."

"Which explains what we can do for Faerie. What do you intend to do for us in return?" I asked, though I was desperately curious to know what magic he meant. I'd certainly never heard of it.

"I would think controlling Lachma's forces so he stops invading your world would be enough," Taelinn said. "You provide me with a reason I can use to compel their loyalty, and I will ensure no elf enters the human world again."

It made sense. It was even appealing. But I didn't like the sound of "compel." On the other hand, what business was it of mine how the king of the elves governed his people? Still... "That's awfully one-sided. It's still humans fighting and dying until we give you what you want."

"Given that humans caused the taint that corrupted Faerie for a thousand years, I think it's only fair you provide some recompense," Taelinn said, smiling in a way that wasn't quite nice.

"Ancient humans. Nobody alive has any responsibility for that," Viv said.

"Even so. Call it a goodwill gesture, if that makes you feel better." Taelinn leaned back now, spreading his hands over his knees like he'd made a telling point. "Well? Do we have an agreement?"

Startled at his abruptness, I blurted out, "Agreement? I can't do that."

Taelinn's gaze focused on me, and I immediately knew I'd made a mistake. "You mean you won't do that? Or do you mean you lack the power?"

I glared at him, my heart racing. Somehow my incautious words had tipped the balance of power in his favor, and all I could think was that speaking more would make things worse.

"Then you can't," Taelinn said. "How is a visionary incapable of making binding agreements? Aren't you the one who rules your people?"

I still said nothing. Taelinn regarded me closely, his overly large eyes narrowing to a semblance of human normal. "I see I've made some wrong assumptions. Who is your leader, then?"

"No one you've met," I said. "But we can take your proposal to her." It sounded weak, like I was begging for his approval.

"I see." Taelinn's voice was neutral. "You don't control the humans' leadership. Which means I'm back where I started."

"That's not true," Judy said. "You have Helena's promise that she'll present your request. The voice of the oracle is an important one."

"I need more than assurances," Taelinn said. "And the fact that you consider it a request tells me you don't intend to take me seriously. My plan is best for everyone concerned."

"You can't force us to act," I said, feeling more alarmed than ever. "You said your duty is to your people—well, humans put themselves first, too. We aren't going to take on the bigger burden here."

"That's enough." Taelinn rose from his seat. "I'm not going to be lectured by a human, even if you are a fellow visionary. Tell me who your leader is so I can treat with her directly."

I glanced at Judy, whose devious mind would see if there was a trap hidden in Taelinn's words. Judy looked Taelinn over. "Her use-name is Lucia Pontarelli," she said. "I'm sure you can find her, you being a visionary and all that."

"Thank you for being cooperative," Taelinn said, though he still didn't sound pleasant. "I'll have someone show you to your rooms."

"Excuse me?" I said, shooting to my feet.

"You are honored guests. I want you to be comfortable during your stay here."

"We're not staying. I want you to send us back to our world." My voice and my hands shook with fury. Being kidnapped was one thing; being treated politely and then told I was a captive was a new level of arrogance.

Taelinn smiled. "I think your Lucia Pontarelli will be more receptive to my requests if she knows her oracle is at stake. Don't worry, we won't hurt you. Personally, I'd love to talk more about how your visionary gift works—"

"Don't you *dare* pretend you're civilized," I snarled. "Send us back, or you'll regret it."

"Regret what? Taking an advantage?" Now Taelinn chuckled, a low, amused sound that infuriated me further. "This is politics. If your leader is clever, she'll understand that."

"That's not what I had in mind," I said, visions of Wardens pouring through a slip into Faerie, with Malcolm, Mike, and Jeremiah at their head. "You have no idea what you're getting into if you threaten us."

"We know we outnumber you," Taelinn said. "I'm not afraid of human retaliation."

Viv launched herself at the king. In a flash, Taelinn stepped out of the way of her attack, too fast for my eye to follow. He grabbed the bell rope and tugged twice. Viv caught herself, spun, and kicked low, aiming for the king's knees. She connected, and Taelinn grunted and staggered back.

The door opened, and a stream of armored men and women led by Carth filed through the door. Two of them took up stations flanking me and Judy, though they didn't lay hands on us. Two more grabbed Viv. They addressed the king in Elvish, and Taelinn, his voice breathy with pain, responded. Carth drew his bronze sword and laid its edge against Viv's throat. Viv froze.

I had a momentary insight that had nothing to do with vision. "Don't," I said. "She fought because you threatened us. She didn't know there's a punishment for touching the king, let alone injuring him. And I swear to you if you kill her, I will use everything in my power to bring you down."

Taelinn massaged his knee and glowered at me. He said something in Elvish that made Carth sheathe his sword. "I choose to forgive you this once," he said. "Make sure it doesn't happen again."

He gestured, and the elves standing behind the couch prodded us to move. Judy turned a fierce glare on the woman, but otherwise didn't resist. I ignored the elf beside me and hurried to Viv's side. Viv shook her head. "I'm fine. I didn't think about that possibility."

"It's all right," I said. To Taelinn, I said, "This is your final warning. If you don't send us home immediately, I can't promise you'll be safe from retribution."

"Your threats won't disturb my sleep," Taelinn replied. A few final words in Elvish had the guards form up around us and march us out of the room.

# CHAPTER TEN

The large ceremonial chamber was empty now. The guards'
booted feet echoed on the flagstones as they led the way back
through the open doorway we'd entered by and down the hall.
The dark stone walls and the green-tinged lights looked sinister now I
knew we were hostages. I walked slowly, hoping for time to see a way
out of our predicament. Carth, walking behind me, prodded me with
his sword, but I ignored it. The king wouldn't let us be hurt, at least
for now.

But no new insights came to me. The blank walls beneath the arches
on either side taunted me, they looked so much like they ought to be
doors we might use to escape. We were still walking too rapidly for me
to summon a prophecy; I'd never succeeded in prophesying while
moving, and since the oracle never gave me prophecies that would put
me in physical danger, I guessed the possibility of tripping or running
into a wall was the reason.

Our elven minders came to an unexpected halt about halfway down
the hall from the ceremonial chamber, and I nearly ran into Judy. I put a
hand on her shoulder to steady myself. I couldn't see anything different
here, but the elf in the lead rested her hand against the decorative

carving of the nearest arch like it was a palmprint reader and spoke three words in Elvish.

A loud grinding sound, stone over dry stone, echoed through the empty hall, and the ancient dark stones of the wall shifted backward and then slid to either side, revealing a jagged-edged opening taller than the tallest elf. The leader stepped through and the others followed, prompting Judy, Viv, and me to move with them or be run over. I glared at Carth, but he ignored me. Carth Ailmach. Taelinn Ailmach. Relatives, but how close? Maybe Carth was Taelinn's heir. It might explain why he'd been sent to find us.

The hall beyond the opening was darker than the main hall, though it was lit by the same weird greenish lights. Here, either the walls were a different color or the lights didn't burn as brightly, but either way it felt creepy, like traveling through an abandoned castle that might be haunted. It was colder, too, chilling my hands to inflexibility and again making me grateful for my coat. If this was representative of elven architecture, no wonder everyone here was so grim.

The hall sloped upward steeply enough my breath came more rapidly and my legs began to ache. I was just reflecting that we hadn't seen any stairs, anywhere in the city, when the slope ended at another hall. Dusty silver light filled the space, and I gaped in wonder at the curved glass ceiling through which the over-large moon was clearly visible, almost directly overhead.

Again, the tip of a sword prodded me from behind. I turned on Carth, snarling, and was surprised to see him twitch as if he was afraid of whatever attack I might launch. Too bad I couldn't think of a way to use his fear against him.

The elf said something in Elvish to the woman in the lead. "Don't bother," I said. Again, he flinched, though he regained control of himself almost immediately. I ostentatiously turned my back on him and followed the elf woman, who hadn't paid our interaction any heed.

I knew I needed to be alert to my immediate surroundings, but the view of the elven city under the grimy moonlight was breathtaking. Towers, spires, arched bridges—if it hadn't been made of that weird substance, it would have been astonishingly beautiful. As it was, its beauty was distorted into something just alien enough to be unsettling, at least to my eyes.

To the right, the city merged with a mountainside, and I watched that because it was a normal mountain, if taller than anything I'd ever seen, and its normality comforted me. More elven buildings grew from the cliffs like those shelf mushrooms Alastair found so fascinating, none of them lit so they were barely visible as buildings.

The mountain and city's distraction meant I was again surprised when our minders came to a halt. I realized we'd stopped at a door similar to the one we'd broken out of before, though the wood was darker and the fittings a silvery metal. It was also barred with an oak plank it took two elves to lift. The elf in the lead unlocked the door with a silver key and gestured to us to go inside. Hating myself for cooperating with my captors, I did as she indicated, following Judy and Viv into a round room furnished with a single backless sofa pushed against the far wall. The last thing I saw before the door shut was Carth's narrow, ugly face sneering at me.

I barely heard the door lock and the bar thump into place before I said, "This is a disaster."

"I hate to be a damsel in distress, but as soon as the Wardens find out we've been taken, our menfolk are going to come riding to the rescue," Judy said sourly. "Which is not going to end well for the elves."

"Do we care?" Viv said. She was prowling the room, examining the other three doors and checking the walls through her illusion-piercing glasses. "They kidnapped us. I don't mind if Jeremiah takes them apart."

"It's still dangerous for them. And the elves do outnumber the Wardens, as far as we know." Judy threw open the door on the right. "Bedroom. One big bed. Great."

"That's fine. I don't intend to be here long enough to need sleep," I said. I sat on the sofa and leaned back against the wall, which thankfully was free of grime. "See what you can find. I'm going to search for a way out."

I closed my eyes and let my mind drift. Distantly, I heard Viv say, "It's... I can't call it a bathroom. I hope that's a toilet," and then I sank deep into a meditative state, filling myself with the question *How do we get out of here?*

My vision surged upward, and I caught a glimpse of a round room like I was floating near the ceiling. It was empty of people, but I knew it was the room we were locked into. I circled the room once, feeling like a bird in flight. With another rush, I flew through the locked door and into the glass-roofed hallway. Now I did see people: two armed and armored elves flanking the door, still as Buckingham Palace guards. Awareness flooded me, the knowledge that even if we could open the door and lift the bar, we couldn't get past the guards.

Frustrated, I let the vision slip away. "That's not much of an answer," I grumbled. I once again centered myself and settled on the question *How can we get rid of the guards?*

The vision was slower to respond this time. Finally, I saw, not the guards, but a stack of children's building blocks painted many bright colors. A hand pulled one of the lower blocks away, making the whole rough tower break apart and fall in a pile. The image repeated itself three times before the vision faded. Judy stood in front of me, looking irritated. "There's no way out that we can find other than the door, though why I thought that was a possibility, I don't know. What did you learn?"

I reflected on the second prophecy. "It wasn't my hand," I mused, "which means someone else caused the blocks to fall—no, don't listen to me, it was metaphorical." I stood and walked to the door. "I think it means we need outside help."

"Great. We're going to be here forever," Judy said.

Viv joined us. "I can unlock the door easily, but it would take a stone magus to lift a bar that size without being able to see it. What kind of outside help?"

I stared at the door like I could see through it. "I don't know. There aren't any windows?"

"No, but I don't think this was intended as a prison." Viv pointed at the back wall. "That's an outside wall, but again, I'd need to be a stone magus to do anything about it. Same with the rooms on either side. Ideally, if we could break through into another room without anyone knowing where we'd gone, we could hide and wait for them to freak out about our disappearance."

"They'd just search the nearby rooms and find us," Judy said.

"If we need outside help, maybe we need to communicate with

someone," I said. "Viv, couldn't you scry into our world or something? Or make a... a sending or whatever? Harriet Keller can manipulate glass and speak through it."

"I could do that, but there's no guarantee someone will see it," Viv said. "I mean, not that I won't try, but we'd have to figure out a place that both has a quantity of glass *and* is frequently used."

"What about Pattern 2.0?" Judy said. "They've got that enormous monitor screen, and people are in and out of there all the time."

"I don't know if that monitor is made of glass. I think it's some other substance. But it's worth trying." Viv tapped her fingers on her arm restlessly. "Let's start with what they've given us."

The bedroom had all the luxury the central room lacked: a thick carpet patterned in blue and gold, an enormous four-poster bed draped in a canopy that matched the carpet, a rosewood dressing table and matching wardrobe, and a washstand with a covered pitcher and china basin. An oval mirror four feet on its longest side sat in a swiveling frame above the dressing table. Viv took it out of the frame and held it by the knobs on either side that had fit into the swivels.

"They can't have been thinking straight, leaving this here," she said. "It's a typical silver-backed glass mirror, perfect for breaking into weapons. Or scrying." She laid the mirror on the bed so it reflected the blue and gold canopy and leaned over it. It took me a moment to realize it wasn't reflecting Viv. I almost joked about vampires, but Viv had closed her eyes and was murmuring too low to make out words, and I decided not to be a stupid distraction.

The surface of the mirror rippled like water and stilled again. Now it showed the cavernous room that held Pattern 2.0. The original Pattern was hundreds of glass tiles Wardens moved around to reflect the incursions of the invaders that used to plague our world. The Gunther Node's resident genius, Rick Jeong, had repurposed the room to show elven incursions instead. A giant screen occupied most of one wall, looming over a number of desks and computers. At the moment, it showed an outline map of the world, with dots scattered across it that indicated where elves were present. There weren't many dots, which relieved my mind that the elves had used our kidnapping as cover for a large-scale invasion.

"Good news. The screen is made of glass, more or less. Enough glass for me to work with." Viv tilted the mirror to show more of the Pattern room. "It's late, but it's like you said, the room's never totally empty. This should shake 'em up."

The mirror tilted back up until the enormous screen filled it. Viv ran her tongue over her lips to moisten them, but she didn't speak. I kept my gaze fixed on the screen. Judy turned her back. "I'll keep watch. Elves might have a way of detecting magic being used."

Viv nodded. She hummed a snatch of a tune—the chorus of "Wonderwall," I thought—and in the mirror, the display screen thrummed in time with the rhythm. Then, with a shimmer of rainbow light, the glass cracked in a web centered on the upper left of the screen and contracted like someone bunching up a handkerchief into a ball. Liquid crystal oozed, drawn by gravity to flow and clump along the bottom of the monitor frame and then drip in an oily, iridescent patter across the smaller monitors on the desks below.

The rough glass ball smoothed over into a perfect sphere that hovered in front of the ruined screen. Slowly, like Viv was sculpting clay, it became Viv's head, or at least what I assumed was Viv's head; the detail was rough, but the hair flip was unmistakable.

Viv cleared her throat. "Hello, whoever is in the Pattern now," she said, speaking slowly and enunciating each word like the diction coach in *Singin' In the Rain*. "This is Viv Haley. Helena Campbell, Judy Rasmussen, and I were taken by elves and are being held captive in Faerie. The king of Faerie wants to negotiate with Lucia and thinks holding us will make her more likely to give him what he wants." Viv glanced at me, her eyes wide and questioning. I figured out what she wanted.

"Tell them not to mount a full-scale rescue," I said in a low voice, in case the magic picked up my words and broadcast them. "We'll free ourselves soon. Play along with the king's demands and find out his weaknesses."

Viv gave me a look that said "you sure about that?" but repeated my instructions. "The king says he's not controlling the elves we've been fighting," she added, "but that doesn't mean he's our friend. Obviously. I will scry this room again in an hour if you have any messages." She released the mirror, and I barely saw the glass head drop and shatter on the floor before the scrying faded. This time, Viv's face was visible, and I gasped and put my arms around her to hold her up as she sagged.

Viv was paler even than usual, but she gripped my arms tightly and said in her normal voice, "That took it out of me. What was all that about us rescuing ourselves soon? Did you see something?"

"I don't know why I said that. It's a feeling based on my last prophecy. Something is coming." I helped Viv sit on the edge of the bed and sat beside her. The bed was tall enough my feet barely brushed the floor.

Judy appeared in the doorway. "Something's happening. I heard the bar lift, and someone's scratching at the lock. I think they're coming to take us somewhere."

We all hurried to the door and listened. It was a metallic scratching sound, irregular and varying in volume. Viv shook her head. "Anyone with a legitimate purpose would have a key. That sounds like lockpicks."

The lock clicked. We all backed up behind the door as it swung slowly open. A hand appeared through the gap, fingers wiggling. It looked deliberate, like sign language, but I had no idea what it meant.

The fingers stopped wiggling. The hand gripped the edge of the door and opened it further. An elf peered around the door, enormous eyes widening further when they saw the three of us huddled there. Viv gave the door a shove, knocking the elf off balance and slamming them into the frame.

The elf let out a *oof* of breath and staggered, then collapsed. Viv jerked the door open again. "Run!"

We hopped over the elf's fallen form and darted past the door. I came to a stop at the sight of two more elf bodies lying unconscious a short distance away and a fourth elf, this one upright and alert, pointing a sword at us. We all froze. The elf with the sword looked very nervous, which worried me. Malcolm always said a scared person with a weapon could be more dangerous than a professional.

Something plucked at my pants leg. I looked down at the elf in the doorway. With a start, I recognized her—she was the elf who'd been so amused by Carth's comeuppance. Blood trickled from her nose, but she was conscious. And she was extending a hand to me.

Whatever this was, a rescue or exchanging one captor for another, I wanted to know what was going on. I clasped the elf woman's hand and once more felt that strange full-body tremor of language passing from me to her.

The elf released me and wiped the back of her hand across her nose, smearing blood across her cheek. "Come with us," she said. "We can send you home."

# CHAPTER ELEVEN

"What makes you think we trust you?" Judy said. "Sure, you broke us out, but that doesn't make you our friends."

The elf woman shook her head. "What choice do you have? You could run, try to find a way out of the city, but our distraction won't work for long, and then you'll have the Ailmach's soldiers after you again. Or you could come with us, and we'll get you away from Faerie safely."

Judy looked at me. "Well?"

I studied the woman, wishing I knew anything about elven body language. Her expression was fierce, though some of that might have been the blood, and although she'd addressed Judy, her attention never left my face. I glanced once at the elf with the sword before returning my gaze to her. "That sword doesn't leave me inclined to trust you."

"We don't trust you either," the woman said. "Humans are dangerous and powerful. How else could you have trapped us here for a thousand years of slow poison? We underestimated your kind once. I swear we don't want to hurt you—the sword is for our protection."

The elf with the sword shifted, a nervous gesture that reminded me of my earlier assessment. "Tell him to put it away. We won't hurt you," I said. "Why are you here? If you're so afraid of humans, why are you helping us?"

The woman nodded at the man and spoke a long sentence in Elvish. The man hesitated only briefly before sheathing his sword. The woman spoke again, and the man visibly recoiled and put his hand behind his back. The woman said something that sounded sarcastic, and I again wondered about similarities and differences between our communications.

"I've asked Siltair to clasp hands so he can join our conversation," the woman said. "He's reluctant."

"I can see that. Is it allowed for you to be so casual about giving us his name?" I asked.

"He's my younger brother, and he follows where I lead. And I hoped to gain your trust by opening ourselves to you." The elf woman cautiously rose, keeping her hands where we could see them. "My use-name is Thandaigh, and our family name is Leath. Please. We don't have much time. If the relief guard comes while we're still here, all of this will be wasted effort."

I didn't stop for a prophecy. "Lead the way, then."

We ran, following the elves, down the hall away from where we'd entered. At the far end of the hall, we came to a spiral staircase going up and down. To my surprise, Thandaigh began climbing. "There's no way out at ground level that isn't observed. We have a different exit."

The spiral stairs went up and up, far enough that my breath came heavily despite my newly-gained stamina. There were no windows, nothing to tell us how high we were, and I was just as glad not to know. I wasn't afraid of heights, exactly, but this felt higher than I'd ever been in a building on Earth.

Finally, the stairs came to an end at a rough wooden door, much plainer and older than any I'd seen in Faerie before. Wind whistled through the finger-width cracks that made the door look seriously unstable. Thandaigh paused with her hand on the knob. "Can your magic make you fly?"

Viv laughed. "Don't I wish."

"Then stay close, and don't get too near the edge. It will take a minute or so for my companions to arrive. I'm sorry about the cold."

She pulled the door open and peeked outside, then waved the rest of us forward.

I stepped past the door and froze. All of the Faerie city lay spread out hundreds of feet below us, gray-lit by the moon that was now half-concealed by the mountain. With few lights and the thick pall in the air, it looked like a submerged city, drowned and dead. I stood on a ridge that ran the length of the steeply-slanted roof and ended at something bulky and dark gray I couldn't make out.

"Keep going, Helena," Judy said from behind me.

I nodded. My throat was dry and my skin felt taut across my skull. I didn't dare look straight down, feeling superstitiously like I might leap to my death to fill the void beneath. The ridge wasn't all that narrow, though, maybe three feet across, and I walked forward, keeping my eyes fixed on the mountain. The wind had died down, but the air at this height felt like ice regardless.

"Go all the way to the end," Thandaigh urged. "They will meet us there."

"Who will?" I asked. I kept walking, though the farther I went from the comforting shelter of the door, the more unsteady I felt, and the less likely it seemed that this was a good idea. "You still haven't said why you care about helping us. Maybe you've lured us up here to throw us to our deaths."

Thandaigh let out a bitter laugh. "Elfkind isn't lock-stepped in its beliefs. Our people tormented yours a thousand years ago, and look where it got us. Clissach Lachma wants us to destroy humanity so we can take your world, but some of us believe we should live with the results of our mistake."

"What, like you deserve to have your world poisoned?" Viv exclaimed.

"Not to that extreme. We figure we've each attacked the other enough that we should call it even." Thandaigh carefully passed me and strode to the end of the ridge, looking as if the height didn't bother her. "Lachma wants to destroy you. The Ailmach—"

"Sorry, does that mean the king, or his clan?" I asked.

"The head of a clan is sometimes called that. It indicates that he or she bears the burden of leadership." Thandaigh shook her head like shooing away a gnat. "It doesn't matter. The king wants to use you to destroy Lachma. My brother and I are part of a group that simply wants Faerie and the human world both to be left alone."

I drew even with her. In the moonlight, Thandaigh's too-pale skin and deep-set, ebony eyes made her look like a ghost from a Japanese horror film, but her expression was calm. "So you're acting against your king."

Thandaigh's lips pinched tightly together for a moment. "We want to prevent him making a terrible mistake. We know our history. Humans erected that poisonous barrier to stop us meddling in their lives. I don't want to think about what they might do to retrieve someone as valuable as you. Visionaries are respected by all elfkind, and I assume the same is true of humans."

"How do you know what she is?" Judy asked. The wind picked up again at that moment, tousling her short hair.

"I was there for the greeting ceremony. The king wouldn't have offered his hand to anyone except a visionary." Thandaigh tilted her head back and surveyed the sky. "There. They are coming."

I looked around, but I saw nothing but the moon and the mountain. Then Viv gasped and pointed, and I swiveled to look at one of the many buildings emerging from the mountainside like odd growths. In the low light, it seemed a flock of birds was headed our way—but they were birds whose wings didn't flap, birds that grew bigger as they approached until they were obviously larger than humans.

It took me a while to recognize that they were actually some kind of glider or one-man plane, but aside from the broad, tapering wings that reminded me of paragliders, they didn't look like anything earthly. They were silent, for one, without roaring engines or flapping wings, just the sound of the wind blowing across their sleek, dark surfaces. Despite the increasingly powerful wind, they weren't rocked by its force or knocked off course; they kept a straight line toward us. I counted six of the flying contraptions, all of them identical.

The flyer in the lead slowed and then impossibly hovered above where we all stood, while the others banked and turned in wide circles like they were waiting their turn. From the belly of the flyer dropped a black bundle attached to a couple of long ropes. Thandaigh unwrapped it, revealing a tangle of net or webbing. "Let me put the harness on," she said, turning to me.

I realized what she had in mind and took an involuntary step back. "You have *got* to be kidding."

"The driftwings are one-seaters," Thandaigh said. "This is the only way to get you quickly and safely out of the king's palace. I promise there's no danger. Elves ride this way all the time."

I glanced up at the flyer—the driftwing—and thought I saw it tremble, like holding the position was difficult. "All right. Show me what to do."

Thandaigh fastened the harness around me. It actually felt really secure, more secure than the time I'd descended in one of the Gunther Node's airjet packs, but then I hadn't had a harness and had just clung to the pilot. The elf woman tugged at the fastenings and nodded as if satisfied. "You'll go first. We will all join you as soon as we can. Once we're out of the city, I'll show you to the cuivuirskeen and open a rift to your world."

She waved, and the driftwing rose, tautening the ropes and then lifting me into the air. I clapped a hand over my mouth to keep from shrieking, either from surprise or terror. Then I was flying.

It only took a few seconds for me to relax. The driftwing wasn't going very fast, and I dragged behind it with no more force than one of those carnival rides where you sit in a hanging seat and it spins you faster and faster until you're practically horizontal. If I'd thought the elf city was beautiful before, seeing it like this, all spread out beneath my feet, was astonishing. Gradually, we sped up until it really did feel like that carnival ride at full speed. It was exhilarating, and I again had to stop myself from shouting, this time with excitement.

The driftwing made a rapid turn to the right, jerking me sideways and flinging me out in a wide arc. I clung to the harness, all my exhilaration gone. Shouting at the pilot was stupid, but in my fear I would have done it anyway if an explosion hadn't gone off not twenty feet away. It wasn't a big explosion, more like a loud pop and a flash of white light, but it startled a cry out of me.

The driftwing jagged right again, and another explosion rocked the quiet night, this one closer than before. I shrieked and gripped the harness tighter. Someone was shooting at us. I'd never felt so exposed, dangling beneath a flying craft that now looked incredibly fragile. I didn't know how far off the ground we were—fifty feet? A hundred?—but if the driftwing was hit, I'd either go with it or fall to my death no matter how high up we were.

Another explosion sent the driftwing plummeting, and for a moment I hung in freefall before being jerked in a different direction. It had been hit. We were going to die. Then its flight leveled out, and it sped up faster than before, dragging me along with it. The thought that I might die from a snapped neck instead came to me, but distantly, like I'd exhausted my terror reserves.

I waited for the next explosion, but when it came, it was too distant for the elves on the ground to be shooting at us. That filled me with fear for Viv and Judy, and I slewed around in my harness to try to see them. Twisting did no good, since we were flying too fast for me to make headway against our velocity, and all I could do was cling to the ropes and pray we'd all make it out alive.

When I opened my eyes, the vast white plain and the dark forest outside the city were all that was visible, and the driftwing's speed had slowed. I again tried to look behind me, with no success. We were also dropping, but slowly, not falling as if the driftwing had been hit. As the ground approached, I was terribly aware I had no idea how not to break my legs when we landed. I didn't even know how parachutists managed it.

But I shouldn't have worried. The driftwing lowered me to the ground until my feet were only inches off what turned out to be snow, after all. I swiftly unhooked the harness, feeling grateful I'd closely watched Thandaigh fasten it, and dropped gracefully to land on my feet without twisting anything. I stepped away from the driftwing and waved, though I couldn't see the pilot. There didn't appear to be a cockpit or windows. But the driftwing rose a little higher, trailing the loose harness, before flying a short distance away, doing a barrel roll, and landing on its back.

Curious, I started toward it before remembering the pilot was an elf and might be afraid of me the way Siltair was. Instead, I searched the sky for the others. The explosions had stopped, and five sleek, dark shapes glided silently toward me. I shivered despite my coat. The snow was, impossibly, warmer than the air, but my toes didn't agree with that assessment.

After barely a minute, Viv landed near me, and I helped her unfasten the harness before hurrying to Judy's side to do the same. Thandaigh and Siltair joined us, and five of the driftwings sailed into the darkness, away from the city, the dangling harnesses drawing smoothly into their bellies.

A hatch popped on the sixth driftwing, the one that had carried me, and a male elf clambered out in a way that told me he'd been lying prone to pilot the ship. He ran to meet Thandaigh, clasping her hand in a comradely way. They exchanged a few words in Elvish, and then the newcomer extended his hand to me. This time, I didn't hesitate. As scary as that escape had been, he'd saved my life with his expert piloting.

The tremor of language passing from me to an elf had started to feel pleasant, which disturbed me, but I didn't have time to dwell on it. The male elf saluted me and said, "My use-name is Dachtein and my family name is Mevair. And we need to run. I didn't think the castle artillery was sophisticated enough to spot a low-flying driftwing, but that just means the king is more alert than I thought."

"It's about a mile to the cuivuirskeen," Thandaigh said. "Not too far."

"Not to be ungrateful, but couldn't we have flown the whole way?" Judy asked.

"The chase is on, and the royal air guard has faster means of travel than a driftwing. We're taking another route." Thandaigh gestured at the trees. "The others will draw the guard off. The abandoned driftwing will make it look like they got one of us and are running scared. But we'll just be running, period."

"Come, now," Dachtein said, and took off running toward the forest.

The snow wasn't deep enough to slow us down, but we did leave deep footprints, which made me half-turn to see the trail we were making. No amount of distraction was going to work to cover that up.

To my surprise, only the footprints nearest us were visible. Farther back, snow filled in the depressions and whisked snowflakes over our path until none of it was visible. I glanced at Siltair, who was running backward with an effortless grace I could never manage. He ignored me, but I could tell he knew I was watching because he stumbled a bit and refused to look my way. I didn't know how old he was, but I guessed he was the equivalent of a young human adult, and for the first time I felt sympathy for an elf.

We reached the forest in less than a minute, but Thandaigh and Dachtein didn't slow their pace beyond what was necessary to not run blindly into trees. I had to slow more than that. The forest grew close together so branches tangled with branches and the foliage obscured the sky completely. It didn't occur to me immediately that if it was winter, these trees should all have lost their leaves, but once I realized this, I couldn't stop thinking about how truly alien Faerie was.

"We can open a slip, but we don't know where it will put you in your world," Thandaigh said. "There's no helping that, but we're sorry."

"It's fine," I said, though I was a bit worried that the slip might open in France or Mongolia. Still, we had our phones, and the oracle, and Viv's magic, so I wasn't terribly concerned. "Thank you."

"It's the least we can do," Dachtein said. "We don't believe in taking revenge on humans who weren't even alive when the barrier went up."

I thought about telling them I was responsible for removing the barrier and decided that was pointless. "So what *do* you want? Now that elves and humans can move freely between worlds, what's next?"

Thandaigh and Dachtein exchanged glances. "Our group, you mean?" Thandaigh said. "We don't want war between elves and humans. That's about the extent of it. Some of us think it's possible for us to rebuild relations with the human world, but I believe that's unrealistic."

"I don't," Dachtein said. "We have records of humans and elves dealing honorably with each other, to the benefit of both. It's not impossible and it's not unrealistic." Thandaigh elbowed him, and he let out an exaggerated *oof* of breath and smiled. The effect on his ghastly, undead face made me shiver, but I controlled myself. "But I agree with Thandaigh that stopping a war is more important," he continued.

"You're the only ones who think that, apparently," Judy said.

"I think the Ailmach feels the same, but he's worried about maintaining his power, which means defeating Lachma with any weapon he can find, which means humans." Dachtein pushed a low-hanging branch out of the way. "We're here."

Gabriel Roarke had told me once how beautiful the cuivuirskeen were in his time. Any trace of that beauty was long gone. The little clearing, perfectly round and free from snow and debris, looked haunted, the trees leaning toward the center in a menacing way, the darkness deeper than it had been beneath the foliage. I shivered again. The thought that these elves had brought us here, had engineered that elaborate escape, only to kill us in this clearing was hard to shake.

Thandaigh walked to the center of the clearing. I watched, curious to see what elf magic looked like. But she didn't do anything dramatic, no chanting or gesturing or wielding a magic wand. Instead, she drew a vertical line in the air from head height to below her knees and stepped back.

A trail of golden light, the first healthy thing I'd seen in Faerie, followed her moving finger so the line glowed like sunlight through a crack in a door. Thandaigh gripped the line with both hands and pulled them apart like she was opening a curtain. The golden glow widened into an oval pointed at both ends and then a lopsided sphere. Thandaigh released the slip and gestured. "It only lasts about three minutes unless we close it. You'd better hurry, anyway."

I hesitated, then held out my hand. "I know you think you owe us, but you risked your lives to help us escape. Thank you."

Thandaigh eyed my hand dubiously, then clasped it. "You're welcome. I'm sorry we can't do more."

"If you're working to stop a war, that's plenty." I shook hands with Dachtein and gave Siltair a friendly nod—he still looked afraid I might contaminate him with my humanity. Then I ducked my head, though the top of the slip wasn't all that low, and stepped into the golden glow.

# CHAPTER TWELVE

My foot came down in something cold and slushy, and I reflexively took another couple of steps forward, trying to avoid whatever it was. The full moon shed enough light that when I regained my footing, I could see I was standing in a low-lying field dotted with shallow puddles that had accumulated in the ruts formed by heavy farm equipment wheels. My right shoe was soaked, and both my feet still felt frozen, but the smell of water and fresh air was so wonderful after the funk of Faerie I didn't care.

Behind me, Judy swore under her breath as, by the sound of splashing, she found the same puddle I had. "This is an improvement."

"Beats being stuck in Faerie," Viv said.

"That's what I meant. Where are we?"

I turned around in time to see the glowing slip shrink back to a golden line and then vanish like a zipper being closed. "I hope it's somewhere close to Portland. It feels like the Pacific Northwest, at least."

Viv had her phone out and was peering at the screen. "This map says we're near Marcola. Where is Marcola?" She messed with the screen a bit and blew out a relieved breath. "It's a little town about seventeen miles northeast of Eugene. We got lucky."

"Lucky in more than one way," Judy said. She gestured at the area around our feet. "If this is a regular slip, and not one they opened the hard way, the Wardens have close access to what's probably the elves' capital city. Talk about an advantage."

The thought chilled me even more than my frozen feet. "I don't know how to feel about that. I mean, the king of the elves did just try to use us as hostages, and I don't feel loyalty to him at all, but does that mean we should attack them in force? Especially if the king isn't behind the elves entering our world."

"He might have lied about that," Judy said. "Though I didn't get that sense from him. But he could benefit from us believing he's not the bad guy here."

"We need to start walking," Viv said, "and talk about politics later. If ever. At least it's warmer here than it was in Faerie. Though—don't you think it's weird it's a full moon in both places? And wintertime there, too? There's no reason our worlds ought to be synced up like that."

"Walk where?" I said. "There's nothing but fields."

"There's a road that way," Viv said. "And we need to make some phone calls."

I trudged in the direction Viv indicated and called Malcolm. He answered so quickly I felt a pang of guilt, like it was my fault I'd been kidnapped. "Helena? Are you all right? Where are you?"

"It's okay, Malcolm, I'm fine. Just cold. Viv and Judy and I were kidnapped by elves, but we escaped—"

"Escaped? Helena, wait a moment." I heard muffled conversation, like Malcolm had covered the receiver with his hand. Finally, he said, "Then the message Lucia received was false. Someone claiming to be the king of the elves contacted her half an hour ago, saying he wanted to enter negotiations and that you would not be returned until he was satisfied."

"That was true. I mean, it was King Taelinn who sent that message, because he told us the same thing. But we're not his captives anymore." My foot went *squelch* as I stepped from the verge to the paved two-lane road. "How did he contact her? I didn't think the elves had the ability to do that."

"We can discuss that later. For now, where are you? I assume not in Faerie, unless our mobile plan is better than I thought."

I laughed. His joke reassured me that he wasn't about to do something rash in his anger at the elves. "We're near Eugene. We don't have our money or ID, just our phones. And we're really cold. Any ideas where we can go to wait for a ride? Or am I really lucky, and there are wardstones nearby?"

"Hang on." Once again, I heard muffled conversation. Nearby, Judy and Viv were carrying on phone conversations of their own. I heard Judy say, "You know how self-indulgent that is, Mike. Wait for Lucia—"

Malcolm came back. "There are a couple of Wardens who live outside Eugene. Mack and Elmira Moreton. Lucia called them, and they're going to come pick you up and take you to the Eugene wardstone."

"How will they find us?"

"Mack is a glass magus. It's no trouble." Malcolm let out a harsh breath. "Helena, when you didn't come home, and we found Judy's car—"

"I know. I'm sorry you had to endure that. Yes, I know, it's not my fault, but I can imagine how upset you were."

"Can you? I was ready to invade Faerie to get you back. Their king has no idea what trouble he's stirred up. It terrifies me that after all these incursions, he somehow figured out who you are and had the resources to snatch the three of you."

"Malcolm, he's not the one behind the elves entering our world. We learned things—I should probably wait until Lucia can hear it, too."

There was a pause. "That screws my curiosity nearly to the breaking point," Malcolm finally said, "but I agree. I'm leaving now for Eugene, and I will be there when you arrive at the wardstone. I need to see for myself that you're all right."

"What about the kids? And Connvuir? Are they safe?"

"We have someone at the house watching them. Several people, actually. Your kidnapping made me afraid someone might go after the children next. So the house is full of Wardens." Malcolm chuckled. "I can imagine the consternation of any elf who tries to breach our defenses."

"I can't wait to see you. I love you."

I put my phone in my pocket and hurried to catch up to Viv, who'd outpaced me. "Lucia's sending someone. A glass magus. I figure we should keep walking so we don't freeze, but he'll find us."

Viv nodded. "I had to talk Jeremiah out of storming Faerie single-handed. He was angrier even than I was about the whole thing. Listening to him, I sort of forgot my objections to Wardens attacking Faerie. How dare they kidnap us!"

"We'll have to do something," Judy said. "I mean, the Wardens as a whole will, not just us. Taelinn Ailmach can't be allowed to believe he can get away with this crap."

"I can't believe I ever thought I could trust him," I said.

"Why would you trust a kidnapper?" Judy demanded.

"Oh—that wasn't the first time I've seen him. I had visions of him, and he saw me too." I flexed my wet toes, but it didn't help. "And in the visions, I had the feeling he was someone who could help, not an enemy. But now... I don't know. He's only an enemy because he tried to use me —us—as hostages. That's not as awful as killing whole villages of humans."

"That still makes him not our friend," Judy said. "Still, maybe Lucia can negotiate with him anyway. It sounded like he originally wanted to make a deal. You know, what he said about believing Helena was in charge. So using us as hostages would have been an afterthought."

"I'm not willing to give him any credit," Viv said. "I don't care what he said about kidnapping being the only way to communicate. That just shows a lack of imagination."

I wrapped my arms around myself. Despite my winter coat, I was shivering. "I hope these people come soon."

"Helena, are you all right?" Judy stopped and made me look at her. "You look like you're approaching hypothermia. It's not that cold out here."

"I don't know. I'm just really cold. My feet never warmed up after walking through the snow, and that makes the rest of me feel frozen." I shook my head and moved on. "I just have to keep walking. It will be fine."

A car passed us, going in the direction we were headed. It didn't slow, and I guessed the driver didn't see us. The road was dark, with very few lamps illuminating it. "We need to be careful," I added. "I don't want some car hitting us."

We walked in silence for a while. Two more cars passed, going in opposite directions. I didn't think I'd ever felt so cold. I couldn't feel my toes except when I wiggled them, and then the sensation was distant, like I was wearing those socks that were like gloves for your feet, complete with individual toes.

Finally, approaching headlights slowed and came to a stop as a pickup truck pulled off onto the shoulder. The front passenger door opened, and a man said, "Mrs. Campbell? I'm Mack Moreton. You all ready to get warm?"

We scrambled to climb into the back of the cab. I silently took back every negative thought I'd had about oversized pickups with their giant tires and extended cabs as warm air blasted me, dispelling some of my deep chill. I sat between Judy and Viv and on a whim kicked off my shoes. With a little acrobatic contorting, I peeled off my wet socks and massaged my feet and felt instantly better.

The woman in the driver's seat looked back at us. "I'm Elmira. You look like you've been through a lot. Lucia wouldn't tell us what, just that you needed a pick up and a ride to the wardstone, so don't feel like you have to talk." She looked to be in her sixties, with curly gray hair and a wrinkled face, but her voice sounded like that of a much younger woman.

Judy and Viv and I exchanged glances. It hadn't occurred to me that the kidnapping of an oracle might be the sort of thing Lucia would want kept secret, at least until she knew how to respond. "Thanks. We really appreciate the help," I said.

"It's no trouble." Mack shut his door, and Elmira wheeled the pickup in a big arc that put us headed back the way they'd come. "We were just watching a movie. Getting older means not needing as much sleep as we used to."

"I'm glad we didn't wake you." I leaned back in my seat. Even with the warm air hissing out of the vents and Viv and Judy close on either side, I still felt cold, like I had an icicle embedded in my chest. It was a gruesome image I dismissed.

Viv leaned away from me slightly to rest her head against the door frame. "I'm also a glass magus, but I don't know how to find a moving target like you did, Mack."

"If we have time, I'll show you the trick. Very useful." Mack turned the car radio on, and faint classical music filled the air. I felt embarrassed. I'd subconsciously pegged the Moretons as farmers and therefore unsophisticated. Then I felt more embarrassed that I assumed classical music was only for high-class people. I was more addled with tiredness and emotional exhaustion than I realized.

We drove without speaking further as the classical music carried us through the night. I didn't have any idea what the different compositions were, but they were pretty and relaxed me nearly into drifting off. Except I was still too cold to fall solidly asleep. I hovered on the verge of unconsciousness, floating between weird semi-lucid waking dreams, or were they hallucinations?

At one point, I sat up, gasping, because I was sure the Moretons weren't really Wardens, they were elves taking us to where the king could kidnap us again. Mack and Elmira were talking quietly and didn't notice my distress. It took me a moment to remember that there was no way an elf could pass as human, and even if they used an illusion to look human, I would see through it.

Viv and Judy had both fallen asleep, so I settled back, closed my eyes, and tried to emulate them. But sleep continued to elude me. I finally settled on watching the dashboard clock tick the minutes past, which was boring but suited my restless brain. The lights outside grew more frequent until the sound of traffic told me we were either on I-5 or near it. The noise of cars passing had never sounded so beautiful.

After about twenty minutes, the ride became rougher, with the truck bumping over what sounded like gravel. I dragged my attention from the dash and leaned forward to see where we were. It was a gravel road, narrow enough I didn't think there was room for two cars to pass each other, illuminated only by the headlights of the Moretons' truck. Fir trees grew close beside the road, making it feel like we were driving through a tunnel with no end. My earlier irrational fears about kidnapping resurfaced. This certainly looked like the kind of place serial killers brought their victims.

Unexpectedly, Mack steered the truck off the road, taking us through the trees. There was just enough room for the vehicle, but fir branches scraped along its sides, the needles sending up tiny whistling, scratching noises where they rubbed the windows. The truck bounced and jolted hard enough to wake Viv and Judy. "Are we there?" Viv asked.

"Almost," Elmira said. "This is public land, so we have to take the back way. Sorry about the rough ride."

As she said this, the headlights flashed across an outcropping of stone, and seconds later we pulled forward into a clearing only about twice as big as the truck. Mack killed the engine. "Looks like you've got people waiting for you."

I saw movement near the rocks and hastily shoved my feet into my damp, uncomfortable shoes, wadding up my wet socks to put in my coat pocket. Viv and Judy were already out of the cab, and I slid out behind Viv and stumbled to where Malcolm ran to meet me. He wrapped his arms around me and said, "You're surprisingly cold."

"I know." I leaned into his warm embrace. "I'm glad it's over."

"It's not over," Malcolm said grimly. "The elves have gone too far this time. We intend to show them why interfering with Wardens, let alone the oracle, is a very bad idea."

"It wasn't—" I didn't know why I was defending Taelinn. "It's more complicated than that. We need to talk to Lucia." I glanced around. "How many Wardens came with you?"

"Five. I'm not inclined to take chances, if elves intend to make a habit of kidnapping. Mike and Jeremiah are en route to the Gunther Node. We're going back there directly, if you're sure you're all right." Malcolm held me at arm's length, studying my face.

I nodded. "Just cold."

I didn't know the stone magus who sent me through the wardstone, which reminded me I still wasn't familiar with half the Wardens in the Pacific Northwest. And yet all of them knew me. It was an odd sensation, being famous. Famous among the Wardens, known to the elf king —I was so used to the oracular gift it sometimes struck me as odd that it mattered so much to people who weren't me.

The familiar transit through the wardstone made a little of my tension fall away, as did my arrival in the central hub of the Gunther

Node. Its solid concrete construction reassured me that here, at least, the elves couldn't get in, and if they did, they would find a terrible welcome.

More familiarity met me in the form of Lucia Pontarelli, custodian of the Gunther Node and, since the dissolution of the Board of Neutralities, the de facto leader of the Wardens throughout the world. She'd never looked more like someone who could go to war against Faerie, with her hands on her hips and a hard, angry look in her eyes. "This King Taelinn had better make his peace with whatever god he worships," she said, "because I intend to make him wish he'd never started this war."

"It wasn't him." I shivered convulsively and hugged myself for a moment. "We weren't hurt—no, don't say it, I know it doesn't matter."

"You're damn right it doesn't. Kidnapping you three and using you as hostages doesn't endear him to me." Lucia looked past me. "Campbell. Is that everyone?"

"It is. I suggest we go to your office." Malcolm gestured to Viv and Judy.

"Debriefing, huh?" Judy said sourly. "I hope our information gives you a way to attack them. We even know what slip opens near the capital city, or whatever the king's residence is called."

"Don't think I won't take advantage of that." Lucia headed out of the transit hub with her usual ground-eating stride. Malcolm put his arm around my shoulders. This made walking awkward, but I felt so comforted I didn't pull away.

Lucia's office, with its many shelves full of file boxes and the familiar melamine and chrome desk, comforted me further. I still felt deeply chilled, but the office held so many memories, good and bad, it anchored me to my world in a way I hadn't realized I needed. Faerie's corrupt beauty felt like a trap, like the barrier was still there and we had all been at risk of being contaminated.

The thought prompted me to say, "Lucia, maybe Viv and Judy and I need to be checked out. Faerie's taint is still strong—it felt like swimming in filth. What if it did something to us?"

Lucia dropped into her swivel office chair and pulled out her phone.

"Like I needed more to worry about—Jeong, I need you in my office. No, as a bone magus. Just get up here."

For once, I didn't protest about rousting people from their beds at nearly midnight. Now that I'd imagined being affected by Faerie, I wasn't going to be able to sleep until I knew it wasn't true.

Lucia set her phone on her desk and laced her fingers together atop it. "Spill."

"It's not what we thought," I said.

I recounted the details of our kidnapping, with interjections by Viv and Judy. Lucia listened in silence, her face expressionless. When I got to the part about being rescued by Thandaigh, she frowned, but didn't interrupt.

"So that's at least three groups of elves with different intentions," I finished, "but I don't know what to do with that. If the king really is capable of supporting our efforts—"

"I'm not putting my hopes on that," Lucia said. "If he has the resources to fight a proxy war, but not a civil war, he intends to use us as his auxiliaries. Cover for his actions. That means he's worried about his people turning against him if he fights other elves directly. I'm not interested in being a pawn."

"We could turn that on him," Malcolm said. "Demand control of his forces. It would put us in power and allow us to use the elves as shock troops instead."

"You sound like you look forward to that." Lucia's frown deepened.

"Elves are formidable fighters. Having them on our side appeals to me. And I think Taelinn ought to pay for kidnapping three Wardens, one of whom is a powerful weapon that could be turned against him."

"I'll consider it. He's lost his bargaining chip, so I'm more sanguine about the possibility of negotiation."

"The slip we came through opens near his capital," Judy said. "That gives us another advantage if it comes to attacking."

Lucia's eyebrows rose. "Interesting. I'll need you to identify it on the map. It's not the one he used to send his ransom note. Notes, actually— he pushed identical messages through fifteen slips across the length of Great Britain and a few in New England, and Wardens at the Peters

Node in Vermont passed the message to me. Misdirection, though it could also mean he doesn't know where we're headquartered."

"Is that how you have to communicate with him? Notes?"

Lucia snorted. "For now. He claims he has magic that will allow for a more direct conversation, but if he means some sort of magical item, I'm not bringing anything into the Gunther Node until I know everything it's capable of. For all I know, he'd attach a tracking device to it."

The door opened, and Rick Jeong stepped in. His shirt buttons were misaligned, and his hair stood up behind like he'd just come from his bed, but this was just how he always looked. "Somebody injured?"

Lucia waved a hand at the three of us. "Campbell, Rasmussen, and Haley spent some involuntary time in Faerie, long enough I'm concerned about infection, or contamination, or whatever you call it. I want you to examine them."

Rick didn't make any surprised noises about Faerie. He took Judy's hand and lowered his head, apparently focusing on his shoes, which I noticed were bright pink Crocs. The rest of us waited in awkward silence, like people in church waiting for someone's silent prayer to end. After about a minute, Rick raised his head. "Nothing. I think someone has to be exposed to the taint for years to show the effects. Like how that elf baby looks mostly normal." He clasped Viv's hand and bowed his head again. "Just to be sure."

I hadn't thought of Connvuir since asking Carth if he knew about the child. I still worried that had been a mistake. "He's all right?" I asked Malcolm.

"He was asleep when I left," Malcolm replied. "Why?"

I shook my head and offered my hand to Rick. "It's nothing."

Rick's scan, or whatever, didn't feel like anything at first. There was just his warm, dry hand in mine, holding me firmly but not painfully. I shivered again from cold. "I feel like I'm never going to be warm again," I joked. "I think I need a blanket and a mug of hot chocolate to melt this lump of ice."

Rick's hand closed hard on mine. "You're cold?"

Surprised, I said, "I was cold after leaving Faerie, and I haven't warmed up yet."

"Your body temperature is normal," Rick said. "Malcolm, hold her shoulders."

"What?" I began.

The chill expanded in an instant, spreading out from my chest and toes through my whole body. I shivered convulsively, again and again, with only Malcolm's grip on me keeping me from falling.

"Sorry about this," Rick said. He sounded dangerously competent, the way he did when he was intent on a serious problem. Before I could stop him, he grabbed the neck of my sweater and pulled it down, nearly exposing my bra. I ducked my chin to look.

A faint blue light pulsed behind my breastbone, like I'd swallowed an LED.

Rick looked up at me. "Helena," he said, "I think you've been bugged."

# CHAPTER THIRTEEN

L ucia swore. "I didn't want to be right. Jeong, what is it?"

My shivering had subsided to a constant tremor, but this sent a spike of fear through me. "They implanted something in me?"

"Looks like." Rick tapped on my chest where the light glowed. "I've never seen anything like it. I didn't know elf magic could do this."

My heart beat faster. "Get it out."

"I will. You should sit down, though. This is going to take a minute."

Lucia vacated her chair for me. I grabbed Malcolm's wrist for reassurance that I wasn't about to turn into some creature, or spontaneously broadcast my thoughts. "Wait. You said, bugged. Literally bugged?"

"I don't know. I have no idea what this does. It's..." Rick shifted the neck of my sweater again, revealing my shoulder and bra strap. "It feels weirdly crude compared to the other elf magics I've studied. Hold still if you can—I know you're shivering, don't worry about that, just don't make any sudden movements."

Malcolm's hands gripped my shoulders more tightly. I sat rigid in Lucia's chair, leaning slightly forward. It was a hard position to maintain, but after Rick's warning I was afraid to relax into the padding. I kept my eyes on Rick, not wanting to look at the weird light inhabiting my chest. I no longer had any sympathy for Taelinn Ailmach, if he thought this invasion of another person's body was acceptable.

Though, having thought that, I started considering who else might have been responsible. Carth, acting without his king's knowledge—though if he was a member of Clan Ailmach, would he even consider moving against his own? The elves who'd kidnapped us? Or even Thandaigh and her friends? None of them had done anything to me that I was aware of, but elves' magic wasn't like ours, and no matter how much we knew from what Gabriel Roarke taught us, there might be a lot more that had developed over the millennium of Faerie's imprisonment.

The chill throughout my body suddenly contracted to a tight knot in the middle of my chest, freezing cold like a lump of ice near my heart. I gasped. "Steady on," Rick said. "This will be uncomfortable."

The ice lump shifted. Slowly, it migrated across my upper chest to my collarbone and then to my shoulder. Malcolm's hand moved away from the spot. I wished I could look down, see if the ice showed visibly beneath my skin, but I didn't dare move.

Something went *pop* beside my ear, and the cold lump was gone. I shivered once more—I still felt unusually cold, but not as badly as I had before—and said, "Did you get it?"

Rick held up a blue pearl. "This is it."

It had felt so much bigger when it was inside me. It wasn't large, maybe the size of my pinky nail, and its surface swirled with darker blue currents across the powder blue pearl. I was afraid to touch it, superstitiously fearing it might be sucked under my skin again. "What does it do?"

"Not sure. This is alien magic. The most I can tell you without a deeper analysis is that there's some kind of sympathetic magic on it, but that's not saying much because we already know elven magic has a strong sympathetic component to it." Rick tucked the thing away into his shirt pocket. "I'll figure it out, Helena. The good news is it didn't leave any, well, residue. You're not in danger."

"*Someone* is in danger," Malcolm growled.

I hugged him. "Time for that later. Lucia, is there anything else to do tonight? Are you going to respond to the king?"

"I was, but now I'm going to leave him to stew," Lucia said, sounding as angry as Malcolm. "This just got complicated, and I need to sleep on it. My instinct is to round up a few hundred Wardens and invade through that slip, but that's all kinds of stupid. Get home, Davies. Get some sleep. I'll need the oracle in the morning."

Malcolm and I were ward-stepped back to our house, to the wardstone we'd installed in a corner of the garage. Malcolm stopped me before I could go inside. "I'm sorry I couldn't protect you. It eats at me when you're in danger."

I held him close again. "I love that you want to protect me. But I'm even gladder that you have good sense. Assassinating the king of the elves isn't a good idea."

He chuckled. "Am I that predictable?"

"After this many years of marriage? Yes."

That made him laugh harder. "All right. Go upstairs and get into bed. I'll bring you something hot to drink. You still feel very cold. I'll send the Wardens home."

I passed through the kitchen with a nod to the three women sitting at the table and hurried upstairs, where I took a moment to check on my children. They were all sleeping, even Alastair, whom I'd suspected would be awake and demanding to be allowed to help. Malcolm must have concealed the problem from him for him to be soundly asleep now.

Connvuir was also asleep, curled up in the portacrib I'd finally borrowed from the Gunther Node day care with Night-Noon snuggled beside him. I paused to look at the boy. He looked entirely human in the low light coming from the half-open door of the dressing room. A pang struck me, memories of caring for each of my children at this age. What would happen to this little elf boy? Maybe he had family, but if Connvuir's father was as dangerous as I believed, his family might not be a refuge.

Then there was the king. If Carth's reaction to his name was any guide, the king might know about Connvuir and have something else in mind for him. And according to my visions, the scary elf—Clissach Lachma—had some relation to Connvuir as well. At least three groups who were interested in the little boy, none of them people I trusted to care for him. Certainly not as well as I could.

I was tired of lying to myself. I cared about Connvuir and I hated the idea of giving him up. And was it so wrong, or strange, for me to love the child? After all, if we couldn't get him safely back to Faerie, something would have to be done for him. Letting him live out his life in our world wasn't that bizarre a possibility.

I stroked Connvuir's blond hair and tucked him in more securely. He didn't react beyond letting out a long sigh, the kind of sound a contented child makes. No. There was no way I was giving him up to anyone who wouldn't love him wholeheartedly.

I was in my pajamas, huddled under the comforter and the soft furry throw blanket that usually lay across the recliner, when Malcolm came in with a steaming mug that smelled deliciously sweet and chocolatey. I took it eagerly and drank deeply, welcoming how the warmth flowed through me. "Thank you. I was this close to taking a hot bath."

"That's still an option if you're feeling cold."

"I am, but this is enough, and a bath would take too long to draw." I set the mug on my bedside table and hugged my knees. "This feels like it's gone on forever. This weird episode, I mean. If the elves know enough to locate me, and have the resources for a kidnapping, why haven't they done it before now?"

"If it's true the king isn't behind the incursions, his actions constitute his first move in the game. Or at least the first move he's made against us." Malcolm sipped from my mug. "But Lucia is right that now isn't the time to worry about the details. Though I've still increased security around our house. I don't like it that the elves now seem to have ways to enter our world at any point. Even if they can't use the slip Connvuir's mother did, there is a lot of secluded territory in this neighborhood that would conceal them if they created another."

The idea scared me, but in a dull, distant way, like I was too emotionally overloaded to react to one more horror. "It would be comforting to know how many of those stones the elves have."

"I don't understand the magic behind them, which is according to our analysts extremely complicated, but there's no way to counter the stones' use to create slips." Malcolm sat on the edge of the bed next to me. "It would mean knowing in advance where a stone was... I suppose 'keyed to' is accurate... and then hardening the area against opening. Not information we have. And reverse engineering them is a waste of energy, given that Rick Jeong's device for opening doors to Faerie at places other than slips is more effective."

"I have so many questions." A yawn distorted my final words. "But they can wait until morning. Come to bed."

"Gladly," Malcolm said.

---

"It's a listening device," Rick said the following morning. I'd been surprised when Lucia said she and Rick were coming to me, but grateful that I didn't have to make the drive after taking the boys to school. Now we all, including Malcolm, sat in our great room while Connvuir and Jenny chased Night-Noon around the chairs and sofa. "But it's not just a listening device. It has dozens of sensory units designed to build up a picture of its surroundings."

"I thought you said it was crude. That sounds complex," Malcolm said.

"Crude by elf standards. Their magic, what I've seen from what we've taken from their fallen bodies, is unbelievably intricate. This has the look of something slapped together in a hurry." Rick held the pearl up between thumb and forefinger, twisting it to catch the rare winter sunlight streaming through the windows to the verandah.

"If it's a listening device, doesn't that make it dangerous?" I asked. "What you describe makes me think of recording devices that transmit secret information to our enemies. I don't like to imagine what the king might do with that knowledge."

"It's inert now," Lucia said. "But we have to assume it sent something to the elf king before Jeong removed it. That's why I came here instead of bringing you to the node. We're in lockdown mode until I'm sure it's safe."

Jenny ran to my side and leaned heavily on my knees. "Can we have cookies?"

"In a minute." I scooped Jenny up and balanced her on my lap. "I don't get it. Taelinn Ailmach thought I was in charge of the Wardens, and he kidnapped me so we could make an arrangement. He didn't know he was going to make me a hostage. Why would he put that thing in me if he believed we might become allies?"

"Security," Malcolm said. "A hedge against the negotiations going wrong. Though I question whether it was Taelinn who did it, based on that. If the device was meant to spy for him, it would do him more good if he sent you back to our world rather than keeping you hostage."

"Okay, but who else is there? Rick, could someone have put this in me without my knowing?"

"You'd be aware of it," Rick assured me. "The implantation would be painful enough to draw your attention."

"The only time I could have missed it was when I was unconscious, right at the beginning," I said. "So it wasn't the... I don't know what to call them. The elves who rescued us? I can't bring myself to say 'good elves.' Anyway, I never felt anything like that when I was with them. It wasn't somebody in the king's court, working against him—same thing. You're probably right that Taelinn wanted security in case his plan failed. Which it did."

"The good thing to come out of this is it gives me a new line of research, now that I know something like this is possible," Rick said. "We could create bugs that record and transmit data on a level no human tech or magic is built to detect."

"I'm not going to stomp on your enthusiasm, but I'm going to suggest that wait for a while," Lucia said. "Right now I need to respond to the elf king, and for that, I need your insights, Davies. Tell me what you made of him. His personality. Anything that will give me a picture of who this elf is, aside from ruthless and devious."

Jenny slid down, and I put out a hand to stop her using my knees to balance as she jumped like an Olympic pogo-stick champion. "He's confident. He takes his privilege for granted, I think—I mean, everyone there deferred to him, and I got the feeling he assumes that means he's got all the power in Faerie. Except he knows he doesn't, because he said Lachma had drawn away some of his support."

"That's an intriguing tension I can exploit," Lucia said. "Did he downplay Lachma's threat to his rule?"

"He said it wasn't a threat at all. That Lachma wanted to leave Faerie behind, along with everyone who didn't see the wisdom in following him. Which means—I didn't realize it at the time, but Taelinn had to have been lying that it didn't matter to him, just because Lachma wasn't physically attacking him. Faerie as a kingdom won't survive if enough elves leave it."

"Right. Anything else?"

I recalled sitting across from the elf king, how reasonable he'd sounded right up until he told me I wasn't going home. "I think he keeps his word, but only the exact letter of it. Like, he'll look for loopholes to get what he wants. That's just a guess based on how he pretended we were his honored guests who just happened to not be allowed to leave, but I think it's right. And I'm sure he's totally committed to the welfare of Faerie. He talked about trying to cleanse it, as opposed to Lachma wanting to abandon it. So—I don't know. I think we can trust him to do what's best for his people, and if human needs conflict with that, we know whose side he'll come down on."

"That tracks with what Roarke has said about elf politics." Lucia clapped her hands and rubbed them vigorously together. "I'll put together a response, now that my response isn't going to be a tactical nuke through that slip. We can't afford not to explore the possibility of allying with the king."

"And if that falls apart?" Malcolm said.

"You already know. At worst, we can't come to an agreement, and we end up fighting two elf factions instead of just one." Lucia rose from her seat. "But this elf has reason to want our help, and I've got leverage."

When she and Rick were gone, I shushed Jenny, whose demands for cookies had gotten louder, and took her and Connvuir into the kitchen. "Jenny, don't be rude. Here, help Connvuir sit at the table and *share* the cookies. No you eating all of them." I poured cups of milk for them and then leaned against the kitchen island, rubbing my temples. "Is it bad that I'm not angry at the king for pulling this stunt?"

"Don't worry, I'm angry enough about it for both of us," Malcolm said.

"It's not that I think he had the right to interfere. It's just that I feel like it wasn't personal. He took a chance that didn't pay off. Like I was a means to an end rather than that he had a grudge against me or wanted to hurt me. And I *am* angry about it, but in a distant way. This is war. If I'd had the means to take advantage of him, I would have. So it's a little hypocritical if I get upset that he did the same thing I would."

"You are much more well balanced than I am." Malcolm dipped a cookie in Jenny's milk and ate it.

"I'm not that well balanced. Will you watch the kids while I take a few minutes to prophesy? I should have thought of it when Lucia was still here, but I was focused on that device and what it might mean."

"Sure. Though, speaking of watching kids, what are we going to do about this weekend?"

"Oh! I forgot." Once a month, my mom took the children for a weekend at Grandma's. "I can't expect her to watch Connvuir. I can't even think of a good explanation for why we're babysitting a stranger's child, even if he looks normal."

"We could see if someone at the Gunther Node will watch him for a few days."

"Oh, I don't want to burden them—"

"Love, you've taken on a burden no one expected of you. You could use a couple of days off. And Lucia wanted him to stay there in the first place, remember?" Malcolm took me in his arms and kissed me. "Don't feel you have to solve all the world's problems."

I sighed. No matter how I felt about Connvuir, the idea of sending him somewhere else that was safe felt comforting. "You're right. Even thinking about the prospect of being child free for a weekend makes me feel lighter. I guess this has been more stressful than I realized."

"You're lucky you have a wonderful husband to point out when you've boxed yourself into a corner." Malcolm kissed me again, more deeply. "And at the risk of sounding selfish, I did make plans for the weekend."

"Mmm. I like the sound of that."

Once I was in my second-floor office, I kicked off my shoes and leaned back in my chair. Thoughts of the weekend, just me and Malcolm, made it hard for me to focus even though I had no idea what Malcolm had in mind. Eventually I calmed myself and let my mind go blank, drifting lazily through clouds of nothing, before filling myself with the question *How trustworthy is Taelinn Ailmach?*

Prophecy gripped me, spinning me up and through the clouds until they opened up to reveal the elf city emerging from the mountainside. It seemed actually seeing the place gave the oracle something to focus on, because the vision contained details none of the previous ones of the city had, such as the forest encroaching on the great plain and the high roof ridge the driftwings had carried us away from. It was also grimy now, the light dull and murky and the buildings dark like I was seeing them through black gauze. The memory of fleeing through those streets made the vision feel sinister, like I might be swept back there through the oracle's power.

I only saw the city for a few seconds, enough to have to tell myself my fears were stupid, before being whisked away. No, it was more like the scene itself had been snatched from my view, like it was a picture painted on cloth, revealing a new scene. This one was the throne room, if that's what the big hall where we'd met the king was called. I saw Taelinn addressing a gathering of elves, and in the instinct of vision I knew he was giving them directions.

From there, a swift succession of images flashed before my mind's eye, all containing the king and one or more other elves. I saw Carth more than a few times and knew with the surety of prophecy that he was the king's trusted man and not just a relation. As if that thought was a trigger, different images appeared, fast enough I could make no sense of them consciously.

When I finally spiraled out of vision, I breathed slowly, letting understanding well up from what I'd seen. The king, and many elves, one or two at a time. My subconscious offered me an explanation: those had been images of swearing fealty, with Carth standing as symbol for the rest. So, the king could be trusted to keep his vows—to elves. Whether he would feel himself bound to do the same to humans was unclear. But I was sure no agreement Lucia made with Taelinn Ailmach would be simple.

# CHAPTER FOURTEEN

I backed out of my parents' driveway, waving at no one. The kids never hung around to say goodbye to me after I turned them over to Grandma; her house was a delight and a treat beyond compare. I always waved anyway. Most of the time, I felt a bit of a letdown when they so happily abandoned me for the basement full of toys, but today, after the week I'd had, I felt nothing but relief.

"It's a good thing I know you love your children," Malcolm said, "because by the way you're humming, anyone might think you'd been given a night off from prison."

I laughed. "Okay, so you were right, I've been under too much stress. It's such a relief to know they'll be cared for and that I can worry just about myself for a little while. Are you sure you don't want to drive?"

"Much as I love to drive, I love even more the thought that if we are attacked by elves, you won't be misled by their illusions. I haven't forgotten how they entrapped you and Viv and Judy."

I couldn't argue with that. "That's so sensible it outweighs how I dislike rush hour traffic on a weekend."

"Then let's drop Connvuir off with Viv, and we'll see where the evening takes us." Malcolm reached back and wiggled Connvuir's foot.

An unexpected giggle escaped the boy, startling me. I tried not to dwell on what it might mean that he still wasn't talking. Gabriel Roarke had said Connvuir ought to speak at his age, so I couldn't help imagining horror scenario reasons why he didn't. Then I considered what it could mean if he eventually started talking. How acclimated to our world, to humans, would he have to be for that to happen? And was that a bad thing?

"Something wrong?" Malcolm said.

"Huh?"

"Now you're humming under your breath the way you do when something's on your mind."

I smiled. Malcolm knew me so well. "Just thinking about what will happen to Connvuir. I know the goal is to send him back to Faerie, to be with his family, but is it horribly, I don't know, human-chauvinistic to think he might be better off here?"

"Because he's free of the taint and free of the war?"

"More or less. I mean, his mother is dead, his father is apparently a danger to him—it's not like he's got a family to miss him."

I regretted saying that instantly. I hadn't shared with Malcolm my thoughts about keeping Connvuir with us, and that made me feel guilty that I was essentially keeping secrets from my husband. I told my inner voice I was simply waiting for the right moment and it should shut up.

"No family that we know of." Malcolm turned to look at Connvuir again. "We know elves have complex clan and family relationships. Maybe someone is missing this little fellow."

"Well—" I still couldn't bring myself to say it, and I wasn't sure why. I shared everything with Malcolm, so why not this? Tentatively, I said, "If it came to it, I wouldn't mind taking him in permanently. The children like him, and he's sweet and well-behaved."

"Helena," Malcolm said. "What are you saying? He's not human. However tainted Faerie is, he's still an elf, and he still deserves to grow up among his people."

"I know!" That came out more forcefully than I meant. "I know," I repeated, more calmly. "I just—I don't know how it happened. He needs me. I don't want to disregard that. And for all we know, there *aren't* any elves who will give him a real home."

"Imagine how you would feel if one of our children went missing," Malcolm said, "and then extend that feeling to whoever is searching for Connvuir. If Gabriel is right about how elves feel about family, someone is almost certainly doing so."

Now I felt awful—guilty and ashamed but still caught up in the heartache of imagining Connvuir gone. "You're right. I'm sorry."

Malcolm put a hand over mine where it rested on the steering wheel. "You have a loving heart, Helena, and Connvuir is the sort of child it's easy to love. But if there's a chance to restore him to his family, we have to take it."

I stole a quick glance at Connvuir in the rear view mirror before returning my attention to the road. "I know. But I'm going to protect him as long as he needs it."

"I agree. And no one is going to simply hand him over to the first elves that ask." Malcolm looked back at Connvuir again. "I wish this were as easy as walking into Faerie and asking to see Connvuir's family. Tionn, was it?"

"That's what Carth said. I feel the same. Wouldn't it be something if elves and humans weren't at war?"

"I hate to say this, but if that happens, it's far more likely that it's because we shut Faerie away for good than because we achieved peace."

"I know." I sighed. "Still. Faerie was beautiful once, still is, in a way, and I can't help thinking we could benefit each other if we could figure things out."

Malcolm put his hand over mine. "I love your optimism."

"That had better not rhyme with 'bless your heart.'"

He laughed. "Of course not. I may not see a path forward, but if there is one, we'll find it thanks to people like you believing it's possible."

That made my heart swell. "Thank you. I love you so much."

"I hope so, because the plans I've made assume you do," Malcolm said.

The sun had set by the time I made the turn onto the winding road leading to Viv and Jeremiah's house. Jeremiah, a wood magus, had chosen the house years ago because it was at the center of an overgrown, heavily-wooded area south of downtown Portland. Viv liked to say an alien dropped into their backyard wouldn't have any idea this was a metropolitan area. It wasn't yet full dark, and the sky was gray with twilight, so even though the streetlamps were infrequent, it didn't feel as late as it usually did after the sun went down.

I hated the short days of winter. My whole body was convinced if it was dark, the hour was late, and seeing the dashboard display the time as 5:44 felt like the world was conspiring against me. I reminded myself that I was this close to a weekend alone with the man I loved. Just a few more minutes.

"I'm glad Viv was willing to watch Connvuir," I said. "She didn't even extort any favors from me. I think she likes him, though I'd never say that to her face. She loves her child-free reputation."

"I told you he could go to the Gunther Node."

"Yes, but he knows Viv, and that makes her house more familiar than the daycare. Plus, it's closer than the access point. Less driving." I slowed to make the turn onto Viv's driveway, which was so overgrown it made my driveway look like manicured parkland.

The two-story house at the end of the drive blended so well with its surroundings it might have been a fairy's home, not the whimsical Tinker Bell kind of fairy, but one who built rustic fortifications of shelf mushrooms and knew the right way to dig a privy. The effect was only slightly ruined by the Christmas lights draped across the pergola—those did look like the sort of thing Tinker Bell would like. Since both Viv and Jeremiah lived here, the combination made sense.

I parked near the front door and got Connvuir out of his seat while Malcolm retrieved all the things young children need for a short stay. Viv opened the door as I approached, letting out the delicious aroma of spring rolls and glass noodles in sauce. "Just in time. Does our little friend want dinner?"

"Thai food? Really?"

"Hey, it's important for children to develop a palate, plus I asked Gabriel if peanut sauce was a problem." Viv stepped back to let us enter. "You know you want some."

"Malcolm has secret plans, but thanks."

The rustic appearance of Viv's house ended at its exterior. Clean, minimalist design was Viv's favorite thing because, as she said, it gave her the best canvas to decorate. What would have been rather cold and soul-less Scandinavian décor was instead a whimsical world of twining flowers painted on walls and ceilings.

Viv's many crafting crazes were represented through the kitchen (old fashioned tole paintings on wooden boards, animals sculpted from clay) to the living room (stained glass window art, upcycled shelving units that looked like wood bark) and came to a peak at the back wall of her dining nook, which was a mosaic of tiny shelves bearing candles, small plants, and odds and ends. Many of the shelves were empty, waiting for Viv to craft something she loved enough to make part of the permanent display.

Jeremiah stirred a pot on the stove and nodded at us as we came in. "I didn't think you'd want to linger, but this is awfully good."

"It smells divine." I settled Connvuir at the table, where a tall stool with a round back had been placed just for him. "Thanks for watching him."

"I like children so long as they aren't mine," Viv said. "They're like the most interesting puzzle you can imagine. The kind of puzzle you can solve and then return to its owner."

"That makes me think—"

The lights in the kitchen and living room dimmed and turned red. Jeremiah dropped the spoon. "Something just triggered the perimeter alarm."

"Elves? Or Savants?" Malcolm asked.

"That warning means the alarm detected magic, so probably elves."

I nodded. Though many Savants were adepts, or had been once, few of them had the ability to wield magic after years of violence and murder.

Viv gestured, and the many windows looking out on the yard, the driveway, and the pergola shimmered. "They're now one-way mirrors," she told me.

Malcolm pressed against the wall to one side of the largest window as if he hadn't heard her. Craning his neck to peer out, he said, "I don't see anyone yet. Viv?"

Viv had hauled a giant aluminum cookie sheet from a rack above the oven and set it on the center island. She swiped her hand across its gleaming surface, and where her palm passed, streaks of darkness appeared. After a dozen passes, she gripped the scrying mirror by the edges and leaned close. "They're mostly invisible, but they're leaving a heat signature. Seven elf warriors—I mean, they're wearing those weird bronze plates and they all have bronze swords, so I'm guessing warrior."

"They didn't pick this place at random," Jeremiah said, his normally cheery expression gone. "This isn't a typical incursion."

I felt sick. "You mean, they're after me again. How? The bug is gone, and Rick said it was inert! And no slips can form here, and—"

"This isn't the time to worry about how," Malcolm said. He pulled out his phone and began texting. "I can have half a dozen fighting teams here in minutes."

"Many minutes. We don't have a wardstone," Viv said. Her attention was still fixed on the makeshift mirror.

"Contact them anyway," Jeremiah suggested. He made a complicated gesture and retrieved his wooden staff from the magical pocket dimension he stored it in. "We can hold the elves off."

"We are going to do more than hold them off," Malcolm said. "Taelinn Ailmach is going to regret testing me. Viv, how close are they?"

"They're two hundred feet from the house on the west and south. Those are the most overgrown approaches." Viv looked up. "Malcolm, you can't go out there."

"Most of my weapons and my night vision goggles are in the car. We don't stand a chance if I don't go." Malcolm squeezed my shoulder and ran for the front door before I could protest.

Instinctively, I picked up Connvuir and held him close. He struggled against my grip, but I was too afraid for Malcolm to pay attention. The sound of the door slamming behind him brought me to my senses. Malcolm wasn't stupid. He knew his abilities and he knew their limits. Standing there paralyzed wouldn't help him. But I could do something that would.

I sank onto the nearest sofa, whispering calming words to Connvuir. "Be still," I murmured. Surprisingly, he stopped fighting and stared at me with his unnaturally large eyes. I managed to smile at him, though it felt strained and I wasn't sure how comforting an expression it was. Then I focused on the question *How do we defeat these elves?*

Vision swept me up and carried me away. I briefly saw Viv's house from a drone's eye view, rising higher and higher until the image transformed into a line map dotted with lights. Seven sickly green lights like diseased fireflies. One bright blue glow moving swiftly from the outline of the house. Three more blue lights clustered at the center of the house, and one unexpectedly brilliant white light.

I guessed the white light was me, the target, but I ignored it in favor of watching the green fireflies advance slowly. Three came from the west, which was the back wall of the house—no windows to give them access, though I didn't think Jeremiah and Viv were stupid enough not to fortify all that glass. The other four approached from the south, heading straight for where our car was parked.

"The four on the south think they're drawing attention away from the three on the west," I said without losing the vision, though to me my voice was almost inaudible. "Those three plan to climb the side of the house and come in from above."

A dog yapped, and one of the green fireflies flickered and went out. I jerked out of the vision and realized that had been a gunshot, not a dog. Connvuir was whimpering at the tight hold I had on his waist. I made myself relax and cuddled him. "Malcolm got one. Viv, I don't think he's coming back."

Jeremiah swore. "He needs backup. Viv—"

"I know. Go." Viv followed Jeremiah to the door that opened on the porch and locked it behind him. Through the window, I saw Jeremiah take two steps and vanish into the viny growth covering the pergola.

I took a couple of calming breaths, though fear gripped me. Malcolm was good, but I'd seen him fight elves before, and they were a challenge even for him. And Jeremiah's skills at moving unseen through the wilderness might not be enough to compensate for him not having a cold iron weapon.

I tried to focus on another prophecy, but Connvuir began crying. I rose and jigged with him, bouncing him gently and trying to quiet him. Viv ignored us and hurried from window to window, pausing at each to trace lines on the glass with her fingertip. They didn't glow, or burn, and I couldn't picture what she had drawn. I hoped it was a strong defense, whatever it was.

Viv suddenly scrambled backwards. "Helena, get upstairs and barricade yourself into one of the rooms. Go now!"

I didn't hesitate. Still holding Connvuir, I ran for the stairs.

I was halfway up when I heard glass shatter. Viv shouted something that cut off sharply. Then the only sound was that of my shoes on the wooden steps.

I dashed down the short hall and into the one interior room in the whole house, the only one without windows. It was barely more than a cubicle, and built-in shelves made it even more cramped. Viv kept her crafting supplies there, orderly as the rest of her domain was not. I slammed the door and searched frantically for a lock or a deadbolt or silver chains or *anything* that might hold it against an elven attack. Nothing.

I put Connvuir down and with a desperate heave that strained every muscle I had shoved an old four-drawer dresser five inches across the floor to partially block the door. I panted heavily, then shoved again, but fear had sapped my first burst of strength, and I had only moved the dresser a foot when something slammed into the door. I shrieked and leaned against the dresser, which had bounced with the blow. The elf struck the door again, shifting the dresser an inch toward me. I put my back against it and braced, but the third blow was more powerful, like more than one elf had joined in the attack.

Terrified, I stared at Connvuir, who looked back at me in perfect calmness. "Good example," I said, and with all the willpower I could muster after more than ten years' experience with prophesying under pressure, I let a question sink deep within me: *What do the elves want?*

My rational brain screamed at me for wasting what was probably the only prophecy I would have time for. Obviously they were after me! But the part of me that was the oracle latched on to the question and carried me aloft in search of an answer. I saw elf faces, hundreds of elf faces, pale and emaciated and undead-looking with stringy, mad hair, all of them intent on—

—not me.

Surprised, I jerked out of the prophetic state just as the dresser slammed into my back and knocked me to my knees. I scrabbled out of the way as it toppled, shielding Connvuir with my body and half crawling, half rolling into a corner. In the small room, the dresser couldn't fall flat; instead, it wedged itself against the opposite wall. With its base now firmly planted, the door couldn't open more than a foot wide, but it was more than enough space for the first elf to slide his narrow upper body through the gap.

I shot upright and grabbed the first thing I could reach from the crowded shelves, which was a two-pound brick of modeling clay. I wound up and clocked the elf over his left ear. In that moment, I recognized him. "Viv better not be dead, Carth," I snarled as the king's right-hand man staggered, clutching an ear which trickled blood.

Carth backed away and drew his sword. "My king is not finished with you," he said hoarsely, like I'd struck his throat and not his head. "You will come with me."

"Nice try," I said. "But you didn't come for me. It's the child you want."

# Chapter Fifteen

Carth recoiled only slightly, his giant, mad eyes widening for a fraction of a second before his usual sneer reasserted itself. "What child?"

I swung the brick of clay again, but he deflected it this time and I overbalanced. Catching myself, I flung the brick at him. Carth dodged, and the clay hit the elf behind him, right between the eyes. Out of the corner of my vision, I saw the elf stagger backward. Anger surged through me, keeping fear at bay. I cast about frantically for another weapon. Bolts of Halloween fabric. Styrofoam in a dozen shapes. Giant bags of poly stuffing. Why wasn't Viv obsessed with ironworking or sword smithing?

Carth pulled himself fully through the gap and reached for me. Instinctively, I backed away. If he had the ability to put me to sleep, him touching me would be game over.

Connvuir let out a whimper, then screamed the shrill, terrified howl only a child can manage. Carth jerked as if the sound had hurt him. My hand fell on something metallic and angular, and I closed my fingers around it and swung whatever it was. It was lightweight and thin, but solid, and I registered that it was a cheap metal bookend, the kind office supply stores sell in bulk, in the second before its sharp bottom corner slashed Carth's face.

Carth screamed, nearly as shrilly as Connvuir, and clapped his hand to his eye. Blood welled between his fingers. That had been a lucky strike with an improbable weapon, and I wasn't going to get many more of those. "Help!" I shouted. "They're up here!" I refused to consider that I might be the only one of us left able to fight.

Breathing heavily, Carth lowered his hand. His eyelid sagged, and his face was covered with blood. "You will not live to tell anyone about the child," he said, and drew his short sword.

I put myself between the elf and Connvuir and wished I had a gun. *Now* fear gripped me. Backing away, I said, "Your king won't like you killing me, will he? Leave now, and you might make it back to Faerie alive."

His lips curled in a snarl. "Brave, stupid words from the walking dead."

My gaze flicked desperately from shelf to shelf. I never dared take my full attention from Carth, but the part of me that had survived monster attacks and the destruction of an alien reality was not giving up. Judy always said anything could be a weapon if you had the right attitude. I hoped she was right.

I feinted right, and when Carth swung at me, I dodged to the left and grabbed Viv's antique grommet press one-handed. It was a cast-iron, angular thing Viv used to fasten rivets and other metal pieces to fabric, it weighed a ton, and if I hadn't been terrified I could barely have lifted it with two hands, let alone one. Fear gave me strength, and I swung the thing so it connected with Carth's right arm with a dull crack.

Bone snapped. Carth howled again and dropped his sword. I let the press fall and snatched up the weapon, gripping it with both hands and aiming a mighty blow at the elf's midsection. Bronze clanged against bronze as I struck his armor instead. Cursing myself, I withdrew a step, all I could manage in the narrow space, and swung at his head.

Carth dropped, curling in on his broken arm, and my strike whiffed past his scalp. "Back away, or your leader dies!" I shouted, realizing in the next second that it was unlikely the other elves spoke

English. Then I realized there wasn't anyone else in the hall. I couldn't even see the elf I'd brained with the lump of clay. Fear surged again, this time for my husband and friends. If the other elves were dealing with them...

Panting, I rested the edge of the blade against Carth's throat. "Call them off," I said, "or I'll test this sword on your jugular."

"I don't take orders from humans," Carth said. He started to get to his feet, but I pressed harder, and he froze.

"You heard me. Call them off." I squeezed the hilt hard to keep myself from trembling. It didn't work. Well, it wasn't as if I expected to bluff Carth.

Carth said nothing. My hand shook harder. I wished he would lunge at me so I could finish him off. Killing in cold blood had never been something I could manage.

Then I heard Malcolm call my name. Carth twitched, and I kicked him in the face. Maybe I was more cold-blooded than I realized. "I'm up here!"

Connvuir began crying, not the horrifying shriek like having an icepick jammed through your eardrum, but a more normal, exhausted-sounding weeping. I didn't dare take my attention off Carth, so I said, "It's all right, Connvuir, everything will be all right."

Carth jerked again when I said Connvuir's name, and the strangeness of this episode finally penetrated my overwhelmed mind. "You want to take Connvuir," I said. "Why? You acted like he wasn't important when I asked you about him in Faerie." When Carth didn't answer, I prodded him again. "Who is he? Is he Taelinn's heir or something?"

Footsteps pounded down the hall, and Malcolm's face appeared in the doorway. "Helena!"

"I'm not hurt—no, don't shoot him! He has answers!"

"I don't give a damn about answers," Malcolm said, but he lowered his gun.

"It's important. Malcolm, the king sent these elves to kidnap Connvuir. We need to find out why."

"*Connvuir*? Not you?" Malcolm's gaze rested on the crying child. "You're right. We need answers."

Viv and Jeremiah came into view behind Malcolm. None of them looked injured. Viv cast her gaze over the ruined storage room and said, "Look at that mess. I had a system!"

"Where are the other elves?" I asked.

"Dead," Malcolm said, "all but one, who fled when she saw the tide of battle was against her. Jeremiah and I let her go when we realized there were two unaccounted for and guessed they made it inside." He extended his gun to me. "Keep this trained on him while we get you all out of there."

"That jackass put me to sleep," Viv growled. "I'm getting sick of being treated like a fainting maiden in a tower. Why haven't you killed him?"

"Because he led this raid to try to take Connvuir, not me," I said. I dropped Carth's sword and held the gun pointed at his chest. The trembling had mostly stopped, but the gun was lighter than the sword, for which I was grateful. Carth didn't need to know it was keyed to Malcolm and I couldn't shoot even if I'd wanted to.

"Connvuir? I hope this isn't the kid's father, because those are not genetics I'd wish on anyone." Viv stepped back for Jeremiah to stand next to Malcolm, and the two men hauled the dresser upright and out of the way. I stood there aiming the gun at Carth and thought how easy it would be, if it were my gun, to squeeze the trigger and end this danger. He would have killed me as easily as squashing a spider, and even the peaceful soul I hoped I was didn't think one less elf in the world was a tragedy. But he knew something about Connvuir, and that ended my desire for his immediate death.

Viv squeezed around me to pick up Connvuir, who subsided into snuffling whimpers and buried his face in Viv's shoulder. Then Malcolm gently took the gun from me and said, "Downstairs. We need to find out if that elf is bringing reinforcements. There may not be much time for interrogation."

"You will be overrun in minutes," Carth muttered. "You ought to run, now, not that it will help, because the Ailmach will send others after me."

A spontaneous prophecy hit me hard enough I had to stop mid-step or run into the wall. "He will not. This was a risk he thought was worth taking, but that's all it was. You're expendable, Carth."

Carth glared at me like he thought I was lying. If I hadn't had the prophecy, I wouldn't have believed it myself. I was sure the king relied heavily on Carth to carry out his more complex and important plans, like searching the elf city for a runaway oracle. But the vision left me certain that in this case, the king wanted Connvuir enough to risk losing his right-hand man and relative for good. The passing thought struck me that we might use this to drive a wedge between Carth and the king, if Carth believed he'd been betrayed, but I dismissed it. It was a good idea, but not something I knew how to use.

Malcolm and Jeremiah hauled Carth to his feet, dragging him past the second elf, who groaned when Carth stepped heavily on his hand. "I forgot about him," I exclaimed. "I guess it was too good to be true for a brick of clay to kill him."

"We'll take care of him, too," Jeremiah said. He aimed the end of his staff at the moaning elf, and whippy tendrils of living roots extended from it, binding the elf's hands and arms.

"I'll take him," I told Viv, extending my hands to receive Connvuir.

Viv gave me a strange look, but gave the boy to me. "Are you sure you're all right?"

"Of course. Carth didn't hurt me."

"I meant—never mind." Viv's gaze fell on Connvuir, then drifted to me. I tried to smile, but I was sure it looked ghastly.

Holding Connvuir, whose sobs had dwindled into shuddering sniffles, I followed everyone else downstairs, where Malcolm and Jeremiah bound our captives to two kitchen chairs with the curtain ropes. The semiconscious elf didn't fight back, but Carth let out a pained grunt when Jeremiah jogged his broken arm. Jeremiah reflexively loosened his grip, and Carth tried to make a break for it. Malcolm pinned him with what I thought was technically unnecessary force, in the sense that skinny Carth was no match for someone Malcolm's size, but I didn't care about the elf being roughed up.

When Carth was secured, I stood in front of him and said, "Why were you after Connvuir?"

Carth glared at me, one eye fierce, the other closed and weeping blood. He said nothing.

I rolled my eyes. "Carth, we could be here all night. Tell me what I want to know, and you can go back to Faerie. You and your friend."

"I don't make deals with humans," Carth retorted.

Malcolm drew one of his steel knives and ran his finger along the edge as if testing it. "It's not a deal. You think this is about your life? I'll feel no remorse about making you suffer for a long, long time."

"Malcolm, that's not necessary." I wasn't sure how this had turned into Good Cop, Bad Cop, but I knew Malcolm would play along. "Carth, just tell me why Connvuir matters. Do you really think we can do anything with the knowledge? It can't be worth your life, or what will be left of it once my husband is through with you."

Carth shot a glance at Malcolm, then back at me as if the word "husband" had startled him, but he didn't answer.

"Thanks, Gabriel," Viv said from behind me. I had a moment's confusion about whether Gabriel Roarke had impossibly teleported into Viv's house, and then Viv came into view, shoving her phone into her back pocket. She knelt behind the other elf and gripped his bound hand, squeezing tightly.

The elf sprang awake, gasping. Viv shuddered and released him. "I asked Gabriel if elves had to choose to take language from someone. He said the less conscious they are, the less control they have over the process. I figured having a second person to interrogate might help." She returned to stand in front of the elf, whose breath was now sobbing in and out of his mouth like he'd been running hard.

"Okay, you." I waved a hand in front of the elf's face to draw his attention. "What's your name?"

"We don't give our names to the enemy," the elf said, his words halting. He sounded like someone just testing out a new language he wasn't sure he liked, which I guess was true.

"That's fine, I'll call you Hermey," I said. "Hermey, why did Taelinn Ailmach send you all here?"

Carth said something low and cutting in Elvish. Hermey lowered his eyes and remained silent. Then Carth said, "You are dishonorable to expect him to betray his superiors."

"*I'm* dishonorable? You were going to kill a child!"

"That's a lie. We came here to take him back to where he belongs. No human should kidnap an elven child."

"We didn't kidnap him! His mother—" I shut up before Malcolm could nudge me into remembering not to give information to the enemy. "Carth. Last chance. I want to know why your king wants Connvuir. Is he Taelinn's heir or something?"

"Carth," Hermey said, then followed it up with a string of words in Elvish, low and urgent.

Carth sneered. "I told you," he said, "my king doesn't believe humans should keep an elven child. Elves belong to Faerie. That's all."

Another spontaneous prophecy struck me, this one wordless knowledge rather than visual. "That's not true. Connvuir is someone important. He's not Taelinn's heir, so who is he?"

"I'm not—"

I slapped him. Not hard, but I was still on edge from the episode in the room upstairs and nervous energy and fear for Connvuir moved my hand. "I'm out of patience, and you're out of chances. Malcolm, take him outside and kill him. I'm sure Viv and Jeremiah don't want blood on their floor."

"Connvuir Tionn is the son of Keilaer Tionn," Hermey blurted out.

Carth nearly wrenched himself out of his seat, shouting at Hermey to shut up—at least, that's what I assumed the hard, vicious syllables in Elvish meant. I turned my attention on Hermey again. "Who is Keilaer Tionn?" I asked, stumbling over the unfamiliar syllables. "Is he important?"

"She is, or was before you humans killed her," Hermey said. "She was Clissach Lachma's sister. Connvuir Tionn is his only heir."

# Chapter Sixteen

"His heir?" Jeremiah said, echoing Malcolm. "Helena, you said Lachma is behind the elven incursions into our world. The same Lachma?"

I nodded. "That's what the king told me. Carth, is it true?" I didn't doubt Hermey—he sounded desperate enough I didn't think he was lying—but I was sure Carth, in the king's confidences, knew more than Hermey. I hoped Hermey's breaking would convince Carth there was no point keeping secrets anymore.

Carth's head sagged. "It's true."

"Then why—" It came to me in a flash, not prophetic insight but simple obvious knowledge. "Taelinn wants to use Connvuir against Lachma, to gain an edge. Lachma's trying to destroy him, indirectly maybe, but it still amounts to Taelinn losing his position and his world."

"And we already know Taelinn won't hesitate to use every advantage," Malcolm said.

My distaste for the elf king grew. War was one thing, and maybe I didn't hold it against him that he'd kidnapped me, but using a child as a bargaining tool was repulsive. On the other hand, Clissach Lachma was actively evil in a different way. If *he* had Connvuir… "How did the king know Connvuir was missing?"

Carth tilted his head so his one good eye could focus on me. "He has informants everywhere. Clan Tionn became agitated about two weeks ago, sending out more than the usual number of hunting and foraging parties. It was enough to recognize they were looking for someone. Then Lachma's forces changed their focus to within Faerie instead of their assaults on this world, and there were rumors about Fiachtein Tionn, Keilaer's husband, disappearing."

"Disappearing? Like, he's dead?"

"Like I said, rumors. Maybe he's only ill or incapacitated. But some people said Keilaer killed him before escaping, and others said Lachma captured him to force him to say where Connvuir went."

Carth's sudden talkativeness filled me with suspicion. "Why tell me this?" I demanded. "Aren't you afraid we'll use this information against you?"

"You can't if you're dead," Carth said.

Malcolm suddenly drew his gun and stepped back, looking wildly around the room. Jeremiah put his staff's end against Hermey's throat, and Viv ran to block the door. "He's escaped," Malcolm said. "Watch the windows. An invisible elf—"

I watched Carth, who was still seated. He shifted like he was working free of the ropes. "It's an illusion. He didn't go anywhere," I said.

Carth's mouth fell open in a comical expression of bewilderment. The ropes securing him to the chair had loosened, sagging so he could easily pull free, but he ignored them. "That's impossible. You're human."

"You need to stop assuming things about what humans can or can't do," I told him. "And I suggest you tell me everything you know about the king's plan to recover Connvuir. How did he know where to look for him? I know I gave away that I knew about him, but that can't have been enough once we got rid of your stupid implant."

Carth didn't fight as Jeremiah tightened his bindings. "You shouldn't have known the child's name. My king guessed there was only one way you could have learned it, which is that you had taken him. He thought you knew what you had and that you'd acted deliberately to gain a weapon against Clissach Lachma. So we used the eistechor to listen to your talk and confirmed Connvuir Tionn was in your hands."

"The eiste—you mean the implant."

Carth nodded. "But you destroyed it. We guessed you would find it, but not that soon." He again sounded bewildered and a little afraid.

I decided not to rub it in that human magic was a match for elven magic, especially since I was sure we'd gotten lucky in some respects. "So Taelinn sent you to retrieve Connvuir. That still doesn't tell me how you found him. You couldn't have gotten into our house, and I bet our wards are powerful enough to block any scrying you might have done." At least, I hoped that was true. The idea of elves spying on me and my family sickened me.

"Our magic didn't perceive the boy in this world. My king was certain of his conclusions, though. So he had people watching and waiting. That paid off faster than we expected, too."

I dismissed a momentary pang of guilt at having exposed Connvuir to this kidnapping attempt by wanting a weekend to myself. Connvuir couldn't stay in my house forever, and if the king was that alert, he'd have discovered the boy eventually. "How was the king planning to use Connvuir against his... I guess Lachma is his uncle?"

Carth gave me another baleful, one-eyed stare. "I don't know. He won't hurt the child. We're not monsters."

His undead face, the gory eye, looked terribly monstrous to me. "Still, that's a vicious thing to do, weaponize a child. War or no war."

"You're naïve. Lachma must be neutralized. I don't know why you don't understand that, given how he plans to destroy your world. If holding his heir hostage will do it, then that's what it takes." Carth said these words in a flat, toneless voice, like he was reciting orders.

"I—"

Malcolm put a hand on my elbow, warning me not to continue. I shut up before I could be drawn into a moral argument with an elf who probably didn't see me as any less an enemy than he did Lachma.

"Jeremiah?" Malcolm said.

Jeremiah nodded. "I'll watch."

Malcolm, still holding my elbow, drew me out of the room and out the front door. Viv, following, shut it behind us. "Now what?" he asked.

"You're asking me?" I said. "I don't know that there's anything else we can learn from him. Do we... should we kill them?" I again wished I wasn't so weak. If Carth and Hermey were a threat to us—particularly a threat to my children and Connvuir—they needed to be eliminated.

"Carth didn't kill me," Viv said. "The two of them teleported past the wards using that short-range shadowstep ability elves have, which is terrifying that they can bypass... anyway, they came at me from behind, and it would have been faster to kill me. Probably safer for them, if they thought I was armed, which I wasn't. But they put me to sleep instead."

"Meaning what?" I asked.

"That Taelinn Ailmach wants to avoid war with humans," Malcolm said. "If he captured Connvuir, he could make the case that elves belong with elves, but if he killed humans to do it, that would be much harder to wave away. He wants to make this an internal matter. And he's not wrong. We really have no business interfering in elf politics."

"But we can't let him use Connvuir as a hostage," I exclaimed.

"Lucia wouldn't let us mount a rescue if Taelinn succeeded in taking him," Malcolm replied. "In truth, we ought to let Carth take him —no, Helena, I'm just saying that's the logical thing to do. I actually think the Wardens are better off if we continue to care for Connvuir. At the very least, it will make the elves think twice about attacking in force. Taelinn strikes me as the sort of political animal who will believe we mean to use the boy against him in our own way."

"And if this Clissach Lachma finds out we've got his heir?" Viv said. "Won't that piss him off enough to come after us?"

"Not if he thinks we could kill the boy if he does," Malcolm said. "Which is exactly what a monster like him would believe."

"That's horrible," I said automatically, but I didn't disagree. The thought of Connvuir in Lachma's control was too awful to contemplate. I couldn't help imagining what the sweet little boy might grow up to be if he was dominated by his uncle.

"Horrible, but we can use it to our advantage," Malcolm said. "I think we should send those two back to their king. Let Taelinn know we're not defenseless and we're not going to give him a hostage no matter how justified he is in believing elves should be with elves. Unless you have a prophecy telling me otherwise, Helena?"

"I don't think I need a prophecy. What you say makes sense. Even so..." I leaned against the door and let myself fall into a contemplative state. No prophecy welled up inside me. "I think the oracle agrees. Or it's a situation where it doesn't matter what we do."

"Call Rick, then, and have him bring the slip key here," Malcolm said. "We won't risk showing them a slip they can access that's near this place."

"Drive them into the countryside and abandon them, you mean?" Viv said. "I love this plan."

I pulled out my phone. "You don't think the king will be angry that we killed his people, given that they spared Viv?"

"He's got no leg to stand on," Malcolm said, "and if he forces the issue, I'm prepared to show him why that's a bad idea."

---

IT TOOK ALMOST AN HOUR FOR RICK TO SHOW UP, AND when he did, it was with Lucia and fifteen Wardens armed with steel blades and pistols loaded with steel rounds. They guided our captives into one of the Gunther Node's signature little white vans with more care than I thought they deserved. Lucia watched the proceedings with a grim little smile. "This is definitely counter to the terms of my agreement with the king," she said, "but I have a feeling he'll lawyer up, or whatever it is elves do when they're exploiting a legal loophole. At any rate, I'll make a big deal about how we aren't going to retaliate, maybe make some threats, and I bet I can squeeze more concessions out of him."

"What did you agree to, in the end?" I asked.

"Mutual non-hostilities. The possibility of augmenting our forces with elven warriors, if Lachma makes a bigger push. I rejected utterly the idea that we would do all the fighting. Taelinn agreed to provide us with information about the enemy's movements. I know he still hopes we'll make Lachma our problem and get the guy off the king's back, and that's even possible, but I won't admit it."

"You mean because Lachma is still directing his attacks at humans," Malcolm said.

"Right. We have to defend ourselves regardless of what it does for the elf king." Lucia shook her head slowly in mock despair. "It's too bad we can't figure out how to turn that around, get Lachma fighting Taelinn's people until they either destroy each other or are too weak to come after us."

"I wish—" I began.

"Davies, your compassion does you credit, but I don't think there's any ending to this fight that leads to humans and elves living in harmony like some kind of Coca-Cola commercial." Lucia patted my shoulder as if to make up for the harshness of her words. "What matters is that humans aren't destroyed by elves. That's where the Wardens priorities lie."

I didn't say anything. That had been a warning: *you are a Warden, too.* And I couldn't exactly argue with her, because she was right. But...

Lucia got into the passenger seat of the van Rick was driving, and the little caravan drove away. Malcolm put his arm around my shoulders. "You know she's doing what she believes is best."

"I know." I sighed. "Let's go. We should get Connvuir home."

"Don't you still want to leave Connvuir here?" Viv asked. "Or are you too worried about his safety? You know we can protect him."

I looked at the little boy, and my heart ached. "Of course. But I—it feels wrong to go off and have fun after all that. Anticlimactic." It wasn't completely a lie, but it wasn't the whole truth. I still felt embarrassed about being so attached to an elf child, and the idea of admitting the truth was uncomfortable.

Viv gave me a playful shove. "Get out of here and relax. You'll get over that feeling."

I stopped myself protesting. She was right. And I knew Viv well enough to know when she needed to be alone with Jeremiah for her own relaxation time. "Thanks," I said, hugging her.

This time, Malcolm drove. "It's going to be all right. Stop worrying that we should have gone with Lucia."

Startled, I said, "I didn't say that."

"No, but you've got the same look you always do when there's a giant spider loose in the kitchen. Even if I'm the one who gets rid of it, you want to watch so you know it's gone for good and you can relax."

I sighed. "All right, it's true that part of me is still worried about elves attacking. But I trust Lucia, and I know Rick is better than competent, and they'll find a place they can shove Carth and Hermey—"

"Why on earth did you pick that name?"

"Hermey? Oh. Like Hermey the elf from the Rudolph the Red-Nosed Reindeer cartoon."

Malcolm started laughing. "Nice way to make him less frightening. That's an elf no one could be scared of."

"Right? Anyway, they'll send those two back to Faerie, and Taelinn will have one more reason not to be dismissive of human abilities." I sighed again. "I'm just having trouble letting go of the fight or flight response."

"Isn't it 'fight, flight, or freeze'?"

"Whatever. It agitates me no matter which of those options I go with. Tell me where we're going? Maybe anticipation of that will take agitation's place."

"Dinner at Giuseppe's, then home. I thought about a hotel, but why do that when our house is luxurious and empty?"

The thought of my favorite restaurant did calm me some. "All right, but I expect our bed to get a real workout tonight."

"You're thinking more clearly already," Malcolm said.

# CHAPTER SEVENTEEN

Lucia called late Sunday afternoon while Malcolm was away picking up the children. "Good. You didn't leave the house with the boy. You have some sense of self-preservation, after all."

"Hi, Lucia. And I do so have self-preservation instincts. I never get into trouble except when..." Memories of a dozen times I'd gone charging into a dangerous situation filled my head, and I shut up.

"Right, Davies," Lucia drawled as if she'd had the same memories. "I need a prophecy, if you're not busy."

"Just a minute." I gathered Connvuir off the tall stool he'd been sitting on at the table, eating banana slices. I'd never seen a child so in love with bananas. Possibly they didn't grow in Faerie. I washed his face and hands and settled him on the floor in the great room with a pile of colorful wooden blocks. "All right."

"Is Connvuir's father dead?"

The bluntness of the question startled me, but before I could respond, prophecy swept me up like a whirlwind. Unlike my previous inquiries about elves, this one was direct and to the point. I saw an elf from before, the one Jenny had identified as Connvuir's father, and gagged at the bloody mess his chest was. He'd been stabbed multiple times, and his face had that empty, vacant look I'd seen on dead bodies before. Then the vision released me, and I gasped for breath, willing away the stink of death that despite being imaginary still sickened me.

Finally, I picked up my phone again. "He's dead. Stabbed to death. I don't know who did it, except I doubt his wife could have caused that many wounds in the condition she was in."

"According to the king, it was Clissach Lachma. Taelinn claims Lachma killed Fiachtein Tionn when the guy wouldn't tell him where he'd hidden Connvuir."

I shook my head, though Lucia couldn't see me. "That doesn't make sense. I'm certain Connvuir's mother was fleeing someone when she came here, someone who'd beaten her so severely she was dying as she ran. And between my prophecies and Jenny's, I'm sure that person was her husband. If anything, he was trying to get Connvuir back, not conceal him somewhere in our world. The king must be mistaken."

"That complicates things. I asked for that prophecy because the way Taelinn talked, I wasn't sure he was telling the truth about Connvuir's father being dead."

"I don't understand."

I heard unintelligible voices in the background, and Lucia didn't respond to me right away. When the voices stopped, Lucia said, "Taelinn wants us to return Connvuir to him on the grounds that humans should not keep elf children away from their kind. He said Connvuir's parents are dead, and as king, he has a better right to care for him than we do."

"But—I hate to point this out, but Lachma is a close relative. If anyone has a right to Connvuir, it's him. Not that I think we should turn Connvuir over to him."

"That's technically true. But Taelinn is right about one thing—we can't steal an elf child—"

"It's not stealing! His mother begged me to care for him!"

"Just listen and stop panicking, Davies," Lucia said, cutting over my words. "The point is that if this was a human child who fell into elven hands, we'd demand that child's return. Taelinn isn't wrong about that."

I put a calming hand on Connvuir's shoulder, shushing him as he made whimpering noises in response to my shout. "All right. I understand. But it doesn't change anything."

"That's right. If we give Connvuir to Taelinn, it solidly puts us in his camp and potentially makes us look like his lackeys. Not to mention it gives him tremendous power over Lachma's crowd. Normally, I'd see that as a good thing, but I can't guarantee that Taelinn would use that power to bring Lachma to heel, or that he wouldn't then turn on us once Lachma isn't a threat. And from what I've seen of Lachma's predations on us, I'm not convinced he wants the best for the kid. I wouldn't put it past him to eliminate Connvuir rather than bow to the king."

I felt sick at the thought. "But Connvuir's his heir."

"Roarke tells me elven lines of inheritance are always well established," Lucia said. "It's likely Lachma has more heirs in waiting."

I rose from my seat and paced the length of the great room, turning in a tight circle when I reached the French doors leading to the patio. "So Connvuir's not safe with anyone but us."

"And keeping him with us is not a long-term solution," Lucia said. "But—"

She stopped speaking so abruptly I checked my phone display to see if she'd disconnected. "Lucia?"

"Sorry," Lucia said. "Taelinn's communication device just lit up. Take care of the kid, and I'll talk to you later." *Now* she hung up.

I cradled my phone in both hands and stared at it as if it could come to life and give me direction. A phone call, a text, anything to show me which thread to pull next. Lucia was right; Connvuir couldn't stay with us forever unless he never left our house, and that was impossible no matter how much I cared about him. The attack by Carth's warriors had proven there would always be someone watching for the boy to leave our warded location, and they only had to get lucky once.

A tug on my jeans leg drew my attention to Connvuir, who grabbed my pants with one hand and waved at the television with the other. "It's not good for you to spend all your time watching TV," I told him. He stared back at me blankly. "But you haven't watched anything today, so I guess that isn't something to worry about. Come on."

I sat on the couch with Connvuir on my lap and turned on one of Jenny's favorite cartoon movies. Then I stared at the screen without processing the images. I didn't need a phone call to get direction. I should prophesy for an answer to my concerns. But Lucia's information had shaken me. For once, I wasn't sure I wanted an answer, because all the possibilities I saw had some terrible flaw. Give the child to Taelinn, and entangle the Wardens in the elven civil war. Give the child to Lachma—I shuddered. No, not that. Keep the child, and be forced into constant vigilance for the rest of his life, or at least until he was old enough to watch out for himself. Even I couldn't justify my way out of that reality. Connvuir couldn't stay with me.

The door to the garage banged open, and my children came running in. "No fair!" Duncan shouted. "I'm supposed to get video game time!"

"Calm down, Duncan, I won't take that from you, and you know you have to read aloud to me before you play." I wiped tears from my eyes and gave him a hug he struggled away from.

"Duncan, be polite," Malcolm said. "Alastair, put your shoes in the cubby instead of kicking them across the floor."

I accepted Duncan's backpack. Homework. Something normal and not at all fraught with heartache. "Why don't you bring me your book?"

"Can I read to Alastair instead?"

"I have to pick the book if you do," Alastair said.

I tried not to laugh. Duncan believed Alastair picked books for him I wouldn't approve of, but the truth was Alastair's choices challenged him beyond what he thought he was capable of. Since Duncan claimed not to love reading, I was fully in favor of this backhanded way of helping him improve his skills. "Well, if you're sure," I began.

Alastair and Duncan raced for the stairs before I could finish that sentence. I never stopped being amazed at how much energy young children had.

Malcolm handed Jenny to me, and I settled her next to Connvuir. "Thanks for taking her with you," I told Malcolm. "Now that she's outgrown naps, I was afraid she'd disturb Connvuir during his. She likes playing with him."

"Does it make you wish we had another child?"

"I feel too old to manage another pregnancy." My gaze fixed on Connvuir, though, and Malcolm noticed it. "I know," I said before he could speak. "We can't keep him. We'd spend the rest of our lives protecting ourselves from elven attacks. I can't tangle my family up in elf politics no matter how much I care about him."

Malcolm's phone rang before he could respond. He glanced at the display, frowned, and said, "It's Lucia."

"She called me just a few minutes ago," I said, but he was already turning away to take the call.

Jenny snuggled into my lap. "I like car rides, but I like cartoons better. Will you watch with me?"

"Only for a minute. I have to get dinner started."

"Helena," Malcolm said. His voice was low and urgent, the way he sounded when an emergency was imminent. "Come in here."

I set Jenny on the couch and joined Malcolm in the kitchen, around the corner by the refrigerator and out of sight of the kids and the TV. "What happened?"

"King Taelinn just contacted Lucia," Malcolm said. "He accused her of sending warriors to attack him and his city."

"That's impossible."

"Impossible that Lucia would do it," Malcolm said. "But she said Taelinn was too angry to be lying, and I believe her judgment. Which means rogue Wardens—"

This time, it was my phone that rang. I snatched it out of my pocket. "Lucia, what's going on?"

"I need to know who those Wardens were, Davies," Lucia said. She didn't waste time telling me what Malcolm had.

"All right." I leaned against the center island and filled myself with a desire to know the truth.

The prophecy came sluggishly, as if the oracle was reluctant to reveal its knowledge. I hated when that happened, because it usually meant I wasn't going to like the answer. Why I did that to myself, I didn't know —after all, I was the oracle, so if a prophecy was difficult, that was ultimately on me—but it was a quirk I'd learned to appreciate over the years, if only because it let me mentally prepare myself.

Finally, a series of images whirled past, pausing in front of me like little windows on reality that showed a scene long enough for me to fully examine it before whisking away. Wardens I didn't know, a city skyline I'd seen in movies, far too many dead bodies, and finally a single face. From the other images, it was a face I'd half expected to see.

"Lucia," I said, "Rebecca Greenough sent a lot of Wardens through a slip somewhere in England. They assaulted the elves' capital city. Lots of people died, elves and Wardens—"

Lucia spat a blistering curse I silently and wholeheartedly agreed with. "That idiot bitch," Lucia said. "She wanted to prove I'm incompetent and that she's a better choice to handle the elves. Now we've got a lot of dead Wardens and an elf king who thinks humans are treacherous, lying snakes."

I didn't know how to respond to that. "Wouldn't this prove the opposite? To the Wardens, I mean."

"It won't matter if Taelinn sends his people through to slaughter humans in retribution. He doesn't get that most humans don't have anything to do with this conflict, and he won't confine his warriors to attacking only Wardens." Lucia swore again. "Thanks for the confirmation. I'll see if I can't talk him down."

"What about Greenough?"

"I don't have time to worry about her now, but you can be sure I'll use this to destroy her support." Lucia let out a bitter laugh. "The way I feel now, I'm not sure I'd deny Taelinn his revenge if he demanded her head on a silver platter." She hung up.

I closed my eyes and hugged Malcolm, welcoming his embrace in return. "This is a nightmare. I can't believe even Rebecca Greenough could be so stupid."

"People who crave power are often shortsighted," Malcolm said, "or see the world through the very narrow scope of their ambition. What infuriates me is that Greenough is unlikely to be the one who pays for her stupid mistake."

"She already hasn't. Malcolm, that was a *lot* of dead Wardens." I blinked away tears. "I shouldn't be so grateful that it wasn't the Wardens I know, but that's the only way I can look at this and not be devastated."

"I understand." Malcolm released me. "Let's make dinner together and try to distract ourselves. I'm sure Lucia will call again tonight for more guidance."

But Lucia didn't call. I went through dinner and the evening's activities and bedtime rituals with my attention half diverted, waiting to hear the ring. Finally, after putting the kids to bed, I cuddled with Malcolm on the great room couch and made myself pay attention to *The Postman Always Rings Twice*. I'd seen it only once before and didn't know it well enough to let it be background noise. Film noir suited my current unsettled mood.

When the movie was almost over, my phone rang. Malcolm sat up, dislodging me. I snatched up my phone from where it lay on the end table. "Lucia?"

"We're not at war yet," Lucia said, "but we're close. I managed to convince Taelinn Ailmach that the attack was unauthorized. He's agreed to hold off attacking us for now."

"Why 'for now'? If he believes you—"

"Just wait, Davies. I had to explain about Greenough challenging my authority, which led to him concluding that I didn't have the power to treat with him so long as she was involved. I had to promise I would deal with her immediately." Lucia sounded weary beyond words. "I think he's bluffing about the extent of his forces. What can you tell—"

Prophecy struck me before she finished her sentence. This time, a sweeping vista of the snow-covered plains beside the king's city appeared, and I gasped and felt the gasp in my own throat, not just in vision. "Lucia," I stammered when I caught my breath, "Lucia. He's not bluffing. I don't know if he can really field all those warriors, but there are a lot of them. More even than Lachma commands."

"I hoped," Lucia said, and fell silent. "Okay. I have to go to London immediately. I'm sending Rick to you with the eistechor. The only other one of Taelinn's demands I agreed to is that you be the one he communicates with while I'm gone. I think he's still convinced that a 'visionary,' as he puts it, is always in a position of power, 'power' meaning 'command.'"

"I thought the eistechor was the thing he implanted in me."

"It means any item that can transmit information over a distance, I'm told. I'm sorry to dump this on you—"

"Don't be sorry. Go beat Greenough senseless."

"It may yet come to that," Lucia said, not joking.

When she hung up, I repeated the details to Malcolm. Malcolm looked grim. "This might be dangerous. Did Lucia tell you how to treat with Taelinn if he makes more demands?"

"She didn't, but I don't need to be told that I should put him off and not commit to anything."

"Fair enough." He turned off the television, where the movie was still playing. "I'll check on the children. Why don't you make some herbal tea? I think we could both use some calming down before Rick arrives."

I nodded and went into the kitchen to set the kettle to boil. The image of dead Wardens on the snowy plain was hard to shake. That there had been nearly as many dead elves didn't comfort me. The whole thing was so *stupid*. If Lachma wasn't a vicious brute... if Greenough wasn't selfish and power hungry... if the king was strong enough to face down Lachma himself... there were a lot of 'ifs' that all added up to this conflict potentially stretching out for years, up until the balance of power was disrupted and one side eliminated the other. Lachma, of course, couldn't be allowed to win. But I remembered Thandaigh and Dachtein, and the idea of Wardens wiping out the elves, all of them including the ones who just wanted to live their lives, didn't satisfy me. If there was another solution, it wasn't one the oracle knew about.

My distorted reflection in the side of the silvery kettle seemed to taunt me. If the oracle didn't know the solution, that meant something inside me refused to answer the one question that might save millions of lives. I hated thinking that way. Being an oracle didn't make me more valuable a human being than anyone else, and I didn't like believing I had that much power. There were so many others involved in fighting this war, and I needed to trust that they, too, had abilities that made a difference.

But I knew on some level, I was lying to myself.

# CHAPTER EIGHTEEN

"I can't believe the king sent us a crystal ball," I said, staring at the thing sitting on the center island of my kitchen.

"It does feel weird to have this concept in common with elves," Rick said, "except who knows if they're the ones who gave the idea to humans? It might not be that farfetched."

I gazed into the orb's swirling depths. The eistechor was the size of a bowling ball and, as I'd learned when Rick handed it to me, almost as heavy. It had no base, so I'd made a nest for it by piling a hand towel in the center of an aluminum baking pan. Rick had assured me it was unbreakable, but I couldn't quite believe him, not with how fragile it looked.

It seemed to be entirely full of creamy, thick liquid, like pancake batter with too much added milk. Pastel colors, pink and baby blue and a very light yellow, wove like filmy ribbons through the liquid, stretching and contracting and at times dissolving completely only for more colors to arise. "It's mesmerizing," I said.

"That doesn't sound good," Malcolm said. He had barely glanced at the thing before turning his attention elsewhere. "Suppose it puts you in a suggestible frame of mind?"

"Eventually you'll get bored of watching. It can't actually hypnotize you." Rick leaned against the island with his back to the eistechor and crossed his arms over his chest. "But it's better if you don't leave it in here."

"What if someone uses it to contact me? If it's in my office, I might not hear it."

"Put your hand against it, like palming a basketball."

I followed his instructions, half expecting a tingle from an electrical zap. Instead, it was cool to the touch, but my palm warmed rapidly until the feeling was almost too hot to bear. I yanked my hand away a second before Rick said, "That's long enough. Now it's attuned to you, and you'll feel a little warning tug when the eistechor is active. Nothing painful, Lucia says, and it's not the kind of connection that lets someone spy on you."

I'd been about to ask that question. "Thanks, Rick."

"Lucia told you what to say if Taelinn reaches out?"

"She called again before she left and gave me instructions that I wasn't to agree to anything, but to answer his questions honestly. I hate that idea. I don't like giving Taelinn information he might use against us. But Lucia gets the political angle better than I do."

"We have to do what we can to keep Taelinn satisfied so he doesn't go on the attack," Malcolm said. "Anything short of a promise is fair game. Besides, we might use communication with him to gain information from him rather than the other way around."

"Fair enough." Rick pushed away from the island. "I have to be getting back. Tomorrow's going to be another busy day. We've stepped up our manufacture of the slip keys in preparation for the worst."

"You mean, if Lucia can't bring Greenough to heel, and if she can't convince Taelinn not to invade in force?" The idea sickened me. "That sounds like we would attack first."

"We can't afford not to. It's not great, fighting a war in enemy territory, but the risk of elves killing civilians if they attack here is too great." Rick grimaced. "What I hate is that the strategy makes sense to me. I never considered myself a military thinker before. It's unsettling. Like I'm going to start seeing people in terms of how I can prevent them from attacking me."

I hugged him. "You won't. You save lives."

"I hold to that." Rick gathered up his coat and headed for the front door.

Malcolm and I saw him out and made sure everything was locked behind him. I hated feeling like we were under siege, but I wasn't about to make things easy on a potential invader. Then I carried the eistechor upstairs to my office, where I set it on my desk like the world's biggest paperweight. Moving it didn't disturb the swirls of color at all. I wondered what might happen if I shook it like a snow globe and decided not to try the experiment.

"It may look like a crystal ball out of a bad '80s fantasy movie," Malcolm said, "but it has a power to it that insists I take it seriously. This is magic the Wardens never dreamed of."

"All of this feels so strange. Elves, magic crystals, those slip-opening rubies. You're right. It should be the stuff of a New Age mystery, but it's nothing like." I leaned against his shoulder. "I'm suddenly very tired. Let's get some sleep, if that's possible. I'm sure I'm going to dream about Taelinn contacting me in the middle of the night."

We cuddled together, but true to my fears, I couldn't sleep. The knowledge of the communication device's presence in my office kept me from doing more than drifting. I jerked awake every fifteen minutes, imagining something pulling at my hand or making my heart beat faster. I wished I'd asked Rick more about what kind of tug he meant.

Finally, I sat up, and Malcolm said, "I can't sleep either."

"Oh! Did I disturb you? I know I was restless."

"No. I feel like I'm waiting for a call that says someone's been rushed to the hospital." Malcolm rolled out of bed in his usual graceful way. "We might as well get something hot to drink, though I'm not sure chamomile tea is going to be enough to relax me."

"Well, alcohol is probably a bad idea, if there's any chance I might have to talk to Taelinn tonight."

I ended up making hot chocolate, not the usual Swiss Miss envelopes but the drinking chocolate I saved for special occasions, made with heated milk and a heaping serving of real whipped cream. We sat at the kitchen table and drank without speaking. My body ached with tiredness, my mind ran round in circles like a hamster on a wheel, and resentment at the elves' arrogance in believing they had a right to our world bubbled up inside me.

"I wish there was someone to blame," I said.

Malcolm's eyebrows rose. "Come again?"

"Sorry. I mean, I wish this conflict was as easy as innocent humans preyed on by wicked elves. Because it is, sort of, no thanks to Greenough's interference, but elves live a long time, and to them, humans building the barrier is still pretty recent."

"Why would it matter if only one side was to blame?"

I smiled ruefully into my mug. "I'd be able to feel justified in hating them all."

Malcolm chuckled. "That's counter to your nature, love."

"I know," I groaned. "And it doesn't matter how I or anyone feels. We have to deal with the problem in front of us." I took another long swig of chocolate. It left a burning, gassy sensation behind my breastbone. I tried to burp it up, but it wouldn't dislodge. The pressure slowly built until I realized it wasn't gas, but something pulling on my chest.

I shot to my feet. "I didn't actually believe Taelinn would make a move tonight."

"Is he—" Malcolm set down his mug. "Let's see what he wants."

We hurried upstairs to my office, where the swirling liquid inside the eistechor was spinning so fast the colors made a muddy blur. "I forgot to ask what to do," I said. "I guess—" I touched my fingertip to the cool glass surface.

Immediately, the roiling stopped, and the ball glowed bright blue with a radiance that reflected off our arms and faces. "Lucia Pontarelli," Taelinn's voice boomed, as clearly as if he was in the room with us. "I demand you reply."

Malcolm and I looked at each other. Malcolm widened his eyes as if to say *what next?* I swallowed and wished I'd had time to brush hot chocolate residue off my teeth and tongue. "It's Helena Campbell," I said. "Lucia left to, um, bring her underling in line." Now I wished I knew exactly what Lucia had told Taelinn about Greenough and what she, Lucia, intended. No promises. I could manage that.

"That's not good enough. I demand reparations. My people have done nothing to humans, and I will not stand for this unprovoked attack."

"Taelinn—"

"You will address me as 'Your Majesty,'" Taelinn interrupted.

That cleared my head. "I will not. I'm not your subject, and if you'll recall, you and I are both visionaries, which makes me your equal." I watched Malcolm, who nodded in approval.

"Equals." Taelinn made a sort of grunting sound I thought was acknowledgement of a telling hit. "That may be. Humans are still responsible for the deaths of elves."

"And elves killed humans in the attack. Can't we agree that both sides acted rashly?"

"Rashly?" Taelinn sounded angry again. "We defended ourselves!"

That, I didn't have an answer for. Weariness threatened to over-whelm me. "Why don't you tell me what you contacted me for? It's late here, and you're keeping me from my bed."

"I want to confirm the location we will meet for you to hand over Connvuir Tionn," Taelinn said.

"The—location?"

"Lucia Pontarelli agreed that elves belong with elves. I am prepared to provide shelter for the child until it's safe for him to join his family."

"Give up Connvuir?" That hit me like a bucket of ice water, dispelling the tired fog filling my brain. "Lucia agreed to that?"

"Of course. She's sensible. If you continue to hold the child hostage, we will have to view that as an act of war. Now, I want your word you won't go back on this promise."

Malcolm's lips pinched tight shut, and he shook his head vigorously. I rubbed my eyes. "You want my word."

"I consider you an honorable ally. I trust your promise." Taelinn now sounded so calm and reasonable it broke through my confusion.

"I don't believe you," I said. "Lucia didn't tell me that was part of the deal. I think you're taking advantage of the fact that she's gone. You want Connvuir—well, it's true an elf child belongs with his people, but you're not Connvuir's relative and I know you'll use him as a tool to further your political goals."

"It's none of your business how I deal with threats to elfkind,"

Taelinn said, still sounding reasonable. That pissed me off, that he could talk about a person as if he was a bargaining chip.

"It *is* my business, Taelinn, because Connvuir's mother asked for my help with her dying breath, and I consider my promise to her sacred. Since we're talking about giving our word. Now, unless you have any other tricks to play, I'm going to sleep." I reached out to touch the sphere again, hoping that was how to terminate a conversation.

"Tricks?" Taelinn laughed. "Oh, Helena Campbell, you have no idea what I can bring to bear against you. In the end, I will take the child, and you will regret not cooperating. Elves have long memories and longer lives. I just have to wait you out."

"Good luck with that," I snapped, and slapped the sphere, making it rock in its nest. The glow vanished, and once more colors wound their way through the creamy liquid.

"I don't like the sound of that," Malcolm said. "We're back where we started. They can't get at Connvuir while he's here, but he can't stay here forever."

"It's worse than that. Malcolm, if they know we have him, and they saw him appear when we took him to Viv's house, doesn't that mean they can track him to the, I don't know, the blank spot that marks our wards?"

Malcolm took me in his arms and hugged me. "That's not how the wards work. There are masses of misdirection intertwined with them, and a couple of magical traps even I don't understand the workings of. Anyone leaving this house is covered by that—you could think of it as the person gradually fading into view, miles from here. The only reason they found Connvuir before is that we took the kids to your parents' house before driving to Viv's."

"That's comforting."

"Even so, it still means—" Malcolm yawned. "This isn't something to discuss while we're both exhausted. We can figure it out in the morning."

I nodded. After all that, I knew I could finally sleep.

# CHAPTER NINETEEN

Things did look better in the morning, or at least I felt more energized and in a mindset to deal with problems rather than fretting about them. I drove the kids to school while Malcolm stayed with Jenny and Connvuir and was able to respond to their usual barrage of conversation with good cheer. There was a solution, and we would find it.

On my way home after drop-off, I mentally went through possibilities for Connvuir's future. Lucia's point about what we would do if our positions were reversed and it was a human child at stake was a good one, but I didn't see an answer. Connvuir had no immediate family except Clissach Lachma, and even if I thought he was a good option, there was no way to reach him that wouldn't result in humans being killed. The king was a possibility, but as far as I was concerned, he would be the last resort. But what about other elves? Elves who weren't part of the political struggle?

I thought about handing Connvuir to Thandaigh and the other elves who'd helped us escape, but had to dismiss the idea after only a few seconds. If reaching Taelinn or Lachma was difficult, reaching Thandaigh was impossible. Even if we could safely get into Faerie, we had no way of contacting her or her group. And I didn't have any proof that Thandaigh and her people were politically neutral, or that they wouldn't turn Connvuir into a bargaining chip as well.

Which meant keeping Connvuir in our world and adopting him was by far the best option.

The idea lifted my spirits. Of course I would take better care of him than any elf, and our world was healthier than Faerie, and... I ignored the little voice that told me I was being stupid and selfish. It wasn't selfish to want to help someone, particularly an innocent child. And anyway, if the other options were better, the oracle would have said something. It was a justification I would hang onto.

My phone rang when I was about halfway home. Gabriel Roarke's name appeared on the display. I answered using the hands-free system. "Hi, Gabriel. What's up?"

"I've been thinking about Connvuir's situation," Gabriel said. "Have the Wardens made a decision?"

"About Connvuir?" I hesitated. Gabriel's question hadn't sounded innocent. "Well, no. But Taelinn Ailmach has demanded we return Connvuir to Faerie. I'm sure that's a bad idea."

"Bad on more levels than you probably realize," Gabriel said. "A clan leader taking the heir to another clan into his custody would spark revolt. Elves take their lineages seriously. It would be seen as an act of interference intended to destabilize the other clan."

"I don't understand."

"It means Clan Ailmach would be declaring their intent to go to war against, in this case, Clan Lachma. That makes this an internal affair, not just Lachma and Ailmach at odds in terms of how to deal with humans."

I automatically signaled a left turn, but my attention was only partly on the road. "But that doesn't make sense. Taelinn as much as said he couldn't fight Lachma directly. And wouldn't that make him unsympathetic to the other elves? They'd all take sides, right?"

"They would, but if he positioned himself as protecting the boy from an unsuitable guardian, that changes matters. If the Ailmach can claim Clissach Lachma's obsession with destroying humanity makes him an enemy to elves, he'd gain a lot of allies."

I made myself focus on driving, though now that I'd reached our overgrown neighborhood, I wasn't worried about traffic. "So you mean taking Connvuir is a backhanded way of gaining support not just for Taelinn's clan, but for his fight against Lachma."

"Precisely. That makes it urgent that the Wardens not give the Ailmach control over Lachma's heir."

A headache had started pressing in on my temples. "Gabriel, we're running out of options. That's why I want—"

"I have a solution," Gabriel said. "I'll take the boy."

"What?" My heart thumped once, hard enough to hurt. "Not to be rude, but how is that a solution?"

"If Connvuir is out of your hands, the Ailmach loses the high ground of being an elf concerned about one of his people. Lucia will be able to negotiate with him from a position of strength. And—we won't make this argument, but it's reasonable—I am an elf, and this means Connvuir will be with his people."

I'd never hated anyone so much as I hated Gabriel in that moment. Immediately, I shoved that feeling aside. I didn't hate him; I hated the idea of someone else taking care of Connvuir, someone who could realistically end up caring for him forever. But at the core of that emotion was the knowledge that Gabriel was right. Keeping Connvuir with me was selfish and stupid and put my whole family at risk, now that I knew Taelinn was able to track all of us.

My selfish heart made one more stab at making Gabriel's suggestion impossible. "But we can't move Connvuir without alerting the king's forces. He'll just come after you instead."

"I have a way of temporarily neutralizing the, well, attention of whatever is tracking the boy. And before you ask why I didn't tell you that before, I've been studying the possibility ever since your first call, and I only just finished working out the details. I didn't want to raise your hopes prematurely. This way, I'll have space to try to locate a better relative to give him to than Clissach Lachma."

His every word felt like a nail pounding the coffin lid shut. I couldn't argue anymore. "Gabriel. This... is the best solution I've heard. How soon can we do this?"

Gabriel laughed. "You sound so eager. I didn't realize how difficult things have gotten."

I wasn't eager, I was heartbroken, but I wasn't about to admit it to Gabriel. "Connvuir can't stay cooped up in my house forever. I want—I want him to be free. I assume Cassie is okay with this."

"It was her suggestion, once we knew Connvuir could be free of the Ailmach's pursuit. I worry more that she'll get attached to him just as we discover a way to return him to his family. She wants children of our own."

Now I resented Cassie for wanting the same thing I did. "Thank her for me." I made the turn into my driveway and drove into the garage, but didn't turn off the car. "What do you need from me?"

"A ride, actually. Cassie and I will be arriving at the Portland airport from San Diego around one-thirty p.m. Then, if you don't mind a longish trip, I'd appreciate it if you drove us to Enumclaw."

"That's no problem. Thanks again, Gabriel."

I turned off the car and sat gripping the steering wheel for a moment. This was the best solution for everyone. It really was. I realized I was crying and indulged in tears for a moment, grieving a loss I wasn't entitled to. Then I wiped my eyes and made myself think. I'd been to Cassie and Gabriel's place outside Enumclaw, Washington, and it was closer to being a heavily-defended compound than a house. I was sure it was warded as thoroughly as my home. Connvuir would be safe there, and Gabriel was right that this put the Wardens in a stronger position. At the moment, I cared more about Connvuir's safety than winning the war.

I found Malcolm reading on the couch while Jenny and Connvuir built a block city on the great room floor and Night-Noon slept on the nearby hearth. "Malcolm, you're not going to believe this," I began.

Words tumbled out of me as I recounted what Gabriel had said, faster and faster as if saying it would make it hurt less. Finally, Malcolm said, "Slow down, Helena. You mean Gabriel has a way to keep Connvuir out of Taelinn's hands for good?"

"I don't know if it's forever, but long enough that the immediate crisis will have passed, and maybe then Connvuir's safety won't be at risk."

Malcolm set his tablet aside. "Helena, you're shaking."

I couldn't think of a good lie. It wasn't that I wanted to lie to

Malcolm; I just wasn't ready for him to know the hopes I'd had were shattered beyond repair. "It's just… this is all so sudden—"

Jenny let out a little sob. "Mommy, don't be sad. There's a fence, there's a fence—"

The fear in her voice brought me to my senses. "I'm sorry, Jenny, I'm so sorry. It's all right. Mommy is sad, but that's not you, remember?" Guilt over unintentionally hurting my daughter filled me, dispelling the awful ache. I was being stupid. Connvuir had other people who would care for him. My children should be my priority.

Malcolm picked up Jenny and cuddled her. "Helena," he said in a low, intense voice, "what is going on?"

I wiped away the few tears I'd shed. "I wanted to keep Connvuir with us. I know, I shouldn't have gotten attached. This was always coming. I just didn't want to admit it."

"Oh, love." Malcolm drew me into his embrace, and the three of us stood together, listening to Jenny control her sniffles. "It's not wrong to wish what you do. He's a sweet, loving child, and you have a generous heart."

"I wish he never—no. That's wrong. I'm glad we were able to care for him. And I think he'll be happy with Cassie and Gabriel." I cradled Jenny's head in my hand. "Sweetie, why don't you play with Connvuir a while longer? He's going to a new home."

Jenny's eyes flashed silver. "Yes, he is," she said. "It has trees and a big moon."

"That's right. Gabriel and Cassie live in a forest."

She shook her head. "Nope, nope, nope. That's not it."

I glanced at Malcolm, who looked as puzzled as I felt. "What do you mean, Jenny?"

"The elves are coming," Jenny said.

---

I WAS PACKING THE LAST OF CONNVUIR'S THINGS INTO A duffel bag when I heard the distant rumble of the garage door opening. I shoved the stuffed caterpillar he'd grown attached to into the bag and hurried downstairs, where I found Gabriel and Malcolm putting the box of toilet training supplies and the portacrib in the back of the land yacht. The daycare hadn't balked at me asking for the portacrib as a permanent loan.

Cassie was holding Connvuir, and I suppressed a stab of irrational jealousy at how she brushed her hand over his shining hair. "Do you know any more about the elves?" she asked me.

"I've tried prophesying several times, but I haven't seen anything useful," I said. "That often means there are too many conflicting futures. But I've seen enough to know Jenny is right, and Taelinn Ailmach is making a more serious push to take Connvuir."

"But he can't find him here," Malcolm said, "and I thought the point of this was that Gabriel can protect Connvuir while he's being moved."

"I can shield him from what they were doing to locate him before," Gabriel said. "I can't predict whether they'll come up with a different plan, and I can't defend against that without knowing what it is. Our best bet is to move quickly and throw up enough obscurations that it won't be an issue."

"What if we waited?" I said. I squeezed my eyes shut. "No, that's stupid. Waiting in one place makes him easier to find, and it will endanger our children if the elves find their way here."

"That's right," Malcolm said. "The only solution is for us to go now. I'll accompany them for extra security."

"I'm going, too," I said.

"Helena, this is dangerous. We need someone to watch the children." Malcolm looked around. "Where are the boys? Shouldn't they be home now?"

Another car pulled up to the house and parked beneath the carport. "I took care of that," I said. "Viv picked the boys up from school, and she and Jeremiah will stay with them. Malcolm, if there's no guarantee the elves won't find Connvuir, we'll need the oracle to stay ahead of them."

Malcolm grimaced. "You said you hadn't seen anything."

"Because we haven't taken action yet. Things will clear up once we're on the road." I was only mostly confident of this. The times when my prophecies were murky almost always coincided with situations that had a lot of possible outcomes, but there was still a chance I was wrong. It didn't matter. I couldn't bear to send them all off and wait at home for news.

Duncan and Alastair raced into the house, followed by Viv. "Where are you going?" Alastair asked. "Aunt Viv says Connvuir is leaving, and I saw elves. Mom, are we in danger?"

"Alastair, I told you—" Alastair's prophesying about things he was too young to deal with was becoming a problem. I hated how ineffectual I felt.

"The elves want to take Connvuir back to Faerie," Malcolm said, cutting me off. "You children are staying here. Alastair, Duncan, Aunt Viv needs your help. Be sure to tell her if you have any prophecies about us. And, Alastair—" He squatted to meet his son's eyes. "Don't ask for prophecies about this. The spontaneous ones will be the ones that matter. Anything you ask to see will only confuse matters, and you'll upset Aunt Viv for nothing. Understand?"

Alastair nodded. Viv managed to keep a straight face.

"Let's go," Malcolm said.

"I'll call when we're headed back," I told Viv. "Thanks again."

"Good luck," Viv said. "I have a bad feeling about this."

"So do I," I replied, "but there's nothing else we can do."

Malcolm navigated us to the freeway and headed north. I sat behind him, next to Connvuir in his car seat, and restlessly drummed my fingers on its armrest. Cassie occasionally glanced at me like she was worried, but she remained silent. Malcolm had turned off the radio, for which I was grateful. Cheerful music would have wound my nerves to the breaking point.

It took me until we reached the Columbia River to calm myself enough to prophesy. I closed my eyes, focusing on the white noise of the car's tires on the road and the swoosh of cars going the other direction until my thoughts were peaceful and empty. Then I embraced the question *Are Taelinn's elves following us?* and let it settle into my bones.

For the first time all afternoon, the oracle swept me up into a dizzying whirlwind filled with vague images, too faint and washed out to be useful. That happened sometimes, and I didn't know what it meant except they didn't seem to influence my actual visions. The images grew brighter for a moment and then faded, dissipating like mist.

"This is so frustrating," I said under my breath. I decided to try something else. Instead of focusing on a question, I filled myself with the desire to know more about our enemy. Again, the whirlwind carried me away, and in the next moment, I saw the land spread out below me like I was a bird looking down on the world. I saw the freeway, and the many roads that branched off it, but there was no sign of our car.

I took hold of the vision like it was a touch screen and expanded it. Now I recognized some landmarks that told me what I saw was much farther north than the Washington border. A patch of glowing red no bigger than a thumbprint marked a spot on the landscape. It wasn't Enumclaw, where Cassie and Gabriel lived, and it wasn't Seattle, which was farther north and west than Enumclaw. The spot didn't seem to mark anything important. I focused on it anyway. My vision swooped, and I was looking at a rest stop, unoccupied and a little rundown. Then the vision faded, and I was back in the land yacht.

"Something important happens after mile marker 80," I said. "I can't tell what, and I don't know how far after, but it has something to do with the elves coming after us."

"So they know where we are?" Malcolm asked.

"I don't know yet." I settled in to prophesy again, this time asking *Do the elves know where we are?*

Again I was shown the landscape, the red glowing mark, and the mile marker. I shook myself free of the vision. "I think it means that's where they catch up to us, or where they finally break through the obscuration—what *is* an obscuration, exactly?"

"It confuses the observer by overlapping perceptions," Gabriel said, but distantly, like he was thinking about something else. "I can't explain it better than that to a non-adept."

"We've been doing it since we left your house," Cassie added in the same dreamy tones. "We can tell it's working, but it's possible for someone to see past an obscuration without that being known to the adept making it."

"Meaning we might already have been tagged by the elves?" Malcolm sounded more tense than he had all day.

"Meaning I have to keep prophesying," I told him. "The only thing I'm sure of is that Taelinn's people haven't found us yet."

Malcolm sped up until he was going a little faster than the speed limit. I started watching for the little green and white mile markers, counting silently when we passed each one. I glanced at Connvuir once or twice in the space between the markers. He was asleep.

We sailed past exits leading to a lot of towns, some small, some... well, not big, but not tiny. I leaned forward like I could make the car move faster with my will. Buildings lit orange by the setting sun lined the freeway on both sides. Gradually the buildings thinned out, and then we were passing a strip of forest and a narrow creek. Ahead was the sign for a rest area. I tensed further. "Do you see anything unusual?"

Malcolm shook his head. "Should I get off at the rest area?"

I prepared to prophesy. "Just a sec."

The car lurched to one side with a dull thump, and we swerved, narrowly missing a car that honked at us. I let out a shriek and grabbed the back of Malcolm's seat to keep myself steady. Malcolm swore and wrestled the car back into its lane. The land yacht continued to make that awful thumping sound. "Tire," Malcolm said. "Hang on."

Connvuir woke up and started whimpering. Cassie murmured comforting things to him, but his cries got louder. Finally, Malcolm brought us to a stop on the side of the road. "Nobody get out. That was an ambush."

"Did you see elves?" I asked.

"No, but having a blowout right where you saw possible trouble is no coincidence." Malcolm felt beneath the seat and came up with a handgun. "If you can tell me anything more—"

I was already deep in contemplation. I didn't focus my prophesying with a question, choosing instead to let the oracle tell me answers I didn't know how to ask for. This time, my bird's-eye view showed me the car, the skid marks where Malcolm had nearly spun out, and the nearby copses of trees that at this time of year were naked of leaves.

And, creeping toward us across the dismal wintry landscape, dozens of sickly green lights.

"They're coming," I said. "Malcolm, there are a lot of them."

"Should we run for it?" Gabriel asked.

"There's nowhere safe to go," Malcolm replied. "This car has protections. I'll call for reinforcements." He didn't sound like he thought this would help, but I recognized when my husband was making the best of a terrible calamity. He would go down fighting, and so would I.

I ignored the argument that broke out around me and prophesied again: *Where will Taelinn's forces strike first?*

The vision that struck me was incomprehensible. It was the usual whirlwind, but a thousand times more dizzying and forceful. I had never seen anything like it, and to me, that made it important. So, instead of rising out of the vision, I clung to it, spinning helplessly until my will overcame the confusion. More elf faces came into view, disappointing me. This wasn't helpful.

Then, as if striding past a crowd of nobodies, a final image came into view, sword drawn and dripping blood. I cried out and mentally scrambled backward, and discovered when I was free of the prophecy that I had physically squirmed into the deepest corner of my seat. Breathing heavily, I shook my head when Malcolm, sounding alarmed, repeatedly asked if I was all right. "What did you see, Helena?"

I gasped and got control of myself. "We were wrong," I said. "Taelinn didn't send these elves. They're Clissach Lachma's people. And he's somewhere out there with them."

# CHAPTER TWENTY

Malcolm swore under his breath. "Did you see how close they are?"

"I couldn't see distances. They're on the other side of the freeway, though. That's a good thing, right? That they haven't got us surrounded?"

"Where can we go, though?" Cassie said. She unbuckled Connvuir from the car seat and picked him up to comfort him. "We can't go to the nearest town. Those elves won't care about not killing any humans they meet."

Malcolm had his phone out and held up one finger to ask for silence. "Dave, we're under attack. In Washington, on the way to Enumclaw." He paused. "You did? How many? Helena couldn't—" A longer pause. Malcolm glanced at me, and my heart sank, because it was the look he wore when things were dire and he didn't see a solution that didn't leave one or more of us hurt, or worse. "That's all right. No, I don't know where that is."

Malcolm fell silent. I could barely hear the sound of Dave Henry talking rapidly. Occasionally, Malcolm nodded. Finally, he said, "We can hold out for that long, yes. But you can't call back. No sense giving them clues to our location. Right." He hung up and shoved his phone into his pocket. "The Wardens are coming. Dave says they have a faster way to get here than wardstones, but it still takes time. Maybe twenty minutes."

"We can't stay with the car," Gabriel said. "We're out in the open. If people see the elves attacking it—"

"I don't see how we can continue to keep this secret," I said.

"I was actually thinking of people stopping to help, or even just gawk, and being murdered," Gabriel said. "If we can draw the attack into the forest, I have advantages to hiding among trees."

"Yes, but so will the elves," Cassie said. Connvuir had stopped crying, but she continued to gently bounce him. "And we can't take lives unless we want to lose our ability to do magic."

I'd forgotten about that. Cassie and Gabriel were adepts, connected to the natural world, and for them, killing humans—and elves, apparently—weakened that connection until they reached a point where it was severed entirely.

"The elves won't have that problem," Gabriel said. He stared out the window across the freeway like he could see through the trees. "If I'd grown up among elves, neither would I."

"You'd also be a few hundred years dead," Cassie pointed out. "We shouldn't fret over things we can't change."

Malcolm shifted like he had come to a decision. "We have to get away from the car. Gabriel makes a good point that it's a target, both for us and for any helpful bystanders. Get away from the car, get into the trees and find a place to hunker down. You can create illusions?"

"Maybe not ones the elves can't see through, but we'll try," Cassie said.

"That's good enough for me. Leave everything. We'll come back when this is over."

That struck me as incredibly optimistic. Even I knew we didn't stand a chance. But I wasn't going to lie down and let the elves kill me.

Malcolm threw open the car door and proceeded to ignore his own advice by opening the tailgate of the land yacht. I started to protest, but then I saw the larger guns he pulled from their hidden, locked compartment beneath the floor, the Smith & Wesson and the big Scar assault rifle, and decided I was fine with him taking a minute.

I climbed past the car seat to get out of the car rather than open the door on my side. We were pulled pretty far over, but I still felt nervous about getting out so close to where the cars whizzed past. Then I felt stupid for being worried about something that harmless when murderous elves were on our trail.

I scrambled down the short hill leading away from the freeway, following the others. The dead winter grass was soggy from the last rainfall, and I slipped and skidded but didn't fall. Despite the setting sun, I didn't cast a shadow; clouds had begun gathering a few minutes after we passed the state border, heavy gray clouds that promised freezing rain. That it would hinder the elves was small comfort when I thought about how much it would hinder us.

The stretch of forest was a few hundred yards south, and Malcolm broke into a run when we were all at the bottom of the hill. Gabriel jogged back and took Connvuir from Cassie, freeing her to run faster. I did my best to keep up, but Malcolm waved to Gabriel to slow for my shorter stride. I didn't worry about it; I might not be fast over short distances, but I could run at a good pace for longer even than Malcolm.

Once we were within the trees, Gabriel told us to stop. "I need to get a feel for where we can hide."

I looked back the way we'd come, and my heart sank. Maybe in summer, this would be a great hiding place, with the trees in full leaf and the bushes and tall grasses big enough to hide behind. Right now, despite the darkening sky and being a good fifteen feet within the copse, I still had a clear view of the car, the slope, and the many obvious footprints we'd left as we ran.

"Helena?"

I startled. "Sorry, Malcolm, I was distracted."

"I asked if the oracle had any advice. Were you prophesying?"

"No, just contemplating our doom—sorry. Not the time for dark humor." I set my back against one of the bigger trees, pretending it was wide enough to conceal me from the road, and calmed my mind so it didn't jitter all over the place. Once I was as relaxed as I was likely to get, I focused on the question *How do we escape the elves?*

The prophecy came quickly, as if the oracle had been impatiently waiting for me to ask that question. Once again I saw the bird's eye view of the landscape. A few seconds' study told me it showed the place where we now hid, though it wasn't the real thing, because I could see landmarks as clearly as if it were noon on a cloudless day. Instead of seeing the tops of our heads, I saw a cluster of blue lights and one bright white one.

As soon as I registered the oracle's way of depicting people, the imaginary bird flew higher, and the "map" expanded to bring the stretch of forest into view. It was bigger than I remembered from my initial vision, not terribly wide, but extending a few miles from the freeway in both directions. A narrow creek threaded its way along the center of the line of trees. It looked like a length of gray ribbon running beneath the freeway and through the trees on either side.

The green lights indicating the elves were closer now, but none of them had crossed the freeway. Yet. I thought about counting them and decided it didn't matter. All the lights were identical, and I wasn't sure whether or not to be grateful that my vision didn't show Lachma's location in contrast to his followers. It might help, but more likely it would frighten me, and frightened people make mistakes.

The vision didn't end there, like the oracle expected me to memorize where the enemy was. I didn't think I could do anything with more information, and I was about to dismiss the vision when more green lights winked into existence, one or two at a time until they equaled the first group.

The newcomers were on our side of the freeway.

Horrified, I tried to focus the oracular eye on this new threat, but the vision faded and was gone before I could do more than assess the distance between us and them.

Gasping, I said, "There are elves on the east side now. Three hundred yards away. We're surrounded."

As if the sky knew a dramatic statement when it heard one, rain began to fall. It wasn't more than a light shower, mostly blocked by the bare branches arching overhead, but the drops were freezing cold and felt like little needles when they struck my exposed face. I put up the hood of my coat and quashed a moment's jealousy at how adeptly Cassie snugged Connvuir into his fleece-lined rain jacket. This was not the time to be stupid.

Malcolm half-extended his handgun to me. It was a Sig Sauer P365 identical to the one I always practiced with. Before I could take it, he drew it back and said, "I forgot. It's keyed to me. It won't fire unless I'm the one who squeezes the trigger. All of them—I wish I'd considered this possibility."

"It's all right. I don't mind being a damsel in distress just this once."

He cracked a half-hearted smile and continued to check over his weaponry. "Everything's loaded with steel rounds, thank God. Helena, if you can tell me where they're moving—maybe they don't know exactly where we are."

This struck me as, again, hopelessly optimistic, but I nodded and again sank into vision. The oracle was cooperating more than it had recently, because I again saw the vista of green lights, slowly moving in our direction. "The ones on the west have reached the freeway and they're hesitating. I bet elves don't know about cars. The ones on the east are moving faster, but they're more spread out. Like casting a net." I held onto the vision as long as I could and felt a twinge of pain at my temples when I finally let go. I'd have to be careful not to overextend.

"That suggests they can't locate Connvuir directly." Malcolm shoved the Sig Sauer into his back waistband and held the Smith & Wesson at the ready. "Which suggests the ones on the east are Taelinn's people, if we assume Cassie and Gabriel's obfuscations worked."

"I hope so, because I'm keeping them going," Cassie said.

"And I am preparing an illusion that will deflect eyes from us," Gabriel said. "It's not guaranteed to work on elves, but it's all I can do."

"You could shadowstep Connvuir away," Cassie said.

"Not far away. And I'm not leaving you to face them without me, not if there's no way to get Connvuir to safety." Gabriel paced a wide circle around the pair of trees we stood between. I didn't notice a difference, but with my ability to see through illusions, I wouldn't.

Malcolm said, "We'll only get through this if we stick together. Separating might buy us some time, but no one of us will be able to stand for long against an army of elves, not even armed as I am. We wait until we see what we're facing. If this is Taelinn's people, maybe they'll have the sense not to start a war with humans, assuming he's still looking for an alliance."

"Or he'll think four humans—sorry, three humans and their elf ally —are easy to dispose of, out here where no one will see," I said.

"I was hoping that wouldn't occur to you," Malcolm said. "All right. Everyone stand ready. Helena, do what you can to keep them all in sight. We want them to pass us. Gabriel, be prepared to take Cassie and Connvuir and run if the elves see us. I'll cover you."

"I'm not without defenses," Cassie said. "As long as I know where we're running to, I can help hold them off."

I sank back into vision. Both groups were much closer, though the ones on the west were spread out in a long line. I hoped they wouldn't cause car crashes, though if an elf could be smushed by an oncoming semi, I wouldn't be too sad. "A hundred yards from Lachma's people on the west. Taelinn's elves are about ninety." I'd taught myself to distinguish distances in vision by comparing things to football fields.

"Hush, then," Malcolm whispered. "They're getting close enough to hear us."

I put my back to the tree facing eastward and stared hard into the distance. Ninety yards was close enough to see even in the dimness, if the trees didn't block my view. The temptation to prophesy was strong, but my fear of being attacked when I was relatively helpless overrode it. So I watched until my eyes felt dry and itchy from not blinking. Nothing moved.

Distantly I heard the sound of car horns honking long and loud, and I cringed inside, picturing hordes of undead-looking elves crossing the freeway with no regard for the cars flying past. Then I pictured Jeremiah playing Frogger on his console emulator, imagined the digital frog as an elf squished by traffic, and I had to cover my mouth with my hand to hold back a semi-hysterical laugh. I was wound too tight. Something had to happen soon.

Far ahead, I saw movement. It wasn't stealthy; whoever it was strode like he was searching for something he didn't fear turning on him. The rain fell more steadily now, but the person didn't act like he was trying to avoid getting wet. After a few seconds, I made out another two figures, all of them pacing together in a loose grouping. The trees obscured them occasionally, so it felt as though they were moving like ghosts in a Japanese horror film, rapidly flitting from one place to another, drawing ever closer.

I let out a breath and froze when it came out as a pale cloud. Had Gabriel thought to hide that? I breathed more shallowly and hoped the elves weren't looking for invisible people. I hoped even more that I was right about this being Taelinn's crew. However Lachma had found us, it was clearly not something we'd thought to defend against.

Rain pattered off my shoulders and ran in drips down my water-proof hood. Some of those drips hit my face, and I blinked the rain away but didn't raise a hand to wipe my face. I had no idea what the illusion Gabriel made looked like from the outside, and I was superstitiously afraid movement would break it.

The three elves were close enough now I could see their faces, bluish-pale and almost skeletally thin. One woman, two men, all of them dressed in their weird armor made of hand-sized bronze plates and the cloaks Viv and Judy and I had seen in the elf city, the heavy ones of dark burlap-like fabric. The two men held bronze swords at the ready. The woman had some kind of projectile weapon I didn't recognize, something between a hand crossbow and a blowpipe. They moved steadily, their eyes scanning their surroundings and occasionally looking across the wet ground.

That reminded me of the tracks we'd made, and I felt sick. Eventually those elves would get through the forest and see the signs of our passing, and they would turn around and follow those tracks to us. We had to be fast once we were outside their search pattern.

The three approached, not close enough together to touch, but well within sight of one another. I made myself continue breathing steadily and shallowly and kept my eyes locked on the female elf, who if she kept on her current course would pass within two feet of me. She didn't slow at all, just continued her careful search. Then she looked directly at me. I bit my lip to hold back a noise that would give me away. It took a few seconds for me to realize she couldn't see me, that she just happened to be looking in my direction. She looked away, not pausing. Then she was past.

My whole body went limp with relief. I reminded myself this wasn't over and continued to watch the elf woman, who now drew closer to her fellow warriors. They had a quick conversation I couldn't hear, though they probably spoke Elvish and I wouldn't understand it anyway.

Then the female elf pointed her weapon at my tree. The explosion was so quiet I didn't at first realize she'd shot at us. Then something *thunked* into the tree trunk at head height, something small that gleamed with wicked silver spikes, and the two other elves shouted and charged the tree.

I froze. Part of me thought *this is a bluff*. They didn't know we were here, and they were trying to flush us out. Then the louder explosion of Malcolm's gun cracked, and one of the elves dropped, blood flying everywhere from a bullet to the head. "Run, now!" Malcolm commanded.

# Chapter Twenty-One

We ran eastward, away from the elves. For a moment, I thought we'd escaped, and then more shouts went up all around us, some of them scarily close. Malcolm led us to a thicket where the trees grew more closely together. "We have to keep moving, but we can't draw them too far from the freeway or the Wardens will be out of position when they get here."

"Anything we can do has to be fairly close range," Gabriel said. "Cassie?"

Cassie thrust Connvuir into my arms. "I can't work magic if I'm worried about him. Are you okay taking him?"

"Absolutely," I said. Connvuir's little body was warm and heavy, and he watched us all with interest, just as if no one wanted to kidnap him and kill the rest of us. I drew his hood more closely around his face.

Malcolm stood with his gun ready to shoot the next elf he saw. "You'll get your wish. There are several coming this way. We need them to be close enough to follow us back around. If we're lucky, we'll lead them into Lachma's forces—"

"How is that lucky?" I exclaimed.

"Because they'll probably fight each other instead of us," Malcolm said. "Be ready—they're almost here."

I stepped back to let Cassie move in front of me just as another four or five elves came into view, running all out. More projectiles fired, but none of them came close, because Gabriel raised a hand and their trajectories took right-hand turns. The projectiles shot into the nearby bushes before they came within ten feet of us.

Cassie didn't look like she was doing anything, but as the elves neared us, three of them shouted and stumbled to a halt as their armor disintegrated and the many bronze plates hit the ground. They looked even more like the undead with their pasty skin and hollow eyes and their thin, almost emaciated chests and thighs. Malcolm took the opportunity to take them out one at a time, with a single shot apiece. I hadn't counted his shots, but I knew Malcolm had a keen awareness of how many bullets he had left.

He drew a bead on the nearest remaining elf, but the creature impossibly dodged, and Malcolm fell back and drew his steel knives from their sheaths. The elf brought his sword down for a killing blow and looked surprised when Malcolm caught the blade with his crossed knives, shoved it to the side, and used the elf's resulting lack of balance to drive the point of a knife home through a gap between the armor plates. Malcolm kicked the body off his knife and whirled to stop the final elf, who was grappling with Gabriel. Malcolm bodychecked the elf, who looked like a stick figure next to Malcolm's well-muscled form, and drove both knives into his fallen opponent's throat.

Cassie knelt beside Gabriel, who'd fallen when Malcolm hit his attacker. "He's paralyzed."

"What?" I hurried to join her. Gabriel was blinking, so he was awake, but his body was rigid and his hands were locked into the position they'd been in when he wrestled the elf.

"Elves can cause temporary paralysis," Cassie said. She was jabbing Gabriel all over, little punches like she was a martial arts master looking for nerve clusters. "It only lasts a few minutes, but it can be reversed immediately if you know where to hit the victim."

"We don't have much time," Malcolm said.

"I know that!" Cassie shouted. "I don't know how to reverse this! You two run, I'll stay with him."

"They'll kill you," I said. "We'll carry Gabriel—"

"They don't want us," Cassie said. "They want Connvuir. I'll create another illusion, and we'll find you once Gabriel recovers. Go!"

Malcolm put a hand on my elbow and guided me away without another word. I didn't look back.

"We need another secure place," Malcolm said as we ran. "It doesn't have to be forever, but I need your intel."

It scared me when Malcolm started talking like a military operative, because when he fell into those patterns, he was remembering being under fire, and that meant we were in serious danger. "I'm not sure we have enough time, but I'll try."

The shouting wasn't as close as it had been, but it was still too close for my comfort. We scrambled through the trees and came to a halt on the stream's bank. "No point using the stream for cover, they're too close to be fooled," Malcolm said. "But we can hide there for long enough for you to prophesy." He pointed at a tree much larger than the ones we'd seen so far, one with a hollow in its base big enough to fit one person. One very small person.

I decided not to waste time protesting about what crappy cover it would provide and ducked into its shelter. Holding Connvuir close to my chest, I closed my eyes and willed myself to see what I now thought of as a battlefield.

We hadn't gone far. There were the two lights representing Cassie and Gabriel, and I felt passing relief that they were both still alive. I barely glanced at the lights showing where Malcolm and Connvuir and I were, because the rest of the landscape was covered with green lights. I didn't even care that the oracle didn't distinguish between Lachma's group and Taelinn's; all I knew was that we were surrounded.

I clung to the one piece of good news I saw. "The elves are congregating to the north and west," I said. "I think they're fighting each other because some of them blink out and don't come back. But there are still a lot of them in our area."

"Where are they the fewest?"

"South and east. Where Taelinn's people came from in the first place." I shook the vision away and rose to my feet.

"We'll go that way. Helena, if anything happens to me—"

"Don't say that!"

"*If anything happens to me,* you need to circle around to the north-west. Yes, I know, that's where they're fighting, but it's also the direction the Wardens will arrive from." Malcolm squeezed my hand. "We're going to survive this."

That scared me even more than the military talk. Malcolm didn't believe in making promises he couldn't keep, and he never said anything like that unless he thought I would need some reassuring last words to remember him by.

I clutched Connvuir closer and followed Malcolm away from the stream. Malcolm moved like a cat, smoothly and silently. I did my best to stay quiet, but my breathing sounded louder than a car engine and I was sure I was stepping on every fallen twig in the forest. I told myself it didn't matter, because the elves would see us long before they heard us. Connvuir whimpered, and I shushed him. The one thing we did not need was the sound of a child's cry telling all the elves where their prey was.

Malcolm abruptly stopped and held up a hand in warning. I managed not to run into his back. He scanned the forest ahead with a slow, deliberate turn of his head, like his eyes could sense things beyond sight. Then he said, "Get down!"

I dropped, cradling Connvuir so I didn't land on him. Again, he whimpered, but I had eyes only for Malcolm. He shoved the Smith & Wesson into his waistband, dropped to one knee in front of me, and let loose with the rifle at the group of elves approaching us. Connvuir screamed at the sudden loud noise, and I covered his ears. I wished I had enough hands to cover mine. The sharp bursts of gunfire were like a knife to the eardrums.

The noise cut off. Malcolm lowered the rifle a little, though it was still at the ready. No elves remained standing. He swiftly reloaded, slamming the new magazine home. "Come on," he said without looking at me. "Stay close. Their formation tells me they know what they're looking for now, and it's not about casting a wide net anymore. We'll get past their line and work our way around north."

Connvuir was still sobbing, though not as loudly, and I whispered calming words to him as we ran. They weren't very effective. I thought back over the afternoon and winced at the realization that he was probably hungry. Poor kid. None of this should have happened to him. The thought of all those adults who should have had Connvuir's welfare at heart angered me. I spared a thought for Cassie and Gabriel, hunkered down in the middle of the battlefield, and for the first time today that thought wasn't tinged with spiteful jealousy. They would care for Connvuir better than anyone else. Including me.

A spontaneous prophecy struck me then, rooting me to the spot. I saw Clissach Lachma standing over a fallen elf body, shouting something the vision didn't convey. He stepped back, and our eyes met. I didn't need his startled reaction to know he saw me. Then the vision ended, and Malcolm had me by the arm and was hauling me along with him. "You can't stop in the open!" he shouted. "You're going to be killed!"

"I'm sorry! It was a prophecy," I told him.

Malcolm dragged me into the shelter of another tree. "What did you see?"

"Just Lachma. But he saw me as well. He knows I'm here, and I think he's coming after me." I was too tired and overwhelmed to be frightened by the thought. With death potentially hiding behind every tree and bush, one more threat didn't matter.

"We're at the perimeter," Malcolm said. He squeezed his eyes shut briefly. "Sorry. I mean the southern edge of the forest. I haven't seen any elves in the last minute, and I think we've made it past their line. We'll stay within shelter for as long as we can, but it's going to be a while before we reach the rendezvous. I make it eight minutes before the Wardens arrive. Can you hold out that long?"

"Of course." It wasn't like either of us had a choice.

Malcolm gently rested his hand against my cheek. "Just a few more minutes. That's all. Follow me. Walk where I do."

He moved between the trees, not quite running, and I hurried after him, letting my movement bounce Connvuir lightly against my hip. He'd stopped crying, but his little face was pinched with cold. I wasn't the only one who had to hold out for another seven and a half minutes.

Malcolm slowed and waved to me to join him. "Something's wrong," he whispered. "What do you see?"

"Nothing." Belatedly I realized what he was asking. "No elves under illusions."

"Good. Stay close. I think they've set a trap."

We edged away from the cluster of bare-branched bushes ahead of us and circled the knot of trees around them. My fingers were numb with cold and fear. An elf trap, if it wasn't concealed by illusions, might catch us before either of us perceived it. I searched the bushes visually until my eyeballs ached with dryness. Still nothing.

We came around the curve of the little thicket, and I was about to ask if Malcolm still felt something was wrong when two elves stepped out from behind a couple of trees about fifteen feet away. Malcolm didn't react, and my heart jolted as I realized he didn't see them. I grabbed his shoulder and screamed, "Malcolm! Straight ahead! *Shoot them!*"

Malcolm responded with an immediate burst of gunfire. One of the elves went down. The other threw herself to the side and brought her weird projectile weapon to her lips. "Aim right and low!" I shouted, wishing I dared grab the rifle and aim it myself.

Malcolm grunted and changed targets, if you could call it that when he couldn't see either of the elves. The shots stitched a line from left to right that intersected with the female elf's chest. She jerked like a marionette cut free of her strings and collapsed.

Malcolm lowered the rifle. "Stupid," he said.

"The noise couldn't be helped. It was that or let them kill us."

"That's not what I meant," Malcolm said. He touched the center of his chest, and his fingers came away bloody. Then the rifle fell from his hand, and he sagged against me, nearly taking me down with him.

I awkwardly guided him to sit on the ground and put Connvuir down. "Stay there," I told the boy. "Malcolm, is it serious?"

"I don't know." Malcolm's breathing was rapid and shallow. He again pressed his fingers to the small wound. "Whatever she shot me with, it's inside me, and—" He grimaced. "And I think it's burrowing deeper."

"What are you talking about?" His calmness frightened me more because I was sure he was doing it so I wouldn't freak out. "That's not possible."

"Elf-shot. All the stories say elves' projectile weapons are deadly for more than just the obvious reasons." Malcolm briefly closed his eyes. "Helena, you have to keep moving."

"I'm not leaving you!"

His bloody hand gripped mine. "At least some of those elves can track Connvuir. If you stay here, they'll find us and kill us both. You have to keep moving, stay free of them—the Wardens are almost here."

My eyes were too dry for tears. "Malcolm—"

"This is the only way," Malcolm said. "Help me get my back against a tree. I can hold them off for a while."

"Then you can protect all of us. It's stupid for me to go out there!"

Malcolm smiled. "I was lying. My only hope now is for you to find the Wardens and get them back here. Please, love. Just go."

I touched his face. "You have to not die on me, promise?"

He smiled again, but said nothing.

I helped him into the shelter of a tree and kissed him, a light kiss that said I would be back soon. It was a lie, too. Then I gathered Connvuir into my arms and took time for one more prophecy. I filled myself with the question *Where is the safe path through here?*

The battlefield appeared again, covered with scattered green lights that shifted randomly with the collisions of two elven forces. Cassie and Gabriel remained where I'd left them. The light that indicated Malcolm glowed as brightly as ever, which I hated because if the lights dimmed when someone was dying—no. I didn't need distractions.

I'd hoped for a line of red dashes marking the path that would take me through this mess without dying. When it didn't appear, I reminded myself that I was unlikely to be able to follow a path I saw from above when I was on the ground. I scanned the space between where I was and the northwest corner. The fighting was worst there, and I almost told Malcolm I wasn't leaving. There was nothing safe about that destination.

Something gripped me, immobilizing my entire body. Terror shot through me that this was some new elf magic, and Malcolm and I were about to be killed. My view of the battlefield shifted and focused in on that knot of fighters battling it out in the northwest corner. I frantically tried to free myself of the vision so I could at least see my killers before my death. The grip tightened, and the vision showed me a little clearing, muddy and torn up by the passage of many feet. It wasn't an aerial view; I saw the clearing from the perspective I would have if I entered it on the southeast. Then the vision faded, and the grip freezing me in place vanished.

I drew in a deep breath and backed toward Malcolm, scanning my surroundings. No elves. No Wardens, though that would be unlikely. "Malcolm," I said.

He didn't answer.

I crouched beside him and leaned close. His faint breath on my face told me he was alive, but unconscious. I swallowed around the lump in my throat and said a brief, heartfelt prayer. Then I ran, leaving him behind.

I tried to stay within the trees, but I wasn't good at knowing when I was concealed, and eventually I moved outside the forest and ran as fast as I could with Connvuir in my arms. He'd stopped crying, at least, but he was heavy and awkward, and he weighed on me enough that my breathing was loud and ragged and my arms and shoulders ached. For once, though, I wasn't afraid. The remnants of my vision told me I would be safe until I reached the little clearing. What happened after that, I didn't know, but I felt more confident than I had since this all started. I could handle anything that came next.

I heard the noise of fighting to the south, mostly swords clashing with swords, and despite my confidence I silently cursed the lack of gunfire. Gunfire would mean Wardens. Then I thought about what it meant that we were all making a ton of noise. If someone stopped because they saw the elves, or wondered about our abandoned SUV, they were sure to hear the commotion. Maybe the sound of sword fighting could be rationalized away, but no human could hear the sound of an assault rifle without getting worried and calling the cops. And the cops, whose guns shot regular bullets and not solid steel, would be overrun in seconds.

The thought of elves slaughtering humans sickened me, but ultimately, it didn't matter. We had to survive this first, and deal with the mundane authorities afterward.

I'd lost track of time. The Wardens might arrive at any moment, but without knowing when that moment would be, I couldn't base my escape strategy on them riding to the rescue. Nothing around me looked familiar. I didn't see anything I remembered from my vision. Connvuir grabbed my hair and pulled on it, whimpering again. "I'm sorry," I whispered. "Just a little longer, okay? And then we'll have something good to eat, I promise."

And just like that, the memory of my vision slid over the three skinny trees in front of me like two pictures of the same place overlapping. I suppressed my feeling of relief. Anything might happen now. It occurred to me that I didn't know if the oracle cared about my ultimate survival. Sure, it kept me out of danger, but things like car accidents or tripping on a wagon Duncan had left in the driveway were ordinary, trivial dangers. Suppose it didn't mind letting me die for a greater cause?

I made myself focus on my surroundings. Now was not the time for philosophical questions. The trees grew more thickly here, with many low-hanging branches rimed with clear ice the rain was slowly melting. Wet muck and the remnants of autumn's leaf fall felt squishy beneath my feet, a thin, slippery layer over the more solid frozen ground below. I found a gap between the trees and slipped through it, brushing the branches and sending a cascade of the cold water clinging to them over myself and Connvuir.

The clearing below was bigger than it had seemed in vision, but it still wasn't more than twenty feet across. The elves had been here, I saw, churning the muck until it was impossible to make out individual footprints. Many of the lower branches had been snapped off by the passage of bodies and now lay ignored on the ground beneath the trees. But the place was empty now of anyone but Connvuir and me.

I paced around the clearing, listening for anything that might tell me why the vision had been so insistent I come here. I could still hear the sounds of fighting, not as close as before. Maybe this was where the Wardens would arrive. I couldn't imagine how they would get here if not with wardstones. Parachutes? I looked into the sky and saw only rainclouds. The rain had dwindled to nothing but fine mist. I couldn't be grateful for this small thing, not when so much else had happened. Thinking about Malcolm, wondering if he was alive, was too painful.

To the east, shadows moved. People were coming, people who

weren't trying to be stealthy. My heart leaped. Wardens! It wasn't too late for Malcolm!

The figures drew nearer, slowing as they approached. I wiped rainwater out of my eyes and blinked so my eyesight cleared. The last light of the setting sun gleamed off bronze. Not Wardens. Elves.

Fear jolted me into movement, but I didn't make it to the western side of the clearing before I knew running was futile. With Connvuir slowing me down, I wouldn't get far before the elves caught me. I turned to face them. Either this was Taelinn's people, and they would take Connvuir and kill me so as not to leave a witness, or it was Lachma's people, and they'd kill me and take Connvuir from my dead body. Either way, I intended to face death boldly.

Connvuir started whimpering again and buried his face in my shoulder. I rubbed his back. "Sorry about not getting you something to eat," I whispered. "It will be all right." Lots of lying promises going around today, I told myself silently. None of the elves saw Connvuir as anything but a tool.

I waited, my heart hammering, for the elves to enter the clearing. I didn't recognize any of them, but that didn't mean anything. What did matter was that the seven elves who passed through the gap and took up positions on either side of it didn't look inclined to slaughter me outright. I didn't let my optimistic heart take that as a good sign.

Which was why I was prepared for Clissach Lachma to step into the clearing.

We stared at each other for what felt like minutes. Lachma's fathomless black eyes fixed on me with an intensity I felt through my bones. His angular white face, blue-tinged where the fading light cast the planes of his cheekbones in shadow, was as terrifying as it had been the first time I'd seen him. Blood stained his armor and his bronze sword, which he held casually by his side.

Connvuir turned when he heard footsteps. When Lachma came into view, the little boy twisted like he was desperate to get away. Fear for Connvuir overrode my fear for myself, and I put my other arm around the boy in a stupid, futile attempt to protect him and said, "You'll have to kill me to take him."

Lachma didn't move. He had the blank expression of someone who doesn't understand the language he'd just heard. Connvuir again tried to get away from me. He twisted his upper body until he faced Lachma.

Then Connvuir laughed.

He reached out his arms to the terrible, menacing elf and said a word I didn't understand, something that sounded like "calla." It startled me so much I nearly dropped him. Connvuir repeated the word several times, all the while struggling against my grip.

I stared at Lachma, whose attention was now focused on Connvuir. The elf spoke something in his own language. It was harsh and rough as all Elvish sounded to me, but he spoke quietly, almost gently. Connvuir laughed again and babbled another handful of Elvish words.

Still, Lachma didn't approach. I swallowed. Then I brushed raindrops from Connvuir's hood and held him close one last time. Without letting myself consider how idiotic this was, I crossed the clearing until I stood within arm's reach of Lachma.

And I held Connvuir out for him to take.

# Chapter Twenty-Two

Lachma regarded the struggling child for a bare second before taking him from me. Connvuir threw his arms around Lachma and said something muffled by how his face was buried in his uncle's neck. Lachma supported him as casually as if he wasn't a hardened, vicious killer of humans. He murmured something to Connvuir, who nodded.

I stayed where I was, not looking at Lachma's dripping sword. If he was about to kill me, I refused to show fear. Or maybe his warriors would do it. Maybe he thought it was beneath him to kill a weak, defenseless woman who'd given away her only bargaining chip.

Lachma said something in Elvish. He was looking right at me, and at first I thought he meant his words for me even though I didn't understand them. Then the seven elf warriors lowered their swords and left the clearing. Lachma continued to stare me down. I didn't offer to share my language with him. He wouldn't accept, and there was nothing he could say I wanted to hear.

Connvuir turned in his uncle's arms and smiled at me. He said something else in Elvish, and I nearly fell over when Lachma's lips twitched in a smile. It was gone almost before I comprehended it.

Lachma spoke at length. This time, I knew he was talking to me. I refrained from saying I didn't understand. He knew that, and I knew he didn't understand me. Then he shocked me utterly by inclining his head, the smallest movement, as much a bow as that twitch of the lips had been a smile. Without another word, he left the clearing.

I found myself on my knees in the muck without remembering falling. My loud, harsh breathing seemed to echo in the little clearing. Finally, I pushed myself to my feet, wiped my hands on my jeans, and stumbled through the trees, picking up speed until I was running.

I didn't remember where I'd left Malcolm. All the trees looked the same to me, and the path I followed had been overrun so many times I couldn't use my tracks to guide me. But an inner force tugged me along, the same powerful feeling that had showed me the clearing where I'd met Lachma and survived, and in no time I leaped over the dead body of an elf and saw a slumped form at the base of a tree.

I threw myself at Malcolm, feeling for a pulse, resting my frozen cheek against his mouth to detect a breath. His pulse was weak, but it was there. For a moment, I gave in to panic. I didn't know anything about elf-shot, didn't know if Malcolm was right about it burrowing deeper, but I pictured the deadly little dart that had slammed into a tree beside my head working its way toward his heart, and I wanted to run away and find a Warden who could save him.

Then I shook myself mentally. I had resources. Malcolm wasn't going to die if I could help it. I gripped his bloody hand in mine and let myself fall into the oracular state, not articulating a question, just willing the oracle to know my need.

Instead of the usual whirlwind carrying me away, a billowing white fog surrounded me, filled with shadowy human figures that never came close enough to be identifiable. I knew in my bones they represented the Wardens searching for us, and the mist was the forest, small in absolute terms but big enough for two people to go unnoticed until it was too late. A crow swept past, cawing loudly, but the sound wasn't a typical bird's call; it sounded like a sharp, explosive bang. Three times the bird called out, and then the vision was gone.

I snatched the Smith & Wesson from where it lay next to Malcolm's hand and pointed it at the sky, but in the next second, I remembered only Malcolm could shoot it. I cursed fervently. I'd thought this was a fantastic idea when Malcolm had told me about it, a wonderful safe-guard against a child somehow getting hold of it and causing a potentially fatal accident. Now I wished I'd been more careless.

Malcolm let out a long sigh and lay stiller than before. Terrified, I grabbed him by the collar and shook him. He didn't respond. I sobbed once, clutching his hand to my chest. His hand—

I grabbed the gun again and wrapped Malcolm's hand around the grip with his finger on the trigger. This time, I remembered to release the safety. I raised Malcolm's arm so the gun pointed skyward, closed my own hand over his, and squeezed his finger over the trigger.

A shot cracked through the silence, once, twice, three times. The recoil was almost too much for me to bear in my devastated condition, and my arms shook so badly I feared I couldn't keep hold of the gun, but I steadied Malcolm's arm until after the third shot. Then I lowered my arm and removed the gun from Malcolm's unresponsive hand. After a moment's thought, I folded both his hands over his chest.

Noises in the undergrowth brought me to myself. The newcomers weren't trying to conceal themselves, and they were speaking loudly. It took me a second to recognize English. "Over here!" I shouted. "He needs help!"

The noises grew louder, and then the undergrowth exploded as if someone had driven an invisible bulldozer through it, sending bushes and saplings flying. I knew stone magus telekinesis when I saw it. Seven or eight humans came through the gap, among them the person I most wanted to see just then.

"The elves shot him," I gasped. "Please, Derrick—I think he's gone."

"We'll see about that, Helena," Derrick Tinsley said. "The rest of you, move out and secure this perimeter. No—two of you stand guard over us." The stocky Black bone magus knelt on Malcolm's other side and put two fingers to the side of his throat like he was checking Malcolm's pulse. I watched him rather than Malcolm, and my heart sank when I saw his expression change to that of a man who was going to have to tell me my husband was dead. The distant sounds of more gunfire and shouting seemed to be coming from so far away I shouldn't have been able to hear them.

"Back up," Derrick said. He rested his other hand over the bloody wound in Malcolm's chest. I scooted back obediently, my mind numb.

The bone magus inhaled deeply through his nostrils. He let the breath out in a huge *pah* that ruffled Malcolm's hair. His hand on Malcolm's chest jerked, looking almost like he'd shot a gun and was controlling the recoil. Then he tossed something silvery in my direction that bounced off my shoulder. In my stunned state, my reflexes were excellent, and I caught the thing before it could hit the ground. It was a bloodstained silver dart.

Derrick dragged Malcolm away from the tree to lay him flat on the ground. He tore the gashes in Malcolm's sweater and undershirt wider and worked his hand into the gap so his palm rested directly against Malcolm's skin. I clutched the dart until it pricked my skin, waking me out of my stupor. Derrick bowed his head as I'd seen him do so many times before, and hope filled me, because he wouldn't do this for a corpse.

Derrick withdrew his hand. Malcolm still wasn't moving. My newfound hope dissolved. "Derrick. Is he..."

"He's alive," Derrick said, and I felt like fainting. "But I can't get him to wake up."

"I don't understand."

"Neither do I. The dart didn't penetrate deeply enough to damage his heart. Frankly, it didn't do much damage at all, though another five minutes and it would have been too late. I think the elves make them seek out vital organs."

"So it was working its way deeper."

"Yes." Derrick rested his hand against Malcolm's cheek. "I've healed him fully, but he's not responding to the physiological command to wake. It might be a side effect of the dart. I hear elves are capable of putting people to sleep for a long time."

"Yes, but—" I was about to protest that I hadn't slept very long when Taelinn's goons attacked Judy's car, but I realized that didn't mean anything, given that Taelinn hadn't wanted me to sleep forever. "What do we do?"

"Once we've secured this place, we'll take Malcolm back to the Gunther Node. Rick may have some ideas." Derrick still didn't look very certain, but I nodded like I believed him. "Was there anyone else with you?"

"Cassie and Gabriel." I'd forgotten about them, what with encountering Lachma and finding Malcolm near death. "Derrick, Gabriel will know what to do!"

"Do you remember where they are?"

I shook my head. "Just south and east of here."

"I'll find them." Derrick rose to his feet. "Redding, Bresnahan, stay with them. Contact Conti and tell him it's a code argent, got it?" He squeezed my shoulder and pushed through the remaining undergrowth, heading rapidly southeastward.

The woman, Redding, nodded and pulled out her phone. Bresnahan took up a guard position, pacing a line a few yards away. His light blue eyes scanned the distance, never settling anywhere for long. I wished I knew what a code argent was. The Wardens rarely used mysterious code words to describe their actions, which meant this was something big and complicated that couldn't be explained easily.

I sat holding Malcolm's hand until more Wardens came through the gap in the undergrowth with Mike Conti at their head. Mike was Malcolm's best friend, Judy's husband, and someone I trusted with my life. "Helena, it's going to be all right," he said, and this time, I believed it.

---

IT WAS FULL DARK BEFORE WE WERE ABLE TO LEAVE. IT TOOK longer than I liked for them to move Malcolm, but eventually a couple of Wardens lifted him telekinetically and steered his inert body carefully between the trees and out into the open. I followed them, my feet slipping now and then on the wet, mucky grass. It surprised me that we hadn't gone very far from the land yacht, only about thirty yards from where Malcolm had brought it to a stop.

It surprised me even more that there was an ambulance waiting at the side of the freeway, its flashing lights casting an intermittent red glow over the scene. I cringed inside at the thought of explaining all this to a helpful EMT. Then it occurred to me that there should have been more emergency response vehicles than a single ambulance. I scrambled up the embankment and stared in astonishment at the traffic jam. Cars crept by, staying in the two right lanes like someone had herded them there while the left-hand lanes remained empty. Cars on the other side of the freeway moved more rapidly, but they still slowed a bit like they were gawking.

I turned to Mike, who had preceded me up the hill. "What's going on?"

"You're going to wish you could see this illusion," Mike said with a grin. "Code argent is a full-scale magnifica illusion of a car crash, complete with police, ambulance, and a couple of collided vehicles. It also includes confusing the emergency dispatchers for the local cops and 911 operators so they don't send any real cops or EMTs. It is one of my more impressive achievements."

"Wow." I watched the Wardens lift Malcolm onto a real stretcher and put him in the ambulance. I recalled the night more than ten years ago when the same thing had happened, only then there had been no Wardens to help Malcolm, and I'd been grateful to the doctors who saved his life. "I need to go with him—no, what about the Tahoe?"

"Somebody was supposed to replace the tire." Mike walked around the land yacht and nodded. "It's fine. I'll drive it back."

"Wait! Where are Gabriel and Cassie?"

"Were they with you?" Mike frowned. "I haven't heard about them."

I turned around and headed back down the slope, but Mike got in front of me and grabbed my shoulders. "Helena, you're in shock. You need to get in that ambulance and get warm. Everything else can wait."

I heard shouting coming from the direction of the forest. Mike glanced over his shoulder. "There's Tinsley now."

Derrick approached at the head of a group of Wardens surrounding Cassie and Gabriel. I shook off Mike's hold and ran to meet them, hugging Cassie. "I was so afraid you were dead."

"Same," Cassie replied. Her brow furrowed. "Where's Connvuir?"

My heart constricted. She was never going to understand this. "He's... he's safe," I said. "It's a long story, and I can't tell it now—Gabriel, what do you know about elf-shot?"

Gabriel grimaced. "That's what those projectiles were. They're silver darts enchanted to seek out vital parts of the victim's body—the heart, or the arteries, anything whose destruction will guarantee death. All it takes is for one to embed itself even partially in flesh, and it will drive deeper into the body." He looked at me fully for the first time. "Where is Malcolm?"

"They got him," I said. "Derrick took the dart out and healed him, but he won't wake up."

"Oh," Gabriel said. "Well, if that's all."

"Gabriel, how can you say that?" I shrieked. All my terror and exhaustion came out in a burst of anger. "He's not responding to anything! What if he's going to be asleep forever?"

"Helena, calm down." Gabriel didn't seem upset by my outburst. "I thought this, at least, was something humans knew about elves."

"I don't know what you're talking about. We know almost nothing—"

"Helena. It's in all your stories, how to wake someone who's under an enchantment. Don't tell me you never read fairy tales?"

I blinked at him. Then I rushed back up the embankment and clambered into the ambulance. Malcolm lay there, breathing shallowly, not making even the tiny restless movements of someone asleep. I brushed the hair back from his forehead, which felt warmer than my own icy skin. Bending low, I pressed my lips to his, kissing him gently.

Malcolm shifted. He put an arm around my shoulders and pulled me closer. "Your lips are so cold," he murmured.

I burst into tears and wrapped my arms around him.

# Chapter Twenty-Three

"You gave him to *Clissach Lachma?*"

Lucia's shout bounced off the concrete walls of the Gunther Node transit hub and brought everyone in it to a halt. I was the only one who didn't cringe. "I did."

"The next words I hear had better be a variation on 'it was the oracle's decision,'" Lucia said. She waved a hand at the onlookers and shouted, "Don't stop on my account. You know how I love people prying into my business."

She grabbed me by the shoulder and steered me in the direction of her office as all around us, Wardens pretended they weren't paying close attention. I pulled away from her and continued under my own steam. "It was the oracle, and it was my decision as well. It wasn't what we thought."

"Lachma is a murderous bastard who might have killed you and taken the kid anyway," Lucia said.

"Yes. And he didn't. Do you want the story, or do you want to go on yelling irrationally?"

Lucia stopped in the middle of the hallway. She pinched the bridge of her nose like she had a headache. "Sorry. This Greenough thing has me on edge. You're right, it can't be what we thought. Go ahead."

"Tell me about Greenough first."

Lucia resumed walking with her usual ground-eating stride. "She tried to brazen it out. Claimed she was acting in the best interests of the Wardens, and that I was too timid to take action."

"Which is when you punched her in the face?"

Lucia let out a low "hah" of mirthless laughter. "You'll be happy to know no blows were exchanged. I pointed out she'd cost us Warden lives to no purpose, and that the king of the elves was on the verge of going to war against us as a result of her stupidity. I reminded her that I am the official Warden liaison with Faerie, if not by human choice, then by the elves' decision."

"But she still thinks she ought to be in charge of the Wardens. I doubt she cares about your authority."

"She doesn't. But it no longer matters. I stripped her of her custodianship and sent her packing."

I gasped. "Lucia! Can you do that?"

"Well, obviously I can, Davies." Lucia opened the door to her office and shooed me inside. "In this case, I held a referendum involving all the Wardens who gave her their allegiance. I pointed out everything I'd said to Greenough and I asked them if they still thought someone that self-centered and rash ought to be giving orders. It was a unanimous vote against her."

I shut the door and took a seat in front of the melamine and chrome desk. "So you really are in charge now."

"It helps that no one else wants the responsibility, especially now that the responsibility includes dealing with at least two factions of elves." Lucia lowered herself into her chair and leaned back. "And now you're going to tell me why you gave a child to our worst enemy."

"Because Connvuir loved him." I recalled the joy in the little boy's face when he realized his uncle was there. "I know Lachma hates humans, and he wants us all dead so he can take over our world, but he was good to Connvuir, and I think he even cared about Connvuir's mother. I couldn't justify keeping Connvuir away from him, not when he's the one with the right to care for him."

"You took a serious risk, Davies. He could have killed you."

"I know." I interlaced my fingers and stared at my hands. "I think he knew I gave Connvuir back because it was the right thing to do and not because I was afraid or intimidated. And I also think Connvuir told Lachma I took care of him. He was so happy, Lucia. I'd never heard him speak before. I think, if we'd kept him with the Wardens or with Cassie and Gabriel, he would always have been a little afraid."

"So Lachma spared your life in recognition of all that."

"Maybe. Yes." I didn't know why I wasn't crying over the loss of the little boy I'd grown to love. Or maybe I did know. "It really was the right choice, Lucia, and I think it's the one I'd have made even if the oracle hadn't implied it."

Lucia nodded. "I don't mind telling you this simplifies matters. Taelinn's no longer in a position to demand concessions in exchange for not forcing us to hand over the boy. And, given that Taelinn sent his warriors into our world to kidnap Connvuir, I'm now the one with the strong position."

"Have you spoken to him yet?"

"He's requested a meeting. In person."

I gasped. "The king is coming here?"

"Not on your life. He wants me to go to Faerie. I know he thinks this gives him the upper hand, but there's no way in hell I'm letting an enemy force into our world. I've set the terms, including ones I'm sure he doesn't see the implications of, but he didn't actually demand all that much. Just that we meet him in Faerie—and that you come as part of my 'entourage.'" Lucia snorted in amusement at the final word.

"He wants me? But he knows I don't support him. I'm not going to plead his case with you."

"He didn't say more than that. I don't know what he has in mind. It's up to you, though I admit I wouldn't mind having the oracle along."

I didn't have to think twice. "I'll go." If Taelinn plotted treachery, I wanted to be there to counter it.

"Thanks." Lucia idly spun a pen around her fingers, something she did when she had already mentally moved on to her next task. "It will be tomorrow afternoon. Meet at the access point at noon, both you and Campbell. He won't let you go alone no matter what I tell him, so I'm bowing to the inevitable. Makes me feel like I'm the boss around here."

I grinned. "What, and ruining Greenough didn't do that?"

"Get out of here, Davies," Lucia growled, but she was smiling.

---

MALCOLM AND I ARRIVED AT THE ACCESS POINT AT FIVE minutes to noon the next day. Since it was during business hours, the gate was open, but Sergio came to greet us anyway. "Hey, Helena, Malcolm. You want me to wash and detail the car while you're gone?"

"Oh, Sergio, I know that's not your responsibility—"

"Yeah, but I love detailing cars. Something about that deep cleaning satisfies me." He caught the key fob Malcolm tossed at him. "And honestly, Helena, it's pretty filthy. You ought to treat your ride with more respect."

I pretended to scowl at him. "I'm not sure a suburban mom with a land yacht has much respect to give."

Malcolm put an arm around my waist and pulled me close. "You are so much more than that," he whispered in my ear, making me blush.

Just then, the door to the repair shop opened, and a lot of Wardens came out, more than I thought could fit inside the office. Lucia, trailed by Dave Henry and Rick Jeong, followed them out. Rick and Dave both held twelve-pound medicine balls painted red and purple respectively. "Let's go," Lucia said.

I kept from asking "go where?" and let Lucia lead the way to one of the repair bays, the only one that was empty. Lucia waved to all of us to stand back so our bodies blocked the inside of the repair bay from view of anyone passing the shop. Dave and Rick stood at either corner of the bay, holding the balls in front of their midsections. They both rotated their bodies until the medicine balls were pointed at the corners diagonal from them. The way they held the balls made me picture lasers shooting from them to intersect at the center of the repair bay.

"On my mark," Rick said to Dave. "Three, two, one, *mark.*"

Both men extended the medicine balls straight in front of them, and to my surprise, beams of red and purple light shot out and met with a sizzle right at the middle of the empty space, creating a tiny sphere of crackling magenta light. The light began extending in both directions from the spot until it formed a vertical magenta line six feet tall that barely brushed the concrete floor.

Two Wardens walked wide around Dave and Rick to the line and, standing on opposite sides, grabbed hold of it and pulled it apart. It reminded me strongly of seeing Thandaigh open a slip on the cuivuirskeen, though hers had been golden light and this looked like gaudy neon. Gradually, the gap widened until it was an oval big enough to fit even the largest Warden in Lucia's team. Lucia nodded, and her people started filing through the slip one at a time.

I asked, "How is this possible? I know Rick's slip key can open slips in difficult places, but this is the middle of the city!"

"It's impossible," Lucia said, "which is why we're doing it. Two slip keys working together can open a slip in what Rick calls 'difficult terrain,' though I don't know where he got that image. Anyway, this gives us more control over where we enter Faerie, and it has the added bonus that when this slip closes, it can never be opened again, not under any circumstances. I like the idea of the access point being protected."

"Is that how the Wardens got to us when Lachma and the king attacked?"

"Sort of." Lucia waved, and Rick and Dave lowered the slip keys. The light of the slip dimmed, but it didn't flicker or waver or do anything to suggest it was impermanent. "We used a slip outside Portland and then cut across Faerie to a slip near where you were ambushed."

"That's clever. And sounds dangerous."

"Yeah, well, Taelinn Ailmach can bring it up if he's got the stones to challenge me after that debacle. I don't think he knows how well and truly screwed his negotiations are." Lucia prodded me on the shoulder. "Go ahead. They'll have swept the area for threats."

"Not to insult your people, but I'll go first," Malcolm said.

I waited until I saw him signal me through the slip, and then I entered.

The air in Faerie was colder than in Portland, and I was glad I'd worn my heavy coat. I stood in a forest that I thought at first was the cuivuirskeen Thandaigh had brought us to. Then I remembered each slip corresponded to exactly one place in Faerie and in our world, so it couldn't be the same forest. Still, it was eerily similar: trees still bearing thick, glossy leaves, snow underfoot that had been trampled by dozens of Wardens.

Lucia came up beside me. "Now we walk," she said. "It's not far, but I hope you wore good shoes."

"What if the slip closes while we're in Faerie? Suppose the elves tricked us, and they wanted access to a slip that puts them at the heart of our city? What if the whole thing is a trap?"

Lucia pointed at Dave. "If the slip closes, Henry or Jeong will open another one and we'll find out where it goes. The slip will be guarded closely—why do you think I brought so many Wardens along? Five to scout the forest, five to guard the slip itself. And if the whole thing is a trap and they kill us, I've left instructions for the Wardens to torch Taelinn's city. See? No worries."

I thought the possibility of being killed was a gigantic worry, but I kept my mouth shut. I had prophesied half a dozen times yesterday and received no warnings of any sort. If there was danger here, it was subtle enough not to require dramatic precautions.

I'd expected at least half an hour's walk, so I was surprised when we emerged from the forest and I saw a golden pavilion only fifty yards away. It became more obviously a temporary thing the nearer we got: it was actually a giant tent with a peaked roof and three of the four sides rolled up. A handful of elf guards wearing swords stood alertly in places surrounding the pavilion. They eyed us as we approached, but didn't react.

More elves gathered beneath the pavilion, among them Carth, who glared at me with his one remaining eye like he wished we hadn't come to parley. They surrounded a stool where Taelinn sat, making a neat semicircle of protection. Taelinn was dressed more finely than when I'd seen him before and wore a circle of gold on his head, bright against his silvery-white hair. He didn't rise when we approached.

Lucia didn't pause to take all this in. She seated herself on the stool opposite Taelinn and waited. No one spoke for several minutes. Despite my coat, I started to feel cold, but I kept from jigging from one foot to the other to warm myself.

Finally, Taelinn said, "These are my advisors. Will you give them your language so they can understand our discussion?"

"Sure," Lucia said.

A trio of Wardens came forward so smoothly I was sure Lucia had anticipated Taelinn's request. They went around offering their hands to the elves. Carth recoiled when it was his turn. "I understand you already," he said, grinding out the words like they hurt him.

When the little ritual was finished, Taelinn said, "You chose to break our alliance by giving Connvuir Tionn to my enemy."

"Right," Lucia drawled. "Do you want to talk about how *you* broke our agreement by sending your warriors into our world?"

Taelinn's expression didn't change. "You refused to do the right thing by handing the child over to me. I simply attempted to right the balance."

"He wasn't yours," Lucia said, "and our oracle divined that Connvuir belonged with his uncle, Clissach Lachma. Go ahead and argue with that, if you want. We both know how this is going to end."

Taelinn didn't respond immediately. "Very well," he finally said. "I consider us even."

"You might, but I don't," Lucia said. "You and I agreed on two things. Humans would not use Faerie as a staging ground for our fight against Lachma, and your elves would not enter our world to do the same thing."

"We entered your world to retrieve the child. It's not the same thing."

"Splitting hairs."

"I call it precision of language." Taelinn smiled. "Okay, then, let's say I agree with your assessment. What do you want from me now?"

"I want your help fighting Lachma," Lucia said. "We need him defeated. You need him to stop being a threat to your rule. We have a common enemy—let's act like that's true."

"I've already told you I can't take action against Clan Lachma. I would lose most of my support, and then I would be unable to help you fight him anyway." The king didn't sound like he was broken up about this.

"You were going to use Connvuir as a tool to gain sympathy for your side by claiming Clissach Lachma was unfit to rule Clan Lachma," Lucia said. "What if you could still do that?"

Taelinn leaned forward. "You have a suggestion?"

"I do." Lucia leaned in to match him. "Let the Wardens heal the realm of Faerie."

I squeaked in surprise. Taelinn's gaze flicked to me briefly and as quickly moved away. "You can't be serious."

"Dead serious." Lucia sounded as certain as I'd ever heard her. "We've been studying Faerie, and the taint caused by the barrier, and we think we know how to get rid of it. Jeong?"

Rick stepped forward, his unnaturally youthful face calm as the king's supporters took a step toward him in a defensive manner. "Sorry. Look, the barrier was originally intended to unravel the magic, and the body, of any elf that touched it. What it ended up doing was unraveling the magic of Faerie itself. Maybe you noticed your powers were weakening over time, maybe not—Faerie generates new magic all the time, so it wouldn't have been obvious. But the thing is that the unraveled magic is still there. It can be persuaded to join together again."

"This is absurd," Carth said. "He's trying to trick us into a final destruction."

"I know you have no reason to trust humans," Rick said, still as calm as if Carth didn't look ready to strike him down. "Just as we don't know if we can trust you. But trust has to begin somewhere. I'm offering to demonstrate that what I describe is possible."

"And once he's done that, we'll offer to teach the skill to elves," Lucia said. "You're not stupid, Taelinn. You know how you can spin this to your advantage. Elves that support Lachma because they think Faerie is hopelessly corrupted will have to think twice in light of this new evidence. You can erode Lachma's support without having to field a single warrior against him."

Taelinn's eyes narrowed. "And what will you get out of this?"

"Fewer enemies to fight, if Lachma loses warriors. It will demoralize him, and I guarantee I know how to spin *that* to my advantage." Lucia smiled, a wicked expression. "And I anticipate, if you position things so Lachma is portrayed as someone working against the good of elfkind, your people won't be so upset if you *do* end up sending warriors to fight him."

Taelinn regarded Lucia in silence for a few moments. "You would swear to this? Swear that you will give us this magic?"

"If you swear you'll use it to bring Lachma in line," Lucia said. "And that you won't act against humans regardless of what happens to Faerie."

"You don't sound certain. It's not much of an oath if you know you can't provide what you say." Taelinn's mouth curved up at the corners.

"I'm just being honest. We know this magic Jeong has developed works. We don't know how well it will work on all of Faerie. It might be a really long-term solution. But I'm willing to swear to our good faith efforts."

Carth burst out in a torrent of angry Elvish. A few of the others surrounding Taelinn murmured agreement, though most of them leaned away from Carth as if physical distancing could show their disagreement. Taelinn let him speak for a while, then held up his hand requesting silence. Carth closed his mouth into a thin, hard line. He glared at me again, like I was the reason for his outburst. I hoped that wasn't true. I disliked Carth, but he had the king's respect, and I didn't want to mess with that.

"Helena Campbell," the king said, and I jerked my attention away from Carth. "What do you say?"

"Um," I said. "I think it's a good idea—"

"As a visionary," Taelinn amended. "Where does this action lead?"

I swallowed. "Don't you have visions, too? Why ask me?"

"I know what my visions say. I want to know if yours say the same." Taelinn's smile broadened. I didn't like the look in his eyes, like he suspected me of lying. "If you tell me the truth, we can have an alliance. And I will know if you lie."

I took Malcolm's hand and leaned against him as he gripped my shoulder, steadying me. I closed my eyes to shut out distractions and let a question sink deep into me: *Will this arrangement bring peace between humans and elves?*

Immediately I was whisked away into darkness. It was the darkness of a moonless night, not a closed room, as I discovered when my eyes adjusted and I saw myself surrounded by a forest. An elven forest, I realized, seeing the glossy small leaves on the trees and the trampled snow on the ground. The air was utterly silent, and I smelled wet grass and the bitter scent of sun-heated concrete, though I saw neither of those things.

As if a volume knob were being turned up, sound flowed into the scene, the faint sound of shouts and screams, gunfire and the clash of metal on metal. The noise grew and grew until it was loud enough to make my chest ache and my ears ring. In a flash of light, the forest vanished, and I saw the battle. Humans and elves fought each other everywhere I looked; elves fought other elves in a vicious, horrible conflict. Nobody noticed me.

I tried to leave the vision. I couldn't believe Lucia's generous plan would lead to this. But the same force I'd felt before gripped me, preventing me from rising out of it. The battle faded away, leaving behind hundreds of dead humans and elves who faded away in turn until I was in a white room with walls that glowed with warm light. The fear and anguish I'd felt disappeared, replaced with a peaceful feeling that made the previous scene seem distant and unreal.

One wall rippled, and I saw the elf king's city and the mountain it grew out of and the broad, tree-lined plain. Faerie. Only not the Faerie I'd fled from. Gone was the grimy taint in the air; sun glowed across the walls of the city and the great copper gates. Birds soared around the mountain peaks and glided over the tall grasses of the plains. It was Faerie as it should have been—Faerie as I hoped it would become.

The force released me, and I blinked until my vision cleared. "It will take time," I told Taelinn, "and there's going to be bloodshed. But in the end, Faerie will be cleansed."

Taelinn nodded and rose from his chair. "That's what I see as well." He extended a hand to Lucia. "Taelinn Ailmach, by right of blood and birth King of Faerie, swears to use the gift you offer to defeat Clan Lachma."

Lucia stood up and clasped the king's hand. "Lucia Pontarelli, by right of conquest—" She smiled a funny sideways smile— "leader of the Wardens, swears to provide the elves of Faerie the means to cleanse their land and to aid in the defeat of Clan Lachma."

I was watching Carth while everyone else had their eyes on the king and Lucia, and it startled me to see the ugly, angry look that crossed his face when Lucia spoke. It was gone as soon as the king released Lucia and turned to speak to his advisors; Carth still looked angry, but that was how he always looked, at least the times I'd seen him.

The king turned back to Lucia. "When will you do it? Excuse my eagerness, but this is something I've promised my people for a long time."

"Understandable." Lucia nodded at Rick. "This is Rick Jeong. He will stay here, with your permission, and show you how the magic works."

"It's possible not every elf will be able to do it," Rick told the king, "so I'll stay long enough to figure out who to teach. If you don't mind." He looked so eager to start I felt like laughing. Finally, something had worked out right.

"You are welcome," Taelinn said. "Once we have proof that it works, I will contact you, Lucia Pontarelli, with more information you can use against Clissach Lachma." He hesitated, then slowly, as if the words were more alien to him than just English, he added, "Thank you."

"You're welcome," Lucia said. "I'll be waiting."

# CHAPTER TWENTY-FOUR

As we all walked back to the slip, Lucia said, "How bad was it? Your vision?"

That killed my good mood dead. "Pretty bad. Taelinn isn't going to bring Lachma to heel immediately, no matter what magic he shows his people. There will be a lot of fighting and a lot of humans and elves dead. I can only imagine it would be worse if we didn't have this deal."

"I'm clinging to that, Davies." Lucia sighed. "If you could see where Lachma will strike next—"

"You know the oracle never gives answers to that question in time for us to get Wardens in place. Better to count on Pattern 2.0 if you're chasing elf incursions."

"Yeah, I know," Lucia said, but not as if she was despondent. "I need a stiff drink and a back rub. If I don't relax soon, I'm going to snap."

"I feel the same. Not about the stiff drink." I wasn't into hard liquor, but a beer would not be rejected.

The Wardens left to guard the slip, the ones scouting around for attackers, stopped us before we could enter the forest. "The word is 'scenario,' Cheng," Lucia told the petite Asian woman who held her gun like she meant to use it on Lucia. Cheng nodded and stepped aside.

"I told you I was cautious, Davies," Lucia said when I gaped. "I considered the possibility that Taelinn might use some kind of elven mind whammy to control me, and I asked Roarke what that might look like. Hence the code word."

Malcolm took the lead when we approached the slip. It was still open and still guarded by the other five Wardens. He stepped through, looked around, then beckoned for us to follow.

Once everyone was through, Dave sealed the slip. It vanished without a trace, but Dave held up a boxy little device like an antique remote control and waved it across where the slip had been. He relaxed when it let out a series of beeps like an electronic stud finder. "Nothing's coming through that slip ever again."

"But how will Rick get back?"

"Would you relax, Davies? You're not the only paranoid one here." Lucia headed for the repair shop office. "Jeong can locate existing slips with the slip key as well as opening them where there aren't natural slips. He'll come back when he's ready."

I started to protest, but then I realized Lucia was right: I was behaving as if nobody else had any common sense. Lucia had it all worked out. I needed to get off her case and deal with the things I was responsible for. Which at the moment meant picking up my sons from school.

Sergio had been right about one thing—a thoroughly cleaned car, one that didn't have French fry chunks lodged in the upholstery and smelled like pine rather than faintly of sour milk, was a delight. Not that it had stunk of sour milk before, and I hardly ever let the kids eat in the car, but it still felt luxurious.

Malcolm drove, and I called my mother to see how Jenny was doing. I'd let her go to Grandma's house as a treat to cheer her up. Jenny had been really upset at Connvuir's not coming home with us, more upset than she had been about the blood on Malcolm's and my coats. The blood had made Duncan demand the whole story and Alastair look at us both with accusing eyes, like we'd deprived him of his right to be shot at by elves. It worried me. I'd thought Alastair was learning good sense about prophecies and not being allowed to fight the elves, but maybe I was wrong.

"You haven't let it go yet, have you," Malcolm said. "You're still humming under your breath."

"Huh? Oh. No, it's not about Lucia. Malcolm, what are we going to do about Alastair? He still wants to get involved in this war, no matter what we or anyone tell him."

"I know." Malcolm didn't say anything more, but I recognized when he was thinking something over and didn't press. Finally, he said, "Maybe we need to give him something to do. Something that will keep him away from the things he's not mature enough to handle, but will still offer him the opportunity to help. He's acting out of fear, you know."

"Yes. He's afraid of the elves hurting him or our family, and the only way he knows to stop the fear is to attack. I can't really blame him."

"I agree, and I think we didn't give that enough consideration. He's smart, and he knows when a threat is real. We can't exactly tell him the elves aren't a danger to him when we come home covered in blood."

"So... what do we do?"

"Let's think about it for a while. Maybe put the problem to Lucia. Tell him we want his help, for one—he responds well to that." Malcolm smiled. "Something he got from his mother."

"There are worse inheritances to give your children," I said.

---

THREE DAYS PASSED AS PEACEFULLY AS IF THE WORLD wasn't threatened by murderous elves. I spent most of Wednesday glued to my phone, waiting to hear from Lucia that Rick was back. Fortunately, I figured out that whatever magic Rick was teaching the elves, it wouldn't be simple, and expecting him to be back in a day was ridiculous. I still kept my phone on me, just in case.

By Friday, I'd almost managed to convince myself to relax. I was back in my usual routine of asking for prophecies on behalf of people who sent in requests via email before tending to all the little details parenthood demanded. I saw no spontaneous prophecies, the kids didn't have any crises, Jenny coped with her empathic abilities well enough I started to believe she could go to kindergarten in two years like any other child. It was so peaceful I suspected something was waiting to strike.

Saturday morning dawned sullen and gray, with clouds threatening rain, if not snow—the weather had turned even colder than usual in the past two days. It left me feeling sullen as well, though I recognized that my mood was more a result of several days of unrelenting tension than the weather. Still, I was cranky enough Malcolm offered to cook breakfast, though it was my turn.

It always surprised me how an unexpected small act of kindness could turn my mood around. I didn't hate cooking, but being relieved of the duty cheered me up. I chatted with the kids over pancakes and cleaned up after breakfast with a light heart, starting the dishwasher just as the first snowflakes fell. The kids all clamored at the door to the patio until Malcolm reminded them they didn't want to use up all the snowflakes before they could accumulate. Then they begged me to let them watch a movie instead.

I started *Coco* and found Malcolm standing close beside me. He drew me into his arms and murmured, "How distracted do you think the movie will make them?"

I laughed. "You know I hate doing that while they're awake, ever since Duncan walked in on us. I'm sure we scarred him for life."

"He seems well-adjusted enough to me." Malcolm kissed the side of my head. "I actually have something to follow up on for a few minutes, if you don't mind me abandoning you. A Campbell Security job from last week."

"I don't mind. In fact, I'm going to be a traditional housewife and bake cookies."

Malcolm raised an eyebrow. "You really *are* in a good mood."

"Mmm. I promise to show you how good a mood later."

I went into the kitchen and pulled out ingredients for chocolate chip cookies. It was one of the few recipes I didn't need a cookbook for, but I always referred to the recipe because the consequences of trusting to a faulty memory, when it came to cooking, could be dire. Or at least inedible.

I was pouring flour into the big mixer when I heard Alastair say, "Mom?"

"Alastair. Don't you want to watch the movie?"

"Not right now. Can I talk to you about something?"

That set off all my mom alarms. "Is something wrong?"

Alastair shook his head. "Not with me. It's not a prophecy. I mean —it is a prophecy, but it's one from a while back." He braced himself, and added, "I prophesied about Connvuir's family."

"Alastair—" I heard how annoyed I sounded and stopped myself. Alastair was watching me with the mulish expression that said he'd done something he believed was justified that I was going to be angry about. That expression softened my heart, and I said instead, "All right. You know we told you not to get involved, and you know you disobeyed. Let's leave that for now. Why did you want to know about Connvuir's family?"

"I overheard you and Dad talking about who he belonged to, and I thought I could find out what happened to his father. Like, so he could have Connvuir back. I didn't know—" His lips trembled for a moment. "I didn't know what he was like."

My heart ached for him. "Can you talk about it?"

"I can now. He... I saw him beat Connvuir's mother, over and over again—I mean, like lots of different times. And his mother was scared, because no one believed her. I didn't understand that part. She looked beaten up, so why wouldn't people believe her husband hit her?"

I understood that well enough, based on things Gabriel Roarke had told me about elf marriages—that elves didn't casually divorce, and they chose their spouses after much consideration, so dissolution of an elf marriage was rare. "Sometimes people don't want to believe evil of someone else. That's true of elves as well as humans, I guess. Was there more?"

Alastair nodded. "Jenny's scary elf. He killed Connvuir's father. He stabbed him over and over again, and the screaming—nobody stopped the scary elf, Mom. It just went on and on."

Quickly, I went to his side and held him while he struggled not to cry. "I'm glad you told me," I whispered. "This is what we feared would happen. It's why we told you not to get involved. Do you understand now?"

"But I can't—Mom, what if that elf comes after you, or Dad, or us? We have to stop him!"

I closed my eyes and hugged him tighter. "Let me tell you something that might help, okay?"

Alastair nodded again.

"I saw Connvuir's father too. Saw him dead, I mean. All I saw was the body, and I didn't know who'd killed him, but I suspected Clissach Lachma—that's the scary elf's name. And before, I thought it happened because Lachma is vicious and evil and likes killing. But now, I think he was avenging Connvuir's mother, because she was Lachma's sister."

Alastair pulled back enough that I could see his surprised face. "His sister?"

"Yes. I think Lachma didn't know what his sister's husband was doing to her, and when he found out, he made sure that elf couldn't do it to anyone else. And the thing is, Alastair, that's not how people are supposed to behave when they see injustice, but you and I both know people don't always do what they should. So I'm not going to tell you I think what Lachma did was right. I'll just say that I saw how hurt Connvuir's mother was when she showed up on our doorstep, and I can understand trying to protect the ones you love."

"I don't understand how he could love anyone. He's killed so many people."

I thought back to facing Lachma in the little clearing, how he'd looked at Connvuir and how he'd looked at me. "I guess that means people aren't always just one thing. But, Alastair?"

"Yeah?"

I held him by the shoulders at arm's length. "Those visions you keep having, the ones you keep secret from us, they may be true, but in one important way, they're lying to you."

His eyes widened. "You said visions are true."

"I did. But these ones lie to you because they've convinced you you're solely responsible for the safety of this family, and that means you're frightening yourself for no reason. Do you believe your dad and I are weak?"

"Of course not!"

"Are we stupid?"

His face flushed. "No."

"Then why do you think you're entitled to break the rules your intelligent, strong parents give you?

The shot hit home. Alastair ducked his head and said nothing.

Instinct told me I was finally getting through to him. "I don't care how smart you are, Alastair. This family is a team, and we can't function if one of our teammates thinks the rules don't apply to him. That's the sort of thing that endangers all of us." I drew in a deep breath. "But let me tell you something else. Your father and I agree that you'll benefit from using your gift to help us win this war. Wait!" Alastair had looked at me with such hope it chilled me. My son was going to be a force to reckon with someday—maybe someday soon.

"I think you understand now what kind of visions we're worried about you seeing, and I also think you agree with us that you're not ready to see such violence." Alastair nodded vigorously. "We haven't talked it out yet, so I don't know where this is going. But I promise you, Alastair, you won't have to feel helpless anymore."

It was the right thing to say. Alastair swiped his sleeve across his eyes. "Thanks, Mom," he said, and hugged me.

I hugged him back. "Why don't you go see if your dad is done with work, and tell him what we talked about? Maybe you can start figuring out how you can help."

Alastair bolted from the room. I felt incredibly weary, but also relaxed in a way I'd thought I might never feel again. I turned on the mixer and stared at the mixing paddle as it churned its way through the cookie dough. I never was one for eating raw cookie dough, because I liked the way cookies tasted when they were hot from the oven. But watching the paddle go round and round soothed me.

Something banged against the patio door, a rattling, insistent hammering that echoed through the house.

Tension gripped me again. I ran for the back door, ignoring Duncan and Jenny's demands to be told what was going on. Three figures huddled on the patio, their faces and bodies obscured by heavy fur coats dusted with the snow that hadn't yet stopped falling. Night-Noon stood before the door, growling a low, menacing hum that sounded more like a dog than a cat's purr. The memory of Connvuir's mother in our backyard struck so hard I hesitated rather than open the door. Whatever this was, it was bad news.

I heard Malcolm approach, and then his hand on my shoulder gently moved me to one side. Night-Noon backed away, still growling. Malcolm flung open the door and aimed a gun at the center figure. "Don't move."

"Malcolm..." The soft voice was unrecognizable, but the fact that these strangers knew my husband's name terrified me. Then the person in the middle, who was being supported by the other two, tossed his head so the hood fell back, revealing his battered, bloody face.

It was Rick Jeong.

Gasping, I hurried forward to support him before he collapsed. I looked up into the faces of Thandaigh and her friend Dachtein. "What happened?" I demanded.

"Get him inside," Thandaigh said. "They worked him over good. He needs a healer, or whatever you humans have."

"He *is* a healer," I snarled, "and you'd better explain. Now." In full light, Rick looked worse than before, his face bruised and distorted. I was sure there were more injuries I couldn't see.

Dachtein and Thandaigh looked at each other instead of responding. Then Thandaigh said, "Thandaigh'Dor Leath and Dachtein'Laiv Mevair officially request asylum and protection from the king of Faerie. Will you grant it?"

"I—" My instinct to protest that I didn't have the authority for what sounded very official was overridden by my sense that this was something these two really needed. "I grant asylum, but why do you need protection from Taelinn?"

Dachtein shook his head. "Not Taelinn. He was assassinated. His cousin Carth'Ayr Ailmach is now king of Faerie. He killed Thandaigh's brother Siltair, and the three of us barely escaped with our lives."

Stunned, I gaped at Malcolm. "Then—what about the treaty?"

"There is no more treaty," Thandaigh said. "Carth rejects all agreements with the human world. He intends to make common cause with Lachma so elfkind can conquer your world and abandon Faerie entirely."

Alastair stood close beside his father, staring at the elves. "What does that mean?" he asked.

"Alastair," I said, "it means we really are at war."

# About the Author

Melissa McShane is the author of many other fantasy novels, including the Warmaster LitRPG series, beginning with *Warmaster 1: Dungeon Spiteful; Burning Bright,* first in The Extraordinaries series; and *The Book of Secrets,* first book in The Last Oracle series.

While her home remains in the Western US, she currently lives in Kerala, India, with her husband, daughter, and two absurdly beautiful Persian cats. She wrote reviews and critical essays for many years before turning to fiction, which is much more fun than anyone ought to be allowed to have. You can visit her at her website **www.melissamc shanewrites.com** for more information on other books and upcoming releases.

For news on upcoming releases, bonus material, and other fun stuff (including kitten pictures), sign up for Melissa's newsletter at **www. melissamcshanewrites.com/contact-me-2/join-my-mailing-list/**

If you enjoyed this book, please consider leaving a review at your favorite online bookseller!

# ALSO BY MELISSA McSHANE

## WARMASTER

## THE BOOKS OF THE DARK GODDESS

## THE LAST ORACLE